Praise for Robert Goldsborough

THREE STRIKES YOU'RE DEAD

"Robert Goldsborough, the man who so brilliantly brought Rex Stout's Nero Wolfe and Archie Goodwin back to literary life, has returned with a new detective, all his own – and that's cause for any mystery fan to rejoice! Goldsborough is a master storyteller, providing crackling dialogue and plot twists around every corner – readers are in for a real treat!" –Max Allan Collins, author of *Road to Purgatory*

MURDER IN E MINOR

"Goldsborough has not only written a first-rate mystery that stands on its own merits, he has faithfully re-created the round detective and his milieu." –PHILADELPHIA ENQUIRER

"Mr. Goldsborough has all of the late writer's stylistic mannerisms down pat." –THE NEW YORK TIMES on *Murder in E Minor*

"A smashing success…" –CHICAGO SUN-TIMES

"A half dozen other writers have attempted it, but Goldsborough's is the only one that feels authentic, the only one able to get into Rex's psyche. If I hadn't known otherwise, I might have been fooled into thinking this was the genius Stout myself." –John McAleer, Rex Stout's official biographer and editor of *The Stout Journal*

ALSO BY ROBERT GOLDSBOROUGH
FROM BANTAM BOOKS

DEATH ON A DEADLINE
FADE TO BLACK
SILVER SPIRE
THE BLOODIED IVY
THE LAST COINCIDENCE
THE MISSING CHAPTER

Robert Goldsborough

Three Strikes You're Dead

This is a work of fiction. Actual names, characters, places, and incidents are used fictitiously with the utmost respect. With those few exceptions, any other resemblance to actual events, locales, organizations, or persons, living or dead, is entirely coincidental.

Echelon Press Publishing
56 Sawyer Circle #354
Memphis, TN 38103
www.echelonpress.com

First Echelon Press paperback printing: June 2005
Originally published in electronic format as "The Year Diz Came to Town"

10 9 8 7 6 5 4 3 2

Cover Art © Nathalie Moore 2005 Arianna Award Winner
www.GraphicsMuse.com

Printed in the United States of America

Dedication

To Bill Granger and Max Allan Collins, two superb writers who have helped me to appreciate Chicago's rich history and traditions.

Dear Readers,

Many years ago I discovered one of the greatest talents of the fiction industry. I read my first Nero Wolfe novel by Rex Stout. Time passed and each book I read drew me deeper into the web of the rotund genius of fiction fame.

Being a mystery novice, I reached the end of the line all too soon…or so I thought. Rex Stout was deceased. No more Nero Wolfe? *Gasp*! Then a gentle little woman in a used bookstore offered me a gift. She handed me a novel by Robert Goldsborough and I found new pleasure.

Now, years later, I can proudly say that I am the owner of the ongoing series of Nero Wolfe novels written by Mr. Goldsborough. So imagine my surprise when a referral brought Robert Goldsborough and me together.

Mr. Goldsborough's talents run as deep as Mr. Stout's, and Echelon Press is proud to bring you the newest novel by this master of storytelling. ***Three Strikes You're Dead*** takes readers back in time to 1938 Chicago and introduces a new kind of hero.

We hope you enjoy this novel as much as we have. And don't miss our other exciting mystery novels, ***Missing!*** by Judith R. Parker and Goldsborough's fellow Chicagoan Luisa Buehler's ***The Rosary Bride*** and ***The Lion Tamer***.

Echelon Press is always pleased to hear your thoughts and suggestions for how we can make our publishing house your publishing house! Please send your comments to suggestions@echelonpress.com.

Happy Reading!
Karen L. Syed, President
Echelon Press

"Today we have Dizzy Dean initiated into the Loyal and Benevolent Brotherhood of Cubs."

–Marvin McCarthy, Sports Editor,
Chicago Times April 16, 1938

PROLOGUE

The rain had stopped, but the cold, damp wind knifed from all directions. Traffic on Broadway had dwindled to the occasional taxi slushing along the wet pavement. The figure huddled against the brick wall of one of the buildings flanking the parking lot, beyond the faint light from a single bulb mounted on a telephone pole.

Neither the wall nor a turned-up coat collar and pulled-down hat kept out the March night. The waiting figure ached, from wet face to throbbing calves to numbed, cold feet that made squishing noises inside soaked shoes. The chimes of a nearby church tolled a single note, marking yet another quarter-turn–11:15.

More than three hours. The blowhard's probably babbling on about how he's going to clean things up. Make the city safe. Right.

The dark green '35 Lincoln Le Baron roadster with its side-mounted spare tire was one of only five machines left in the dingy parking lot wedged between two darkened buildings. The rest of the local do-gooders must have taken taxis or streetcars. Not everybody had the kind of money in these hard times to afford a car, let alone a Lincoln. Now if he only came out by himself...

As the chimes struck the half-hour, footsteps came from the direction of the restaurant. The figure drew in air and struggled to keep from shaking, then tensed when a man reached the circle of light. Slender...wearing a fedora...him? Yes! No, not tall enough. The man walked toward a black Chevrolet coupe as the waiting figure edged back into a recessed doorway of the building. The Chevy started with a cough and pulled out onto Broadway, and the figure relaxed the grip on the cold, nickeled steel nestled in a coat pocket.

Another quarter hour passed. More footsteps. This time it had to be him. Yes. The confident, self-assured stride, long arms swinging at his sides, his ego fed by the mindless adulation of the group in the restaurant. The love of being at center stage and hearing the applause. He headed for the sporty roadster. And he was alone.

The figure emerged from the alcove, slowly but with purpose. The shivers of a few minutes ago had passed, replaced by resolve, and the hand that gripped the automatic was dry and steady. Any lingering doubts were erased by memories and hatred.

The tall man stopped just short of his car and cocked his head as if he'd heard something. The waiting figure's hand tightened on the gun. The tall man pivoted deliberately, noticed the figure, then leaned forward at the waist, raising a hand tentatively, as if in recognition.

The heavy, damp night muted the single shot.

CHAPTER 1

I awoke at 10:30 on New Year's morning with a headache, which surprised me. True, I had rung in 1938 at Kilkenny's just down the street, but I nursed only three beers in that entire stretch, from about 9:00 p.m. until past 1:30. Plus I took seconds and thirds from the big spread that the Killer had laid out, in his own words, "as a way of thanking all my regular customers, who are also my dear and cherished friends, for their enduring patronage and their tolerance of my myriad foibles." That's how the Killer talks.

"Oh, noblest of Gaelic publicans," I had responded in kind, lifting high my glass, "we do indeed tolerate your varied foibles, bizarre though they may be, for we–and I speak for all in this august assemblage–have at one time or another found solace in your understanding and sympathetic ear and your hospitable nature, a nature that befits one whose roots go deep into the Old Sod."

"Malek, sit down and shut up, or better yet, have yourself another drink," Morty Easterly bellowed. "One gasbag in this joint is enough, and as he happens to own the place, we can't very well tell him to button his yap."

"Point taken, albeit reluctantly," I said amid a chorus of jeers, waving and sitting down. I kept on eating and socializing as the old year slipped away, but I declined the champagne poured with a flourish nearing midnight, and I was home and asleep by 2:00. The moral, if one is to be found: Next time, two aspirin before bed. I rolled over and turned on the squawky little radio on the nightstand to get a weather report, but all I could find was music–Crosby and Kate Smith and Rudy Vallee–plus one station where a bass voice somberly recited the major events of 1937: FDR's second inauguration…the crash of the Hindenburg dirigible at Lakehurst…Japan's invasion of China…the continuing Spanish Civil War…Amelia Earhart's plane lost in the Pacific…Joe Louis knocking out Braddock at Comiskey Park for the heavyweight title.

"Tell me something I don't know, like the temperature, will ya?" I muttered, turning off the radio and easing out of bed, making sure my feet landed on the small island of rug where I'd parked my slippers. I padded across the wood floor to the window. The sun had punched through the clouds, and the predicted flurries never showed up.

Most of Chicago was still asleep, or at least inside likely nursing its collective hangover. Three stories below me, Clark Street was empty save for a red streetcar that lumbered by, clanging its bell at nothing in particular. A few weeks earlier, after we had spent a Saturday night in Kilkenny's, Walt Carlin from the copy desk at the *Tribune* decided he didn't want to go all the way south to his two-room flat on 67th Street, so he bunked on my sofa. He got up in the morning griping about how noisy my place is, what with all the traffic on Clark, particularly the bell-happy streetcars. But in the two years I'd lived there, the racket had never bothered me. Maybe it's because I'm a heavy sleeper, or maybe it goes back to the three-flat in Pilsen where I grew up. It had railroad tracks right behind it that rattled the china in my mother's kitchen cupboard at least once every half hour, day and night, or so it seemed to me. As my father liked to say, "If you can fall asleep here, you can doze off at State and Madison the Saturday after Thanksgiving with a Salvation Army band playing five feet away."

I measured coffee into the pot and shuffled to the front door. The *Trib* was in the hall on the mat, neatly folded rather than thrown down with its inside sections spilling out, as was usually the case. The talk I had with the newsboy when I gave him his year-end tip seemed to be paying off, at least for now. Sitting with a Lucky Strike and a cup of black coffee at my small kitchen table, I went through the paper. The banner story, as it is every January 1, told how the New Year's Eve crowd jammed the Loop, and what a wonderful time they had. I figure the type for this piece just gets saved and reused year after year.

A few pages back was the headline HITLER MAKES A NEW YEAR VOW–GREATER ARMS, under which the guy calling himself Fuehrer was quoted as saying "Expansion of German fighting forces is a political necessity." As I worked through the front section, I grinned for the first time in 1938. My day-old piece about a raid on a South Wabash handbook ran almost as I had written it, including the lead: "Bookie Carl 'Ace' McCabe had a deuce of a time Friday when a trio of Chicago Police in four minutes wrote him up on five separate charges of illegal gambling." I never thought it would clear the copy desk, although that cretin of a slot man on the day side, Jasper Cams, made sure there was no byline on the story.

The lead editorial warned that "There will be no comfortable coasting in 1938" and that "Times call above all for fortitude."

"Just what I needed to hear," I muttered into my cup. "A stiff-upper-lip lecture to break in a new calendar." I silently mouthed the name of the *Trib's* chief editorial writer and followed it with several of the words the paper refuses to print.

Turning the page, I groaned at the three-column photo printed there–the city's number one publicity hound and self-proclaimed do-gooder had struck again. The man who reporters privately refer to as "Goody Two-Shoes" had held another of his "Let's Do Battle Together for a Clean Chicago" rallies, this one on the sidewalk in front of City Hall on New Year's Eve afternoon. The extended caption (there was no story) read: "Some 100 or more interested citizens and casual passers-by listened attentively as reformer and heir to a steel fortune Lloyd Martindale exhorted them to 'get rid of those despicable vermin known by the all-too-polite label of *organized crime*.' Martindale, who many speculate is setting his sights on running for mayor in 1939, urged his listeners to demand 'better police protection, better government leaders, and a better year ahead for all residents of our great city.'"

He closed by lambasting Mayor Edward J. Kelly as "a tool of the Nittis, the Riccas, and all of those other repugnant throwbacks to the Capone era who think it is their birthright to ply their nefarious businesses: gambling, white slavery, and drug dealing."

It sounded familiar, and for good reason. On a blustery fall afternoon some three months earlier, Martindale had pulled the same stunt in front of Police Headquarters at 11th and State, and all of us in the pressroom begrudgingly–and under orders from our city editors–trudged outside to cover his harangues.

"Goddamn windbag knows how to get publicity, I'll give him that much," Anson Masters of the *Daily News* muttered to me as Martindale, tall, with salt-and-pepper hair well-barbered and impeccable in a three-piece blue serge suit, stood on a crate on the sidewalk and spoke into a bullhorn. He gave the newspaper photogs his sharply etched profile and berated the police for, among other things, "cavalierly allowing the crime syndicate to operate unchecked and unfettered throughout the length and breadth of our great metropolis."

The 15-minute diatribe, delivered with the style and fervor of a sawdust-trail evangelist, drew applause and cheers from a couple of dozen spectators, most of them middle-aged women, who almost surely had been brought along by Martindale and his sidekick, a red-haired fireplug named Lumley.

About ten uniformed cops stood off to one side watching the performance, shaking their heads and making behind-the-hand comments to one another. As we trooped back into the building, I asked a lieutenant I knew casually what his opinion of Martindale was. "Well, what do you think?" he shot back, rolling his eyes. "Don't quote me, not that anyone would be interested in my opinions, but he's a bullshit artist, and if he ever becomes mayor, which I seriously doubt, I'm moving to the suburbs. And I *hate* the suburbs."

I looked again at the photo of Martindale, fist in the air and jaw jutting like the prow of a battleship as he stood in front of City Hall, and I wished I had the same doubts about Martindale's success as the police lieutenant. It seemed to me that Martindale really *could* end up running the city. After all, look at what good old-fashioned stem-winding oratory got Huey Long down in Louisiana: a governorship, a Senate seat, and a bullet.

I tossed the paper aside and proceeded to waste the afternoon. None of the football games on the radio interested me, although I'd read a lot in the sports pages about Whizzer White of Colorado and how good he was and that he should have won the Heisman Trophy instead of some Yale swell named Clinton Frank. So, while I had a can of tomato soup and an apple, I listened to some of the Cotton Bowl game; however good this Whizzer may have been, he wasn't good enough this time because Rice beat Colorado.

This was Saturday, which meant I had the next day off too, and around 7:00 I decided to catch a movie at the Chicago Theatre–"Wells Fargo" with Joel McCrea and Frances Dee. I peered into the bathroom mirror and poised my comb, trying to decide if the patch of gray behind my left ear had begun to spread. Given that the rest of my hair is sort of dusty-colored, it didn't seem to stand out all that much anyway. I put on a white shirt and my navy blue suit, and the bright red tie with swirls that Norma used to say made me look like a floorwalker at Marshall Field's. As I slipped on my overcoat, I noticed that the right sleeve was fraying. I snipped off the loose ends with the kitchen scissors and went to the front closet, where I grabbed the new dark blue Dobbs hat–my Christmas present to myself.

Down on the street, the wind swirled and had teeth. There were no cabs in sight; maybe all the hackies were hung over like the rest of us. I waited 10 minutes for one, then gave up and grabbed a southbound Clark streetcar. I was one of just six riders, and three of the others–two old geezers and a double-chinned woman in a brown babushka–were asleep. The woman snored softly, the purse she clutched to her mountainous bosom rising and falling with each breath. A young couple held hands and gazed unblinking at each other, their mutual enamor blocking out the mean surroundings.

I settled into a cold wicker double seat and started in on the *Trib* sports section I'd brought along for company, but the bare bulbs gave off so little light that I finally gave up. As we clattered toward the Loop, I looked out on a succession of darkened storefronts–butchers, dry cleaners, drug stores, auto mechanics, currency exchanges, grocers, haberdashers, and a Woolworth's five-and-dime. Other than the austere and depressing lobbies of the transient hotels, only the saloons were open, their neon window signs for Schlitz and Pabst and Blatz cutting through the murk like welcoming beacons.

I grew up in the comfortable boredom of Pilsen, a well-scrubbed Bohemian enclave of apartment buildings and small houses on the Near Southwest Side. After I got married, we lived in a brick six-flat in the Logan Square neighborhood up Northwest. Now, for the last two years, I'd had a taste of what I felt was the *real* Chicago: North Clark Street. If any thoroughfare throbbed to the rhythms of the city, this was it. I hated living alone, but at the same time, I loved Clark Street.

The streetcar bulled through the Fullerton intersection. On the right a couple of blocks farther south was the warehouse where Bugs Moran's crew got machine-gunned at point-blank range on Valentine's Day 1929, and it had to have been Capone's men–dressed as cops, by God. Only in Chicago. The St. Valentine's Day Massacre, the papers called it, and why not? It was a massacre, all right. I already was working for the *Tribune* then, but I was stuck inside on rewrite. When word came in to the local room about the shootings that Thursday morning, I tried to persuade Bob Lee, the city editor at the time, to send me up there to lend a hand with the coverage. But his snappy reply was that the p.m. papers were going to beat us on the story for their home-delivered editions anyway, and that I should stay put and take phone dictation from the battery of reporters he'd dispatched to the warehouse. I did what I could to liven up their flat copy, and I made it a lot peppier at that.

Pardon the horn-tooting, but by then I was the best the *Trib* had at writing news features–human interest stuff, but with solid reporting behind it–and if I'd been up there at the site, I would have turned out a better piece than the whole damned bunch combined. They were reporters, but so was I, and I was something none of them was–a *writer*.

The red streetcar had crossed North Avenue, passing the two big German gathering places called the Red Star Inn and the Germania Club, which faced each other like blocky sentinels proclaiming Teutonic glory. But another few blocks farther south, in the shadow the downtown skyline, the street changed its character again, for the worse. Stooped men in rags, many bare-headed and seemingly oblivious to the cold, sat on the sidewalks with their backs against the walls of flophouses and saloons or stood in alleys, silhouetted in the Styxian glow of fires in salamanders, those 40-gallon drums whose blazes were likely fueled by newspapers or oily rags. Some nipped from pint bottles wrapped in paper sacks, which they passed to eager neighbors. This was skid row. Not *the* Skid Row, which was a mile or so away on West Madison, but real enough in its degradation. The editorial writers were always wringing their hands in print about these stretches of misery and what should be done about them, but nobody had yet come up with a good answer. Maybe there wasn't one, at least not as long as this Depression had its fangs dug into us. According to the *Tribune*, FDR definitely wasn't the solution, but then I never thought the paper had given the guy a fair shake, although you wouldn't hear me saying it within a cannon shot of Tribune Tower.

We clattered across the river on the Clark Street drawbridge, which put us in the Loop. I got off and walked two blocks east to the Chicago Theatre at State and Lake–the biggest movie house in the world, somebody called it, probably the Balaban & Katz chain, which ran the place. Whether or not it was the biggest, it was grand with its mirrors and gold railings and wide, sweeping staircases and thick carpeting and chandeliers. I'd been going there for movies and stage shows almost since the day it opened, which was the year after I graduated from high school in 1920. And that's where Norma and I had our first "downtown" date in 1923–to see Richard Barthelmess and Dorothy Gish in "Bright Shawl," followed by a vaudeville show that bored both of us.

On this New Year's night, not even a quarter of the seats were taken. I had liked Joel McCrea in other movies, but you can have "Wells Fargo." It was too long, with too many slow spots. He was better in "Barbary Coast." After the movie, the screen went up, the curtains parted, and Ted Weems and his orchestra started playing on the stage, so I got out fast. Several years before, Norma and I had danced to Weems at a downtown hotel, I forget which one, and I didn't need that kind of memory.

At twenty past eleven, I stood under the marquee of the theater and paused to absorb the warmth of its hundreds of small light bulbs. I hadn't eaten since early afternoon and decided to treat myself to a late supper at Henrici's. I went the half block south and turned west onto Randolph, where the Rialto's movie palaces trumpeted in three-foot-high letters their starring performers: Carole Lombard and Fred MacMurray, John Barrymore, Mae West and Nelson Eddy, and a young comedian named Red Skelton, who was live on stage.

The Randolph Street sidewalks that twenty-four hours earlier had overflowed with revelers now were almost deserted. Henrici's wasn't crowded, either. I gave my coat and hat to the checkroom girl and turned to the tuxedoed maitre d', whose supercilious grin had been frozen onto a long, sallow face. He sniffed twice and led me across the black-and-white checkerboard tiles and past a half acre of starched linen on empty tables to a spot near the back of the paneled, high-ceilinged dining room. Dropping a menu on my plate as though it, and I, were tainted, he executed a snappy about-face and returned to the comfort of his rostrum.

After ordering a Schlitz on draught from a marginally friendly waiter, I saw her, alone at a table under a landscape painting, reading and sipping coffee. Her short brown hair framed that delicate, famous face, which I had in right profile, and she wore a pale blue, two-piece outfit that probably cost more than I made in a month.

I ordered the roast beef plate and sipped beer from a pilsner glass as I watched her. I had known she was in town, of course, what with all the publicity and the reviews. But I never expected to see somebody like that alone without an entourage or bodyguard or escort as a buffer against the masses.

I can't say what made me decide to go over to her–maybe it's what Norma had often called my "essential brashness." I walked the 20 feet and stood beside her table, waiting to be noticed. She looked up, her intense blue eyes questioning but not hostile.

"Pardon me," I said, making an awkward attempt at a bow. "I don't mean to disturb you, but I just had to tell you how much I liked you in *Victoria Regina*–I saw it two weeks ago, right after it opened. It's the only play I've seen in at least a year. And I'm awfully glad you brought it here at last."

"Why, thank you very much," Helen Hayes said as if she meant it. She smiled primly. "And please don't apologize. You are most definitely not disturbing me, Mr.…"

"Malek. Steve Malek." I spelled it.

"Which would make you a Czech, isn't that so?"

"Sure is. Both of my parents were born in Bohemia."

"Were you, as well?"

"Afraid not. I'm 99 and 44 one-hundredths percent Chicago."

"And you should be proud of it. This is a great city," she said with conviction, dabbing her lips with her napkin. "Tell me, Mr. Malek, would I be too bold if I asked your line of work?"

"Not as bold as I am for intruding. I'm a reporter, a police reporter. With the *Tribune*."

Her smile grew to a laugh, but I could tell it wasn't at my expense. "I should have guessed!" she trilled with unsuppressed pleasure, clapping once. "I've known a lot of newspapermen, including my own husband, and all of you have

11

something in common. It's a certain…"

"How about 'essential brashness'?"

"Well…I might not have termed it that way exactly, but I suppose it comes pretty close to describing…"

"Is everything all right, Miss Hayes?" The maitre d' was breathless from sprinting across the room.

"Oh yes, Emil, of course it is, although you're sweet to look after me, as you always do." She touched his arm in affirmation. "I've just been getting reacquainted with an old friend. Have you met Mr. Malek, from the *Tribune*?"

Emil furrowed his brow and looked with uncertainty from the actress to me and back again. "I…don't believe I've had the pleasure." He turned to me, nodding stiffly. "Sir."

"Emil." I dipped my chin in return to show there were no hard feelings about the way he had high-hatted me when I came in.

"Are you having supper?" Helen Hayes asked, and when I told her I'd just ordered, she urged me to join her, patting the chair at right angles to her own.

"But it looks like you've already finished," I protested.

"I just had a snack. That's all I usually eat after a performance. But I need more coffee, Lord, several cups more, to get me through *this*," she said in a stage voice, shaking a sheaf of papers she had just picked up. "And I would very much like the company. Emil, have Mr. Malek's meal and drink brought over here."

"Yes, Miss Hayes," he responded, doing another about-face, this one not at all snappy.

"I don't believe Emil cares a whole lot for me," I said as I sat down.

"Oh, don't worry about him," she replied gently. "He's not nearly as stuffy as he puts on, and he's very protective of me. I'm here several nights a week after the performance, usually by myself–I often like being alone after working–and Emil views himself as my guardian, my protector. Actually, almost nobody ever approaches me. Maybe they don't recognize me, or if they do, they choose not to come over."

"I almost didn't come over myself. Thanks for pretending that we have known each other."

She tilted her head gracefully in what may have been a practiced gesture, although with her it seemed natural and spontaneous.

"Not at all, Mr. Malek. Now if you'd been, say, an accountant or a stockbroker or an optometrist–not that those are bad professions, mind you–I almost surely would not have invited you to join me. But a newspaperman–that's different. You as a group are among the most interesting people in the world. And in candor, I was feeling sorry for myself. Also, as I told you, I welcome the company."

"Feeling sorry for yourself? Why?"

"This!" She stuck out her lower lip and shook the sheaf of paper again. "Mr. Malek, when we left New York and took *Victoria Regina* on the road in the fall, I got this crazy idea that this cast could rehearse another play, *The Merchant of Venice*, as we go across the country and then give a few performances of it, *very* few, in certain cities. I told myself, and everybody else, that it would keep us all fresh and stimulated. But that was a bald rationalization on my part; I am thirty-seven years old, and I have always wanted to do Shakespeare."

"You never *have*?"

"Never. Not once. Be very careful what you wish for, Mr. Malek, because you might get it," she said with feeling. "I'm playing Portia"–she tapped what I now realized was a script–"and we're supposed to give our first performance of 'Merchant,' a matinee, right here in Chicago at the Erlanger two weeks from today. Never in the history of the American theater has a cast been more unprepared, and I include myself, particularly myself, in that indictment.

"Well, you've heard quite enough of my problems. Let's talk about you and newspapers. My husband, Charles–Charles MacArthur–worked as a reporter here some years ago, before he moved to New York and we got married. We live up in Nyack, not too far north of Manhattan. He's back home now, working on a screenplay. When he lived in Chicago, before I knew him, he was on the *Examiner,* and also your *Tribune.* I suppose you're too young to have known him?"

I smiled. "For the record, you and I are just about the same age. I'll be thirty-six come March. But I didn't get onto the *Trib* until your husband had gone East. Of course I've seen his and Hecht's play, *The Front Page*, and I do know him as a reporter by reputation. God, the stories they still tell about him in the local room–that's what the *Trib* calls its city room. He's a legend."

"Oh?" Her eyes danced and she clapped her small hands. "What kind of stories?"

"Well…here's one, although I'm a little fuzzy on some of the details. Apparently, he was sent by the paper to a small burg over in Michigan to cover a trial. I think it was when Henry Ford sued the *Trib* over something they wrote about him that he didn't like. Anyway, so the story goes, MacArthur– your husband–commandeered a streetcar, tossed the motorman off, took the controls, and ran the thing at full speed to get to the courthouse, which sat up on a hill overlooking the town. The police chased after the trolley, so MacArthur got off at the top of the hill, took some cannonballs that were piled up next to a Civil War statue, and rolled them down on the town coppers like bowling balls, which sent the cops racing for cover while the locals stood around and cheered."

"Come to think of it, I believe Ben–Hecht that is– mentioned that episode once. To hear Ben and Charlie talk, and how they both do love to talk, those were boisterous days on the Chicago newspapers. Is it still like that?"

"I wouldn't say so. Since the Crash, everything's been, well, more serious."

"From what I've seen, that's the case just about everywhere," she said solemnly, sipping coffee as the waiter arrived with my dinner and more beer. "How did you get started in the newspaper business, Mr. Malek?"

"When I was a kid, I figured I'd be a streetcar motorman, which is what my father is and always has been, at least as far back as I can remember. But in high school, my junior year it

14

was, I volunteered for the school paper because it seemed like that's where all the good-looking girls were. And I ended up liking it, the paper, I mean, the reporting and the writing. Well, when I graduated, I knew college was out of the question. There was just no money either for me or for my sister, she's three years younger. The advisor on the school paper was impressed with my work and said he'd put in a good word with a guy he knew at the City News Bureau. That's mainly a police reporting service that the papers all use, and…"

"Oh, yes," Helen Hayes said. "I'm sure I've heard Charlie talk about the City News Bureau."

"Sure, you would have. It's been around forever, and almost every reporter in town gets his start there. Anyway, I signed on, and it was pretty rough at first. The pay is terrible, and the police out in the precincts make fun of you and play tricks like stealing your notes and things like that. But if you're serious about your work, and good at it, the coppers end up accepting you–most of them are pretty good guys, actually. And it's great training; you cover murders, auto crashes, fires, the works. Besides, putting in your time there is almost a necessity for getting a job on one of the dailies."

"What do you do at the *Tribune*?" Her eyes fastened onto me, suggesting that what I had to say was important.

"I cover police headquarters, which is down at 11th and State. I've got the day shift."

"Sounds impressive. Are you happy?"

"It's a job."

She considered me with a thoughtful expression. "You don't seem terribly enthusiastic for someone in such an exciting line of work."

Looking back on that evening, I am still surprised by how much I opened up to her. I like to think I'm good at getting other people to talk about themselves, but I hadn't talked much about my own life for several years, with reason. But here was someone–and not just anyone–who seemed genuinely interested.

"I've had better assignments than this," I told her. "I

covered both City Hall and the County Building several years ago. I don't mean to brag, but I was considered one of the top young reporters on the paper, particularly when it came to news features and human-interest stories. Then, well…I got so I was drinking more and more. It sort of snuck up on me. And I'll be honest–it affected my work."

"The newspaperman's curse," Helen Hayes pronounced sympathetically. She looked down at her coffee cup, then glanced fleetingly at my almost-empty beer glass. I'd heard enough stories about Charles MacArthur to know that he had his own demons.

"I'm real careful these days," I put in quickly. "No more of the hard stuff. None. I limit myself to beer now, and not too much of that, either. A few people have tried to get me to look into this new thing called Alcoholics Anonymous, but I don't need it. I really have cut way back."

"That's good to hear," she said with conviction. "Do you have a family?"

"I did until two years ago. A wife and a son. I'm divorced. That happened mainly because of the drinking, too."

"*Mmm*. And do they live in Chicago?"

"On the Northwest side, Logan Square. Norma works at a bank up there; she's an assistant to the head cashier, a good job. And my son, Peter, he's almost twelve, in the sixth grade. I see him weekends, usually Saturday. Except this one. He and Norma are visiting her parents over in Indiana near Fort Wayne, where she comes from. I've been telling Norma how I've cut back so much on the drinking. I'd like for us to get back together, but she has said no unless I quit totally. She's one of those who wanted me to try this 'Anonymous' thing. The others were an editor at the paper and my parents, who still live in the same building where I grew up. But like I said, I don't drink much at all anymore. I'm okay."

She gave me a nod and an understanding look. I talked some more about myself and went into detail about a few of the stories I'd covered, like the big to-do over Sally Rand and her famous fan dance at the Century of Progress World's Fair in '33 and the John Dillinger shooting outside the Biograph Theatre on Lincoln Avenue the next year. After Dillinger got gunned down by the G-men, I went up there in a cab and wrote a terrific feature, lots of color and quotes, about the mood around the movie house and how people were coming from all over town just to see the spot, even though Dillinger's body was long gone to the morgue. I even recited a few sentences from the story to Helen Hayes, who was nice enough to act like she admired the prose.

It was now well past midnight. Henrici's was almost deserted, and at the opposite end of the big dining room, busboys were putting the chairs upside down on top of the tables and mopping the floors. "I've so enjoyed myself, Mr. Malek," the actress said, reaching across the table and giving my hand a squeeze. "Thank you so much for joining me."

"I'm the one who should be doing the thanking. I barged in on you, and not only did you welcome me, you let me run off at the mouth."

That drew another of her pleasant laughs. "Ah, but you made me forget all about *The Merchant of Venice* for most of an hour, and I can't even begin to tell you how much that means. Would you be interested in seeing the performance? It may be the only one we ever do! I'll have two tickets left in your name at the Erlanger box office, but I won't guarantee the quality of the production."

"I'd be honored to go. Before I forget it, I was amazed at the way you aged–what was it, fifty years?–as Queen Victoria. How long does it take you to get all the makeup off?"

"Not as long as you'd think. But then, after all this time, I've got the routine down pretty well," she said, calling the waiter over. She asked him to give her my check.

I jumped up. "No, I can't let you do that. I want…"

"This is my treat, Mr. Malek. I really must insist."

"Miss Hayes, we have had a wonderful conversation, and you did let me run on about myself, which I appreciate. I feel really good right now, and I want to hold onto that feeling. But I can't unless I pay for my dinner. Besides, you have already offered me two free tickets, which I plan to use."

"I won't try to argue with that logic," she answered merrily. "And I certainly don't want to risk losing a potential member of the audience. There may be few enough of you in the theater as it is."

"I don't believe that for a minute," I answered as we rose to leave. "A dollar says you get great reviews."

"No bet! I wouldn't put it past you to bribe your own paper's critic–Charley Collins, isn't it–just to win the wager."

We continued bantering as we got our coats from the girl in the checkroom, who was glad to see us leave. Realizing for the first time how short she was, I helped Helen Hayes with her coat. At that moment, I felt very much the bon vivant. Even Emil eyed me with respect, albeit grudging, I'm sure. "Where are you staying?" I asked her.

"The Palmer House. It's a nice, short walk, and I need the exercise."

"Only on the condition that I escort you as far as the lobby," I insisted. "I will not have a national treasure walking our rough, dark streets alone after the witching hour."

"A handsome speech, sir, but State Street is hardly rough and certainly not dark," she riposted. "However, I shall welcome the company."

So it was that I strolled south along State Street with America's most famous stage actress on my arm. I would have liked to run into someone I knew at that moment, but I had to settle for the beat cop at State and Washington, who touched the brim of his cap when we passed. "Evening, Miss Hayes," he said, beaming.

"Good evening, Mr. Garrity," she responded with a mock formality. "Pleasant night for the season, don't you think?" When we were beyond his hearing range, she turned and winked up at me. "See, I'm perfectly safe. I have friends in high places."

"I'm impressed."

"As well you should be. By the way, that hat makes you look very debonair."

"Thanks, it's new. I like hats a lot. Almost always wear one. That's how I got my nickname, 'Snap,' as in snap-brim. As I like to say, a man is known for what's on his head as well as what's in it."

"I can't decide whether that is glib or just plain corny. Probably both," she concluded.

"Probably," I agreed. I felt agreeable. "You've surely heard this a thousand times, but I thought you were wonderful in *A Farewell to Arms*. I saw it right here in the Loop, in '32, I think it was."

"Mr. Malek, most of us who work in the theater and in films never tire of hearing praise. I know I certainly don't. I adored making that picture, and I thought it turned out well, never mind that Mr. Hemingway grumbled about the ending. Working with Gary Cooper was grand–especially the love scenes. Oh, my! I truly believe I was envied by the entire female population of Hollywood, and that included Hedda Hopper and Luella Parsons!" We both laughed.

"You know, I have come to enjoy this city so much," she said, turning to look up and down State, with its department stores looming on both sides, their darkened hulks interrupted by the lights of an occasional bar or restaurant, plus the marquee of the Roosevelt Theatre. "The people are so warm and friendly here; they don't seem to have a lot of pretensions. But I know it's got a reputation as a brawling gangster town, or at least it did, to hear Charlie and Ben go on about it. Is that the case now, too?"

"There are still plenty of gangsters around, God knows, and plenty of rackets, too. But these guys today are nowhere near as flamboyant as they were before Prohibition got repealed. Most of them, at least the smart ones, try to avoid notoriety now. We–the press, I mean–still try to make them sound more legendary and colorful than they really are. We even tag them with nicknames, or at least take the names somebody else gave them and make sure we always use them in print. Like Jake 'Greasy Thumb' Guzik, Murray 'The Camel' Humphreys, Hymie 'Loud Mouth' Levine. But honestly, most of these guys are lowlifes…nothing more than bums."

"I'm not surprised to hear that. Still, there's quite a history, isn't there? Here's one story I can tell *you*. Several years ago, when Charlie and I were living in Manhattan, we threw a small party for our daughter Mary's first birthday. Charlie had told some of our guests that Al Capone was going to show up. When they learned it was just another one of his gags, everybody laughed it off except an Italian opera singer named Lucrezia Bori, who had really believed Capone was going to be there. She was angry, and to calm her, Charlie somehow got hold of Capone's number in Chicago and telephoned him. It turned out that Capone was a big fan of Lucrezia and her singing, but he wouldn't believe she was on the line until she sang an aria. She did, and then Capone knew it was her and everybody was happy."

"That's quite a story," I told her as we got to the hotel and went through the revolving door into the lower lobby.

"I'll never forget that evening," Helen Hayes said. "And this has been a very pleasant evening, too, Mr. Steven 'Snap' Malek. You are engaging company, and I wish you the best in your work and in your personal life. By the way, on top of everybody else you've met in your interesting life, I don't suppose you knew Al Capone, too, did you?"

My answer was a smile, and we shook hands like old friends in the lower lobby of the Palmer House.

CHAPTER 2

I knew Al Capone.

In March of '34, the year Dillinger got killed, I was at my desk one morning in the County Building pressroom working the *Examiner* crossword puzzle when I got a call from Michael J. Ahern, who was in the café across the street and wanted me to join him. When I asked why I was being so honored, he cryptically replied, "I'll tell you when you get here. And I promise you won't find it a waste of your time."

"Iron Mike" Ahern had been the lead defense attorney in Capone's well-publicized federal tax trial three years earlier, and I was one of the *Tribune* team covering the trial. My assignment was to do color pieces–human-interest stuff, like describing the courtroom, the judge's mood, how many jurors fell asleep (the record was three in one session), who of note was in the audience, and so forth.

One day the British actress, Beatrice Lillie, in Chicago to be in a stage play, showed up in court and stayed most of the afternoon. When she left, I caught up with her in the hall and was pleased with the quotes I got for the next day's edition. Among them: "I thought the whole proceedings lacked passion" and "I was a bit put out that Judge Wilkerson didn't have one of those powdered wigs like they do back home–I think he would have looked adorable in one."

I was a damn sight less pleased when the *American* carried almost the same quotes, along with reproductions of sketches–good sketches–that Miss Lillie had drawn of Capone, the judge, and the state's attorney. To quote my father, "Never trust a limey."

I had of course gotten to know Mike Ahern during the weeks of the trial. He was natty, urbane, and always ready with good quotes and historical or literary references. He knew what made for good copy, and in the courtroom had once described Capone as "a modern mythical Robin Hood, a creation of the newspapers." On another occasion, he used the name of the Roman soldier and statesman Cato to underscore a point he was driving home. Nevertheless, I always felt he and his partner, Albert Fink, had done a second-rate job of defending Capone.

I hadn't seen Ahern since Capone got sentenced, but I recognized him through the haze when I entered the café, a favorite hangout of lawyers and politicians, even though he was in the booth farthest from the front. In his vested pinstripe, he was easily the best-dressed patron in the place, and possibly the most distinguished-looking, too. With his well-tended hair, rimless glasses, and benign expression, he could have passed for a Presbyterian minister at a very large and very prosperous North Shore church. But he was by no means a ministerial type.

"Mr. Malek, thank you so much for taking time out of your busy schedule," he said amiably, rising to shake my hand. "And so good to see you again, you're looking well. Sit down, sit down. Care for some breakfast? I'm about to order eggs and sausage. As I'm sure you know from working across the street, the link sausage here is absolutely the best in the Loop. Maybe in the whole city, for that matter."

"Coffee is fine for me, thanks, Counselor. Haven't been hearing much about you lately. You still making a career out of defending the indefensible, the vicious, and the venal?"

"Ah, Mr. Malek, you have not changed an iota since last we met. Still as tart-tongued and outspoken as ever. As to your question: Would you, a member in good standing of the Fourth Estate and as such a supposed defender of our Federal Constitution and the American system of jurisprudence, honestly deny legal representation for any citizen?"

"I'm all for giving everybody the opportunity of legal representation, Counselor. But here's what interests me about your clientele: maybe it's coincidence, but you often seem to have mobsters as clients."

Ahern spread his arms, palms up, and looked at the ceiling. "It was George Barrow who said 'Follow your calling, however various your talents may be.' Mr. Malek, what humble talents have been bestowed upon me by the Almighty seem best suited to defending those whom society has chosen to damn as members of the underworld–often without reason or adequate evidence for making such a judgment. These men, many among the most earnest and hard-working members of the populace, are entitled to an adequate defense in our courts, which I try to provide to the best of my limited abilities."

"You know, I could listen to you go on like that all day, even if at least eighty percent of it is bilge," I told him, grinning. "You could charm the hard-earned shillings out of a Scotsman's purse. But as you mentioned earlier yourself, I have a busy schedule. To what do I owe this summons?"

Ahern shot his cuffs, crossed his arms on the table, and leaned forward, looking at me intently. "It has to do with Alphonse," he said, lowering his voice despite all the babel around us.

"One of your better-known cases," I remarked dryly. "You still in touch with Capone? I thought he was pissed off at you and Fink after the way you handled–or mishandled–his tax trial."

The lawyer colored slightly and cleared his throat. "I think Alphonse has come to the awareness that defending him was a more difficult task than he realized. Not long ago, he hired a supposedly high-powered Washington attorney named Leahy to get him out of prison, and Mr. Leahy failed. And now…well, he has rehired our firm."

"For what? Does he want you to help him tunnel his way out of the big house down in Atlanta?"

"Oddly enough, he's trying to do precisely the opposite," the lawyer remarked, dropping his theatrical tone. "I assume that you've read about the new maximum-security prison the federal government is planning to open later this year out in San Francisco?"

"Out on that island?"

Ahern nodded gravely. "It's called Alcatraz, which is Spanish for 'the Isle of Pelicans.' And I also assume you've heard via your very efficient grapevine that Alphonse may be headed for the new penitentiary."

"You assume correctly, Counselor. I've also heard the feds are sore because ol' Scarface has too damn much freedom down in Atlanta, which is embarrassing for them. They want to rein him in, or so the word is."

"Nonsense!" Ahern barked, slapping a palm on the tabletop. "He has been a model prisoner, no trouble for anybody. You must have figured out it's that goddamn publicity-seeking warden, Johnston, who's setting up Alcatraz; he wants to build a reputation for the place and for himself. To do that, he needs big-name inmates, stars you might call them, and what bigger star is there than one Alphonse Capone?"

"Interesting," I said, sipping coffee. "And just why are you bothering to tell me all this?"

Ahern leaned forward and lowered his voice once more. "Alphonse, not surprisingly, doesn't want to go to this Alcatraz. And for that matter, the warden down in Atlanta doesn't particularly want to see him go."

"Of course not. Having Capone there gives the place some status. The Atlanta turnkey doesn't want to lose that cachet to some upstart hoosegow out on the West Coast. I think Al should be flattered–everybody wants him as a house guest."

"Mr. Malek, Alphonse respects you, he trusts you," Ahern said, shifting gears smoothly to his courtroom-earnest voice.

"What the hell are you talking about?" I shot back. "We don't even know each other. We've never met, not even once."

"He remembers you from his trial," Ahern persisted. "He always thought you were fair to him, unlike the other reporters who went out of their way to be insulting and derogatory in their stories. You know what he said during the trial, he said 'That *Tribune* kid is OK.' And, Mr. Malek, he repeated those very words last week when I saw him in Atlanta, those very words." The lawyer leaned back and folded his hands across his vested chest as if having just scored a major point in court. I was not impressed.

"In the first place, Counselor, I doubt very much that Capone ever knew who I was. Second, I find it hard to believe that he referred to me as 'kid'–I don't believe he's even three years older than I am. And third, he hated the *Tribune* and Colonel McCormick so much that I can't believe he'd ever have anything good to say about anybody at the paper."

"Wrong on all counts," Ahern countered. "One, he read every word about the trial in all of the Chicago papers, and knew all the bylines–he can still name all of the reporters. Two, he calls a lot of people 'kid,' regardless of their age. And three, he may dislike the *Tribune* and its owner as you suggest, but he's smart enough to know that it employs many good people."

"All right, for the sake of moving this conversation along, I'll stipulate those points. So?"

"Mr. Malek, I am about to offer you the journalistic coup of the decade, perhaps of the century. As I said, I was in Atlanta last week visiting Alphonse. Although he bravely claims, to use his own words, that 'the fix is in' in his favor and that he'll never be sent to Alcatraz, I know him well enough to realize he's terrified of the possibility that he may land on that new Devil's Island. And as I said, the warden down in Atlanta doesn't much like the idea either. But both of them are willing to let you–and no one else–interview Alphonse face-to-face for up to two hours so that he can talk about what his life is like in the Atlanta penitentiary."

I hadn't seen that coming and it knocked me off balance, something that rarely happens. Capone was famous for his hatred of the press and for not sitting still for interviews. I lit a Lucky and studied Michael Ahern, saying nothing for a half-minute or more while I rearranged my thoughts.

"So I'm supposed to go down there and write this fairy tale about how Alphonse Capone has transmogrified into a choirboy who is an asset to the great Atlanta penitentiary, right? And the public, which of course adores Scarface, will be so delighted to learn of his rehabilitation in Georgia that they will rise up *en masse* and march on Washington and every other major city protesting any attempt to move him to this new hellhole in San Francisco Bay? A brilliant plan, Counselor. Absolutely brilliant."

Ahern flashed a sardonic smile. "You have a way of placing the worst possible interpretation upon an opportunity."

"Nah, I'm just a realist. I've been around people like you long enough to have developed what is commonly termed a healthy skepticism. You say Capone specifically asked for me on this so-called story? I don't know whether to be flattered or insulted, but I'm leaning toward the latter. Why don't you request a sob sister? Every paper in town has at least one on the staff, including us, and they're perfect for this kind of thing. God, any one of them could wring so much emotion out of this assignment that there'd be a run on the handkerchief counter at the Boston Store."

"If you weren't so maddening, you would actually be quite entertaining," Ahern said, undaunted by my reaction and maintaining his beatific smile. "Mr. Malek, it's you or nobody on this story–I repeat that Alphonse specifically requested you. And I have to wonder how your editors up in Tribune Tower would respond if they learned that one of their veteran reporters turned down a chance to interview the most famous inmate in the world. I myself would not want to be on the receiving end of what most surely would be a strong reaction."

The city editor's eyes bored in on me through black-rimmed glasses. "Let me make sure I've got this straight, Malek," Bob Lee snarled from behind the desk in his cluttered office just off the *Tribune's* two-story local room. "Mike Ahern guarantees you an interview with Capone, and the warden actually goes along with the idea? Sounds wacky to me. Do they actually think any kind of a story, no matter how sympathetic, could keep that thug from becoming a charter member of Club Alcatraz?"

"Ahern seems to think so, although it sounds crazy to me, too."

"Ahern!" Lee brushed him aside with a hand and a sneer. "He and Albert Fink couldn't keep Capone out of jail. Besides, does he actually think you'd write the kind of piece that he and Capone want?"

"He couldn't have gotten that idea from anything I said to him. What bothers me is that they both must think I'm inherently sympathetic to Capone."

"Well, you're a decent writer, I'll give you that, and you're balanced—at least you certainly were during the trial—so they probably feel that you'd give that scum a fair shake in print, which you would," Lee commented in a rare burst of praise. "You know, what we've got here is one hell of an opportunity. And we'd be crazy to pass it up, right?"

"Right!" I echoed, heart pounding.

"Wait here," Lee said, jangling the keys on his chain, which he always did when he was agitated. "I'm going to see Mr. Beck." He went out to the square center desk in the midst of the local room's pandemonium, where the top editors sat, one on each of its four sides, manning phones, reading galley proofs, shouting for copy boys, and otherwise directing the flow of news as it came in from reporters in Chicago, the Middle West, and around the world.

The city editor leaned down to talk to one of the four, a distinguished-looking gray-haired man in shirtsleeves and suspenders. This was Edward Scott Beck, the managing editor, who had ruled the *Tribune's* news operations for twenty years and was a symbol, at least to most of the reporters I knew, of dignity, honor, and good, if conservative, news judgment. As I watched from Lee's alcove of an office, Beck rose and the two men, their heads nearly touching, talked for several minutes, both occasionally glancing in my direction.

Finally, Lee nodded and returned to his office. "Mr. Beck gave his approval," he said. "But he had several thoughts about this venture and so do I. Take notes."

And that is how I came to occupy a bedroom on the Dixie

Flyer as it pulled out of Dearborn Station for Atlanta a little before midnight on the first Wednesday of April in 1934, with Mike Ahern occupying an adjoining bedroom. My instructions from Beck, as relayed by Bob Lee, had been simple and basic: Talk to Capone for as long as I was allowed and learn as much as I could about his existence as an inmate for the last two years, as well as asking about his overall reflections on his life. Lee was diplomatic enough not to lecture me about being taken in by the man's supposed charm–not that I would have been anyway. And although neither he nor Beck were happy about Ahern's insistence that he go along to pave the way, they accepted the condition as long as the *Tribune* paid all the expenses, Ahern's as well as mine

To my surprise, I was glad for the velvet-tongued lawyer's company on the long ride into the Deep South. Both in the lounge car and the diner, he played the raconteur with flair and relish, describing cases he had tried and characters–underworld and otherwise–he had come to know and represent in court. But he didn't want to talk about Capone. "You don't need me prejudicing you one way or the other about Alphonse," was his reply to my queries.

The train pulled into Atlanta in the evening, and we went straight to the Dinkler Plaza Hotel downtown. The next morning after breakfast, a chauffeured black LaSalle that Ahern had hired–and that I insisted having the *Tribune* pay for–took us through a steady rain to the great gray federal penitentiary southeast of town.

Once inside, we passed through several sets of barred or solid steel barriers, at least two of which slid open by electricity, and after being patted down for weapons, were ushered into the office of a deputy warden whose name I almost immediately forgot. I learned that the warden himself, probably not wanting to be directly associated with my visit, had traveled to Washington on what his assistant termed "official prison business."

The deputy warden, a prim-looking specimen with a bald head and a pince-nez, sat behind his desk and favored Ahern and me with a dour expression. After we sat, he cleared his throat, cleared it again, and pulled some sheets from his center drawer, then began reading from one: "I, Steven Malek, an employee of the *Chicago Tribune*, have been allowed precisely two hours with inmate number four-zero-eight-eight-six. I understand that said inmate and I will be in one of the private visitation rooms, with a guard present throughout. I also understand that the guard is not there to eavesdrop on our conversation, but that he has express instructions to prevent the passage of any object between said inmate and me. I also understand that if I attempt to pass to, or receive from, said inmate any object whatever, my visit shall at that moment be terminated."

The deputy warden gingerly placed the sheets on his blotter and cleared his throat again. "Mr. Malek, do you fully comprehend what I have read, and do you agree to the conditions?"

"I do."

"Then please sign both the original and the two carbon copies and date them where indicated," he droned, pushing the three sheets across the desk along with a pen. "One of the carbons will be given to you for your files upon your departure from the premises."

After I had signed all three, the turnkey checked my John Hancocks, slid the sheets back into the drawer, and rose. More throat clearing. "You may see the inmate now. Mr. Ahern, you may wait in the visitors' lounge down the hall, where there are newspapers and magazines. The guard just outside the door will direct you."

Ahern gave me a thumbs-up, and I followed the deputy warden through a labyrinth of gray-walled and shadowy corridors. After making several right-angle turns, we came to a steel door, next to which a uniformed guard stood, hands behind his back. "He's inside now?" the turnkey asked, and when the guard said yes, the bald man nodded curtly.

The guard turned a handle, pulled the door open, and gestured for me to enter. The room's walls were as gray and blank as those in the corridors, and the only pieces of furniture on the concrete floor–also gray–were a square wooden table, maple and about five feet on a side, and two straight-backed wooden chairs that looked like they had descended from the same tree as the table. In one of these chairs, facing me, sat Alphonse Capone.

He gave me a half smile as I walked toward the table, then nodded as I took the chair opposite him. "Yeah, kid…you're the one all right," he said in that husky voice. "I told Ahern I remembered you from the courtroom, even your name. How ya doin'?"

He was as I remembered him in the courtroom–arrogant, round-faced, thick-lipped, balding, flat-nosed, and with those probing gray eyes hooded by dark, thick brows. And, of course, the feature that gave him his moniker, that famous scar on his left cheek running from ear to jaw. His body, however, seemed shrunken within the blue prison denims, although maybe that was because I had previously seen him only at the defense table, and then wearing perfectly fitted suits that covered the color spectrum, including purple, light green, and even yellow.

"Y'know, kid, having you come down here was Ahern's idea," Capone rasped, lowering his eyes and throwing a glance in the direction of the guard, who had silently entered the room behind me and was standing, back to the door, some fifteen feet away. "Says the word's out they're gonna send me to that new island pen out in California, but I'm tellin' you now, it ain't gonna happen. Besides, he's tryin' to get in good with me after the way he and Fink screwed up my trial."

He leaned his thick arms on the table. "I shouldn't even be in here, y'know. But what can ya expect when a whole community's prejudiced against ya?" I've given the public what it wants. I've spent my best years as a public benefactor. Y'see, ninety percent of the people of Chicago and Cook County drink and gamble, right? And my offense is that I gave them amusements. So how do I get repaid? Shit, I'll tell ya; I get blamed for everything bad that happens anyplace near

Chicago, that's how. I been blamed for crimes that happened as far back as the Chicago Fire. The reason I'm in here–the rotten bastards set me up, including your goddamn Colonel McCormick at the *Trib,* never mind that I helped him when his circulation drivers was gonna strike back in '28. I got those guys back in line, and McCormick thanked me personally, told me I was famous–like Babe Ruth, he said." Capone seemed to puff up as he recalled the incident.

"I got nothin' against your paper now, or even against that mush-mouthed old colonel of yours. And by the way, kid, I was clean on the Lingle rubout, too. I liked the guy." He was referring to a *Tribune* reporter, Jake Lingle, who supposedly had ties to the syndicate and who got shot dead in a downtown pedestrian tunnel in 1930.

I didn't believe him about Lingle, but I didn't give a damn whether what he said was true or not. I felt strangely, eerily, detached, as if I were hovering somewhere outside looking in at this cubicle and its three figures: cop, crook, and snoop.

"Ah, hell, that's enough history," Capone said when I didn't respond to his Lingle pronouncement. "Hey, how's things in Chicago, kid? How are the Cubs gonna do this year?"

"So-so, maybe third place. Giants and Cardinals both look too good for them," I said.

"Yeah, those damn Cards with them hillbilly Dean brothers they got. How the hell did they learn to pitch like that down in the backwoods?" Capone gave a chuckle and slapped a beefy paw on the table. "Aw, you didn't come down here to talk about baseball, didja? Okay, maybe Ahern's not so dumb after all. Like I said, it's a sure bet that I ain't goin' to that Alcatraz place, but maybe it's not such a bad idea to hedge the bet anyway. You were okay at the trial, didn't insult me like that other guy the *Trib* had there or those bastards from the Hearst rags, they were the worst. So Ahern says maybe a story on me, on how I'm doin' down here, might be a good thing right now."

He leaned forward on his hairy arms, eyes fastened on me. "What do *you* think, kid?" The words were more than a question, less than a threat.

I met his gaze. "I think a good feature story on you would get more readership than a Presidential assassination or another Lindbergh flight," I said evenly. "You're still big news in Chicago, and across the country for that matter. Even around the world. Everybody wants to know about you."

"That right?" He was puffing himself up again, but struggling to not show his pleasure.

I decided to lay it on even thicker, as it seemed to be working. "Absolutely. I get asked about you all the time, damn near every day, because I spent all that time at the trial. People really want to know what life is like for you here."

"Okay, then, let's tell 'em, dammit," he said with relish, shifting in his chair and leaning on the table with one elbow. "Start askin' stuff."

I flipped open my reporter's notebook and took out a pencil. "First off, do other inmates ever try to get tough with you?"

He guffawed and thumped his chest with a fist. "If they do, kid, it's only once–Alphonse here can still take care of himself."

"So this means fights? And if so, with knuckles, or knives? And…"

For almost two hours, I posed questions about every aspect of prison life I could think of, including Capone's work as a cobbler of shoes and his newfound interest in tennis, a sport he had taken up in prison. Capone answered most of them directly, except when I asked about special privileges. At least twice, he paused and either shook his head or tried to change the subject by giving me a colorful anecdote about some other inmate, such as Lefty Scaldo, the one-armed bank robber and former minor-league baseball player who pitched for the prison team and once hit a home run, so Capone claimed, that cleared the outer wall of the prison yard, a blast reckoned at 400 feet. "His only arm's bigger'n a goddamn tree trunk," he said, holding up his palm as if to give an oath.

Halfway through the session, lunch was brought in for

both of us on metal trays–beef brisket, boiled potatoes, green peas, apple pie wedge, coffee. It was passable, although Capone muttered something about "lousy stir grub." That attitude didn't keep him from finishing everything, however.

Near the end of my allotted time, I got more pointed–and daring–with my queries. "So, do you keep in touch with any of your old associates?" I asked.

"What old associates?" Capone's tone hardened.

I shrugged with what I hoped was nonchalance. "Oh, the guys you were in business with over the years–Nitti, Torrio, Lucciano, Schultz."

"Don't know anything about 'em anymore, not a thing," he snarled.

"You mean you don't ever…"

"Goddamn it, I said I don't know 'em anymore, are you deaf? That's not what this interview was supposed to be about." He rose, flexing his big shoulders, and nodded at the guard. "I'm done, got to get back to the cobbler shop," he barked. "So long, kid."

"So long. And good luck," I told him, although a wall had formed between us, and he gave no indication that he had heard me. And I didn't care.

I was escorted back to the deputy warden's office. He looked up from his desk when I entered. "Ah, yes, Mr. Malek, how did your visit go?" he asked, expressionless.

"Okay. Before I go, I'd like to see Capone's cell."

He pursed his lips. "I'm afraid that's impossible. Against regulations, you understand. Sorry."

"Yeah, well at least I'd like to get a quote from you about what kind of prisoner he's been."

The deputy warden raised his eyebrows, which for him was an animated gesture. Ah, now that I can help you with, yes I can, yes sir. The warden anticipated your desire in this matter, and he has prepared a statement solely for you. Yes he has." He reached into a drawer and pulled out a sheet, handing it across. Typewritten and double-spaced on Atlanta Penitentiary letterhead, it was a single paragraph: "Since he has been in the Atlanta facility, Alphonse Capone has shown himself to be respectful and peaceable. He works diligently in the cobbler shop and gets along well with his fellow inmates. He obeys every order when it is given."

Beneath the statement was the warden's signature. "Do you have anything you want to add to this?" I asked his underling.

"Oh, no, no, the warden has very nicely summarized the situation," he said, handing me a carbon copy of the agreement I had signed earlier. He rose to bid me goodbye.

On the way back into Atlanta in the chauffeured car, Mike Ahern tried to pump me about the interview, but my responses were noncommittal. He kept at me on the train home as well, until I finally closeted myself in my bedroom. Actually, I had planned to stay in my room on the trip north, anyway. I took out the portable Royal I'd brought, and as the train steamed north through the Appalachian night toward Chicago, I wrote the first draft of my article, then a second, and finally a third. When we pulled into Dearborn Station in the morning, I'd gotten only two hours' sleep but had wrestled the article into the shape I wanted it.

The editors apparently agreed, because the piece ran at the bottom of Page One three days later under the headline EXCLUSIVE–OUR REPORTER VISITS CAPONE IN PRISON! And nobody messed much with what I wrote, either. My lead was a single sentence: "I had lunch with Al Capone last Friday."

I went on from there to describe his physical condition and mannerisms, and to quote him on his daily routine ("I'm just an ordinary guy here"), his living conditions ("Hell, I've got seven cellmates, nothin' special about me"), his fears ("I'm nobody's prisoner when I'm asleep, sleeping is like escaping"), and his claims on unjust imprisonment.

Jack Stewart, another *Tribune* police reporter, had located a guy who'd just gotten out of Atlanta, and he wrote a sidebar to my piece anonymously quoting this ex-con, who painted a different picture of Capone's life behind bars. "Ah, he's livin' like a king down there, and don't let nobody tell you otherwise. Sure, he's in an eight-man cell, that's true enough, but he's got everything there–two rugs, mirror, typewriter, tennis gear, alarm clock, and even a whole set of that *Encyclopaedia Britannica*. Let me tell you about the privileges he gets…"

Together, the articles got plenty of reaction–lots of letters to the paper, most of them angry that Capone was living so well, but others from people who actually felt sorry for him. About a week after the pieces ran, I got a call at my desk in the County Building pressroom from Bob Lee, telling me to come over to the office immediately.

"What for?" I asked. I set foot in Tribune Tower as little as possible–too much internal politics.

"Never mind what for!" Lee barked. "Just get over here now. Take a taxi and expense it."

I was in Lee's office fifteen minutes later. "I told you before that was a helluva job you did on the Capone thing," the crusty city editor snarled. "Mr. Beck thought so too–called it the single best piece of writing the paper's had all year. Don't know that I'd go that far myself, but anyway the Colonel wants to see you right now."

"Geez, why?"

"Malek, I don't know why. I'm just the damned messenger here. But I do know that when the Colonel wants to see someone, he wants him *right then*. Better get your ass upstairs."

I had never met Colonel Robert R. McCormick, only seen him at a distance once or twice when he came down to the local room to talk to Beck. As I rode the elevator to the rarified altitude of the 24th floor, I turned over the possibilities: He was going to reward me for the story. He was going to can me for being too easy on someone he detested. He was going to have me demoted to working nights. He was going to…

The elevator doors opened onto a paneled, carpeted reception area bigger than most living rooms, and some ballrooms. I gave my name to a pleasant-looking woman with blonde, marcelled hair who was sitting behind a mahogany desk. She spoke a few words into a phone, then smiled at me and gestured toward a paneled door. "Go right on in, he's expecting you," she said, her voice barely above a whisper in keeping with the sedate surroundings.

I felt as if I'd wandered into somebody's castle, and I suppose in a sense I had. The office had high, coffered ceilings, dark paneling, a chandelier, and a fireplace, and it could have held six pool tables with room to spare. On the windowsill were several sculptures, including a bust of Lincoln. At the far end, working at an oversized desk with a polished marble or granite top, and with a German shepherd dozing on the carpet beside him, was Colonel Robert Rutherford McCormick, editor, publisher, and, so I always assumed, sole owner of the *Chicago Tribune.* As I approached, he looked up from his paperwork and nodded off-handedly. He had a full head of white hair and, in his tweed, vested suit, he looked like my conception of an English nobleman, although I was aware that he detested almost everything about the English, their country, and their culture.

"Mr. Malek," he said, and I immediately understood why Capone had called him mush-mouthed. "Sit down, sit down." He indicated a chair facing his desk. I sat.

"Read your article on Al Capone last week. Most interesting."

"Thank you, sir."

"Never liked the fellow, you know. Bad for the city, very bad. He tried to muscle in when we were negotiating with the circulation drivers years ago. I ordered him out of the room and told him to take his plug-uglies with him. I also suggested later to the federal law enforcement people that the way to get Capone into jail was through his failure to pay income taxes. And they listened to me."

I tried to swallow, but my mouth was too dry. "So I understand, sir." Actually, I understood the story somewhat differently, but this did not seem like the time or the place to refute the McCormick version.

"But whether I like the man or not is totally beside the

point," the Colonel continued, reaching down to stroke the German shepherd. "The *Tribune* always deals fairly with everyone."

"Yes, sir," I responded, curious as to where we were heading.

"And you, Mr. Malek, have proven to be a paragon in that regard. Your interview with Capone was sensitive and even-handed, not to mention extremely well-written. You brought out the human side of the man and made no judgments about him. I like that. Further, Mr. Beck tells me that almost no rewriting was necessary. He also says this high caliber typifies much of your work."

"Thank you, sir."

"Mr. Malek, it is I who thank you on behalf of the *Tribune* and its readership, and please accept this as a token of the newspaper's gratitude." He handed me an envelope with my name typed on it. It was unsealed, so I reached in and pulled out a company check for $200, made out and signed by R.R. McCormick.

"I'm…I really appreciate this," I sputtered, standing and trying to string together the words to thank him. Two hundred was more than I made in a month. The Colonel had turned his attention back to the papers on his desk, clearly dismissing me, so I rose and pivoted to leave. But I could see no door–the entire wall surface of the big room was paneled in wood. I went to two of them and pushed, but they were solid. I turned back to the Colonel, but his head was down; he was signing papers.

I looked around the room again, baffled. Without looking up, he spoke. "Kick the plate."

"What?"

"Kick the plate."

I finally spotted it. One panel had an unobtrusive metal plate at floor level. I nudged the plate with my toe, and the panel swung silently open. As I turned to look back at the man, who was still concentrating on his paper, I thought that I heard a low chuckle.

However well done my interview with Capone may have been—and it was damn well done—it didn't let him avoid the dreaded Isle of Pelicans. According to James Bennett, director of the U.S. Bureau of Prisons, he had become "too big a problem for our officers in Atlanta to handle." Late in the summer of 1934, Alphonse Capone became one of the 53 "incorrigibles" given the signal honor of becoming the first inmates in the new federal penitentiary in San Francisco Bay known as Alcatraz.

Chapter 3

Logan Square...I've never completely gotten used to going back. At the start, just after I moved out, I wasn't surprised that my stomach tightened up every time I rounded the corner and turned into what had for almost ten years been referred to by Norma and me as "our block." But that feeling had never gone away, never diminished in all the times–it must be close to a hundred times now–that I've gone back to the apartment to pick Peter up for our times together on weekends. And it was no different on this second Saturday morning of the new year–the dryness in my throat, the perspiration even in freezing weather, the urge for one last Lucky Strike, even just a few puffs.

I climbed the eight concrete steps to the door of the brick two-flat and rang the upper bell with the typewritten N. MALEK under it. The buzzer sounded, unlocking the door, and I walked up the carpeted stairs, which squeaked in all the usual places. Norma was silhouetted in the doorway at the top, also as usual.

"Hello, Steve," she said. "Peter's been talking about the museum for three days now."

"Glad to hear it," I answered, thinking how good she looked in the brown housedress with white trim on the collar and sleeves, which I had never seen. "How've you been?"

"Fine, fine." She nodded and brushed a strand of auburn hair from her cheek as she backed into the living room. "And my folks are well, too. Dad's back at the plant on a regular schedule again; the doctor says his heart is strong, that he could easily live to be 90 despite the stroke."

"I'm glad to hear that, I really am. He's one heckuva guy. You said hello to both of them like I asked?"

"Just like you asked. And they said to wish you a happy new year. Oh, and Peter could hardly wait to get home to start playing with that Erector set you gave him. It's his favorite Christmas present, by far. He really loves it. But now he says he has to have more girders, whatever they are."

I laughed. "Yeah, I figured that was going to happen. I should have given him a larger set. Me, I had a nice quiet New Year's Eve," I volunteered.

"We did, too. But then, so does everybody back home, as I know you recall. We listened to the midnight countdown on the radio, Peter too, and we played 'Twenty Questions' and were all in bed by 1:00."

"No surprise there. I did have one interesting thing happen myself last Saturday, which was New Year's night," I said, pausing for effect. "I had dinner with Helen Hayes."

"Helen Hayes!" Norma's brown eyes widened. "*You* and Helen Hayes? Only the two of you?"

"Yep, only us chickens. At Henrici's. I'd gone to a movie, and I just ran into her there, after her play."

She put her hands on her hips and shook her head in wonderment, smiling. "Steve Malek, you've been 'just running into people' all your life. You really are something, do you know that?"

I returned the smile. "It must be that essential brashness of mine, as somebody I know once termed it. But just so that you know, I was very much the gentleman."

"How could you be anything else with Helen Hayes, for heaven's sake? She'd even bring out the gentleman in that gorilla over at Lincoln Park Zoo–what's his name again?"

"Bushman. And thanks a lot for the comparison." Norma and I hadn't had such a lighthearted bit of conversation since the divorce, and it made me feel good, very good. I almost asked her to have dinner with me sometime, but I felt this wasn't the time, not yet. "Where's Peter?"

"In his room–where else–with that Erector set. I'll get him."

"No, I will. I know the way, remember?" I went through

a dark living room too filled with furniture and memories and down a corridor past our–Norma's–bedroom to Peter's room at the back of the flat. He was sitting cross-legged on the floor fastening a nut onto a bolt near the top of a three-foot tower of miniature steel beams. "Looks a lot like the Parachute Jump at Riverview," I remarked approvingly from the doorway.

"Oh, hi, Dad," he said over his shoulder. "This set is really super, except I'm running out of girders." He stood up, grinning. He was short for his age, and he had Norma's brown eyes, which was a lot better than getting stuck with my watery blue ones. His light brown hair, which stuck up something like Dagwood's in the *Blondie* comic strip, was somewhere between hers and mine in color.

"Tell you what, you've got a birthday in April. We'll make sure you get some then. Think you can wait that long?"

He nodded thoughtfully. "I guess so. Sure. Are we going to the museum now?"

"That's the plan, my man. Get your cap and coat. We've got places to go and things to do."

Peter loved riding the streetcars, so the day was off to a fine start. We needed to transfer twice to get to the Field Museum out on the Lakefront, and he kept his nose pressed against the window for the forty-five minutes it took: east on Diversey, transfer, then south on Clark and transfer again to the line that runs all the way out into Grant Park. "Dad, remember the time I spent the whole day with Grandpa on his streetcar?" he asked as we walked up the long flight of steps at the museum entrance.

"I sure do. He and I both figured you'd get bored silly riding for that long. But you fooled us."

"Uh-huh. We went all the way down to the end of the Western Avenue line and back again a bunch of times, maybe four. And Grandpa even let me put up the trolley pole when we changed directions."

"Yeah, I remember him telling me how good you were at that. Well, you ready to see some mummies now?" His sixth-grade class was studying Egypt, and Peter had gotten enthusiastic about the pyramids and the mummies and how people lived along the Nile thousands of years ago. The class had made one field trip to the museum already to see the Egypt exhibits, but they didn't stay long enough to suit him. He could really get interested in his studies, unlike me when I was in school. He took after Norma in that respect.

"You have a good time in Indiana?" I asked him two hours later as we ate ham sandwiches with dill pickles and peach pie in the museum cafeteria.

"Uh-huh, it was okay," he said with his mouth full. "The train ride was really neat. We took the Pennsylvania Railroad, and Grandpa and Grandma met us at Fort Wayne. On the way there, Mama and I had lunch in the diner, and they gave us these funny little silver dishes to wash our hands in before we ate."

"Yeah, finger bowls. Didn't drink out of yours, did you?"

He laughed. "Hey, that's a good joke, Dad. Mama had told me what they were for."

"Sure, she would have. Are you taking good care of your Mama?" This was a question I asked each time we were together.

His expression now serious, Peter nodded. "I just wish she didn't have to work so hard. I think I'm the only one in our class whose mom works."

"Well, she has a pretty important job at the bank," I reminded him. "Is she home when you get back from school?"

"Most of the time. But she has to work on Saturdays, you know. She waits until you come to pick me up, then she leaves." I knew; she had worked Saturdays at the bank even when we were together.

"Is she still seeing Mr. Baer?" This was a question I rarely asked him.

"Uh-huh," he said, concentrating on his sandwich.

Then a question I had never asked: "Do you like him?"

"He's okay, I guess," Peter responded flatly, not looking at me. "He drives that neat car I told you about, that red Packard roadster."

I felt guilty about grilling my own son, but unlike past occasions, I couldn't seem to stop. "Where do he and your Mama go?"

"Movies, restaurants, stuff like that, I think."

"And a sitter comes to stay with you then?"

He made a face. "Yeah. Usually Mrs. MacAfee, you don't know her. She moved in next door a few months ago. She's fat and she stinks, like she doesn't take baths or something. I'm really old enough to stay at home now, Dad. I don't need somebody there."

"I think you're right about that–I'll talk to your Mama. It sounds as if she really likes Mr. Baer."

He shrugged. "I guess so. After we eat, can we go and see the stuffed elephants and the dinosaur skeletons?"

Norma had been seeing Martin Baer for several months. I first heard about him from Peter just after Baer had taken both of them on out to Brookfield Zoo in the suburbs in his red Packard. All that I was able to learn from him at the time was that Baer used cologne ("He smells sort of like a Christmas tree") and owned a men's clothing store in the Lincoln-Belmont-Ashland shopping district on the Northwest Side.

I walked around that area a week or so later and spotted a fire engine-red Packard cabriolet parked at the curb in front of a shop, "Martin's Haberdashery & Fine Men's Footwear." I went in, pretending to browse for a necktie, and saw him across the room talking to a customer. I figured it was Baer even before I heard one of the sales clerks call him by name. His appearance screamed retailing prosperity. He had black hair slicked down and parted in the center and a thin moustache, neatly trimmed, and he wore a double-breasted gray herringbone suit that was a twin to the one in the window that cost forty-four bucks. I had to concede this was a good-looking specimen, about six feet, lean, and with a profile that would have stacked up well against the great Barrymore himself.

I never went back to the store, of course, but a few times after that when I stopped by to pick up Peter, I asked Norma what she did with her free time. Her answers were always short and vague, like "Oh, once in a while, I'll go to a movie." I never let on that I knew about Baer.

It was almost 3:30, with light snow falling in the near-darkness, when we left the museum. I was ready to collapse, but Peter seemed to possess endless energy. "Can we stop by Field's toy department, Dad?" he asked in a plaintive tone.

We caught a streetcar within two minutes and were on State Street well before the big store's closing time. If Marshall Field's didn't have the largest selection of toys in the world, I couldn't begin to guess who did. The highlight of all my Christmases as a boy was the whole family's annual pilgrimage to the toy department in that big and wonderful building. I looked forward to it for weeks, even though my parents never had the money to get me what I wanted, variously an Ives mechanical train, a Radio Flyer wagon, and a Schwinn bicycle. But that did not diminish my excitement that time of year. Besides, none of the other boys in the neighborhood ever got much more than we did. If any of us were deprived, we weren't aware of it.

Even now, a full generation beyond my own childhood and in the backwash of another holiday season, the toy department worked its special magic on me. It stretched into room upon room filled with bicycles and tricycles, Shirley Temple dolls and doll houses, Lincoln Logs and Tinker Toys, scooters and wagons, Chinese Checkers and chemistry sets, and of course trains–but now the brands were Lionel and American Flyer.

With Peter leading the way we wound up, hardly to my surprise, in a corner where an Erector display, including a Ferris wheel and a double-arch bridge, gave testimony to what could be fabricated by aspiring civil engineers. "Aren't these swell, Dad?" he said, eyes wide as he studied the constructions. "I just want to stay a minute and see how they're built, okay?"

"May I be of help to you gentlemen?" a grandfatherly sales clerk asked, peering over dark-rimmed glasses perched halfway down his nose.

"Indeed you may, sir," I answered. "My colleague here and I are in dire need of some extra parts for our Erector set–girders, nuts, bolts, the works. Have we by chance come to the right place?"

He nodded and winked, moving to a shelf behind him, and Peter smiled up at me.

Chapter 4

Either it was false modesty or Helen Hayes had sold herself and her troupe short: The single matinee performance of *The Merchant of Venice* was pronounced an unqualified success by the only theater critics in Chicago who counted– Collins in the *Tribune* and Lloyd Lewis in the *Daily News.* For what it's worth, if anything, I liked it, too, although this was the first time I had seen any Shakespeare since high school, when the junior class performed *Hamlet* and the cardboard set of the castle fell over on Billy Murakowski, who was playing a sentry. He crawled out from under the fallen citadel and bowed to the audience, easily getting the biggest applause of the evening.

True to her word, Helen Hayes left two tickets–ninth row center–in my name at the Erlanger box office for that Saturday performance in late January. I took Peter, figuring a little culture couldn't hurt him. Actually, although he seemed to have as much trouble as I did with some of the language, he came away impressed by the experience.

"She was really good, Dad," he said as we walked out of the theater. "And so was that guy who played Shylock. I guess Shakespeare didn't like Jewish people, huh?"

"Why do you say that?"

"Well, I couldn't understand a lot of what they were saying, but it seemed like it was very important that Shylock was Jewish. Remember, somebody said he was a devil in one place, and almost everybody in the play called him 'Jew,' like it was a bad word."

"To be honest, I struggled with some of the phrases, too. But I thought Shakespeare gave Shylock some sympathy when he had him talk about how Jews bleed when they're pricked and die when they're poisoned, and so on like that."

"Yeah, I suppose so. Do you like Jewish people, Dad?"

"I haven't known very many, Peter. Almost none."

"Mr. Baer is Jewish, I guess."

"I assumed he was. That's often a Jewish name."

"Oh. I didn't know. Well, one day a few weeks ago, he and Mama picked me up from school in his red car, and the next morning, James Keller, he sits right behind me in class, told everybody that I got a ride from a kike. That's a word for somebody who's Jewish, isn't it?"

"Yeah, and not a very nice word," I said, recalling how often I'd mouthed it myself over the years. I remembered how a bunch of us in the fifth grade shouted it as we chased Sammy Horowitz, the grocer's kid, home after school, throwing stones at him all the way to the store. "I hope you never use it," I told Peter.

"I won't, Dad. I promise."

On Monday mornings, the day side reporters in the pressroom at Police Headquarters invariably spent the first half hour or so recounting their weekend escapades. At least a third of the stories may have held some kernel of truth.

"I ran into the goddamndest broad Saturday night at the bar in the Chez Paree. A blonde with hair like Jean Harlow, you know, real smooth and soft, almost white, and like cotton candy. She was a looker in this red, silky, low-cut job that stuck to her like flypaper." It was Eddie Metz of the *Times*, all five-feet-four of him, disheveled and semi-shaven as usual, sitting on one leg at his desk and sucking an Old Gold between slurps of coffee. "She was dy-NO-mite, a real prize."

"As in booby prize, Eduardo? That's about where you'd come up to on her," cracked lanky Dirk O'Farrell of the *Herald and Examiner*, who was a master at pulling Eddie's chain. "You've got to switch brands of smokes–those things are making you hallucinate, for God's sake. No Harlow look-alike would go within a furlong of you unless–wait, I take it back, I take it all back, my apologies. Now I see." O'Farrell snapped a suspender and threw his hands up in mock surrender. "She probably wanted to use the top of your flat head as a table for her highball."

That brought the expected horselaughs, and before a flushed Eddie could begin to mount a counterattack, Anson Masters of the *Daily News*, the dean of the city's police reporters, ran a hand over his freckled, balding pate and weighed in. "Edward, Edward, you shouldn't be wasting your time on these lamentable floozies who drape themselves across the bar at the Chez. How often have I counseled you about the high-quality women who can be found…"

"Oh, Christ, Anson, not that old go-out-and-get-yourself-a-classy-call-girl spiel again," jeered Packy Farmer of the *American*, the town's other Hearst paper…as if we needed two. Packy, who like Masters had long been divorced, leaned back, stroked his thin moustache, and grinned. "Bear in mind, Anson, that I've met some of those 'quality women' of yours, like that one you introduced me to with the gold tooth who drank scotch and Coke–and drank it through a straw, yet. And who insisted on being called Nefertiti or some crap like that, even though her name was Agnes…or was it Maud?"

"Now, Cyril," Masters parried haughtily with Farmer's despised middle name, "you fail, not surprisingly, to appreciate true individuality and uniqueness in a woman."

"Yeah, Farmer," Eddie Metz jumped in relieved he was no longer the target. "If your name was Agnes or Maud, you'd change it to Nefertiti, too."

At his junior-sized desk in the corner, the kid from the City News Bureau, the local reporting service owned by the daily papers that also supplied police news to the radio stations, looked wide-eyed from one speaker to the next. He was a skinny redhead no more than 20 whose name none of us knew– City News shifted its young, underpaid reporters around like chessmen–and he was new enough on the beat that he likely thought he was seeing the flower of Chicago journalism indulging in witty repartee. He'd realize soon enough that all these flowers were wilted, and that their repartee wore very thin very quickly.

Each pushing sixty, O'Farrell and Masters were solid reporters who knew their beats–and the city–well; but both were simply playing out the string. Farmer had worked on papers across the country, leaving–so the talk went–a trail of bad checks and angry women in his erratic wake before he landed in Chicago just after the Fair in '33; Metz, who had the Headquarters beat only because his older brother was an assistant city editor on the *Times,* would never go anywhere on the tabloid, a loud and scrappy little imitation of the New York *Daily News* that itself didn't seem to know where it was going.

Then there was me, the youngest of the five regulars and the most talented, at least as a writer. But my battles with the bottle had cost me the assignments I once had and sent me to this gray room in this gray building at 11th and State on the dingy southern fringe of downtown, which might rate as okay duty for some reporters, but not for me.

Would I ever break out? I asked myself that question every day. In truth, I'd blown a lot of assignments in my partying days and I knew I had a lot of atoning to do. Bob Lee, the managing editor since Beck's retirement in '37, told me when he sent me to Police Headquarters that "If it hadn't been for that Capone piece that Mr. Beck and the Colonel had liked so much, you'd be out the door." And I got the clear message that if it were up to Lee, he'd be the one pushing me out that door.

"What about you, Snap, you've been awful quiet," O'Farrell drawled. "Do anything interesting over the weekend?"

I should have let his question pass, which would have been easy, but discretion has never been my strength. "Went to the theater with my son. We saw Helen Hayes in *The Merchant of Venice*."

"Hot damn!" Metz slapped his thigh. "That's Shakespeare, now, isn't it? This boy here's up and gone Shakespeare on us. Whaddya think of that, Dirk?"

O'Farrell did a practiced eye-roll. "Perhaps you do not

understand, Mr. Metz. Colonel McCormick, suh, expects all of his loyalists to be cultured, and don't you forget it. Comes with any job in that grand Gothic citadel on North Michigan Avenue that we ordinary folk know as Tribune Tower. None of that low-life stuff that we lesser minions engage in. In fact," he leaned forward and lowered his voice, "it wouldn't surprise me one bit to learn that our Mr. Malek here has white tie and tails squirreled away in his closet for such events as the noble Tribune expects him to attend."

"Ah, the secret and exciting life of Steven Malek, bon vivant and boulevardier, first-nighter and swell," Farmer intoned between drags on a misshapen cigarette that he had rolled. "And to think, we all toil side-by-side, cheek-by-jowl, with this social lion." Anson Masters delivered a bass rumble from deep within. "Much as I hate to disrupt this enlivening badinage, we have a public that clamors, yea *demands*, to be informed. Let's get to work." As senior man in the pressroom, he was its unofficial–and self-anointed–chairman of the board. He also liked to view himself as its conscience, which was amusing, since he was easily the laziest among us. Nevertheless, pressroom reporters were slaves to form and habit, and far from the cutthroat competitors that some novelists and playwrights–including Hecht and MacArthur– liked to portray Chicago journalists.

The hoary practices in all the pressrooms in town, including Police Headquarters, was share-and-share-alike, or sink like a rock. Consequently, almost every story to come out of the building at 11th and State was pooled. For example, a reporter would get the particulars on the arrest of a suspect in the strangulation of a prostitute and shuffle back to the pressroom, where he'd mete out the details to his scribbling "competitors." Each then would phone his respective city desk to dictate the story, and nobody would get into trouble with his editors for being scooped.

Occasionally, though, a young buck, in most cases a newcomer to the beat, would play Lone Ranger like I did my first week at City Hall back in '30 when I phoned in an exclusive on an alderman who told me that he planned to run for city clerk. The morning my story ran, I was met with silence from the other reporters in the pressroom. After an hour of being pointedly frozen out of all the usual banter, I went to the men's john, and the *Examiner* reporter, a stocky grouch named Clyde Crockett, who'd been around since before the Columbian Exposition in '93, followed me in and bellied up to the urinal next to mine.

"Malek?"

"Yeah?"

"What you did, that was jackass stupid."

"That so?" I answered, hoping I sounded tough.

"That piece of yours on Considine running for clerk."

"But…"

"Shut up and listen, hotshot." He didn't turn his head or raise his voice, but he didn't have to; each word sliced like a knife. "You try that once more, Malek, just once more, and by God, we'll freeze you out of every fucking story worth having that comes out of this building, right down to a press release announcing the replacement of an assistant custodian. Your high-and-mighty starched-collar bosses up in that damn tower of theirs will think you're sitting in some bar all day getting plastered instead of working, and they'll fire your ass inside of two weeks. Understand what I'm saying, or do I have to repeat myself?"

I looked straight ahead and nodded.

"Good," Crockett rasped. "Don't ever forget it." Thus I was indoctrinated into the sharers' club.

At Police Headquarters, the responsibilities were divvied up. I had got the Homicide Division for two reasons. First, I had an in with its top dog, the curmudgeonly Chief Fergus Sean Fahey, because I'd done a long Sunday feature on him that he liked back in '35 when I was a general assignment reporter. Second, and more important, as low man in seniority among the reporters for the dailies, I was nominated for that beat because nobody else wanted it–too much work. A lot of news came out of Homicide, and the others preferred to let me dredge it up and deliver it to them on a plate, which I more or less faithfully did.

Besides, as Eddie Metz had said with irrefutable logic, "You *should* have that beat, Snap. Your paper has the biggest news hole in town, and we all know that Homicide generates the most stuff. It's only fair–as long as you deal us all in, of course." And deal them in I did, of course.

As we started dispersing to make our rounds of the building that January Monday, Packy Farmer stopped us with a bellow. "Wait! We've got to do a pool on Martindale, remember?"

"What's that all about?" the City News kid asked, wrinkling his nose in puzzlement.

"Oh yeah, you're new, you wouldn't know," Farmer said, not unkindly. "We decided in December that we'd each toss in a fin–you don't hafta, of course, not on your salary–and guess what date this year the good and great and noble Lloyd Martindale announces that he's graciously consented to run for mayor of this here burg. Whoever comes closest takes the pot."

"Martindale? Why would he want to be mayor? Isn't he a millionaire?" The kid's face was still a question mark.

"Who the devil else the poor Republicans gonna run?" Anson Masters snorted. "Right now, the best they can do is Dwight Green, whose claim to glory was putting Capone away, which any second-rate prosecutor could have done given the caliber of Scarface's defense. The only other possibility is Big Bill Thompson, horrible to say, and this town had more than enough of him in City Hall when they tossed him out on his fat ass in '31. That pathetic old fraud doesn't know when to quit."

"Kelly'd knock either one of those two off easy," O'Farrell put in. "City's solid Democratic now; about the only way the Republicans can win is with a reform candidate, which is what Martindale purports to be, whether you buy that or not. So he's probably their logical choice. As far as his being a millionaire, kid, you're right, but don't hold that against him. He never earned a cent of that himself. It was his grandfather and then his old man who built up the family steel business. I doubt if Lloydie himself has ever even been inside that big mill out in South Chicago. He's not one to get his hands dirty. In fact, he's what you might call a dilettante–heavy into culture, opening night at the opera with his society wife, stuff like that."

"The guy's pretty damn pompous too," Farmer weighed in. "I don't see that side of him playing well with the hoi polloi; the rank-and-file voters in this town don't have any use for snobs. Hell, when Martindale was out in front of this building last fall blowing hot air around, I went up to him afterwards and asked if he had his eye on the mayor's chair. And you know what his answer was?"

"I believe we've heard the story before, but I don't suppose that will stop you from regaling us with it yet again," Anson Masters snorted.

Farmer ignored the sarcasm. "Here's what he said, and this is verbatim: 'I am here to serve my city, and if at some future time it is the wish of the populace that that service be in elected office, I have no choice but to accede to those wishes.' Talk about somebody who stuffs his shirts."

"Agreed, the guy's stuffy and arrogant, and probably more than a little naïve, too. But look at what he's got going for him," O'Farrell countered, holding out a hand and ticking off reasons on his nicotine-stained fingers.

"First, he's tall, wavy-haired, and I suppose handsome in a nose-in-the-air kind of way, while Ed Kelly's short and dumpy and always looks like he's slept in his suit. So stuffy or not, right there Martindale's got a lotta the women's vote, right?

"Second, unlike the mayor, he's articulate, even if he is spewing bilge most of the time. Hell, he's big-time college stuff, Harvard and then Yale Law, isn't it? That makes him strong on Lake Shore Drive, Astor Street, plus Sauganash and Beverly Hills, at the very least.

"Third, although he's Episcopal–what else?–his wife is a Catholic, same as Kelly, so the mayor don't get too much of an edge on that count out in the parishes, right?

"Fourth, even though he's not active in the steel company, the guy *is* part of a successful family worth millions, and some of the smarts of the previous generations figure to have rubbed off on him. Stack that up against a mayor who's been in office for what–five years–and hasn't proved he can run anything well.

"Fifth, and most important, Martindale appears to be as clean as a nun's habit on Easter morning, while Kelly–well, calling Ed shady doesn't even begin to describe the man."

"Yeah, Dirk, but offsetting everything you said, Kelly's got the machine behind him," Eddie Metz piped up. "And it's his *own* damn machine, his and Pat Nash's, with Nash pulling all the strings that make our dear mayor dance. You said yourself the city's solidly Democratic. With all the pork they can hand out, that's gotta be worth thousands of votes."

"Pork?" It was the City News kid, frowning again.

"Patronage," Metz said impatiently. "As in city jobs, handouts, and shit like that."

O'Farrell waved a hand dismissively. "I still say Martindale can counter that. Kelly's not all that popular, even with a lot of the old-line hacks in his own party. You know damn well the only reason he's got the job at all is because Tony Cermak caught that bullet supposedly meant for FDR down in Miami."

"Yeah, our martyred, grand, and glorious late mayor, rest his soul," Farmer hissed.

"Admit it, Cyril, Cermak was really an okay guy–a little dumb and maybe just slightly crooked, but okay," Masters said. "If he'd lived, he would have turned out to be a decent mayor– not brilliant, maybe, but decent. You're just cynical about everybody."

"And you're *not*?" Farmer retorted. "And what's this 'just slightly crooked' crap? You got a short memory. If Cermak had been in City Hall much longer, people woulda started wishing Big Bill was back."

Masters cleared his throat, as he always did when he was about to place himself above the fray. "Mine is a measured, healthy cynicism, Cyril, born of years as a passionate observer of the human comedy. And I–"

Farmer pushed back his chair and stood. "Oh, shove it, Anson! You are as sour as I am, probably sourer, and you damn well know it. Are we going to do this pool, or not?"

"Well, it's your show, Packy," I said impatiently. "Let's get going before our city desks start wondering how we're justifying these princely salaries."

"Okay, here's how we'll do it," Farmer said, reaching for a pad of half-sheets of copy paper. "Everybody put down their name and the date they think Martindale's going to announce, and we'll save the sheets until the big day, when the one of us who was closest gets twenty-five Washingtons."

"What happens if Martindale never decides to run?" Metz asked.

O'Farrell threw up his arms. "Eddie, for God's sake, what the hell d'ya think happens? Then there's no wager, of course– no pool, no money, no nothing. Do we have to spell everything out for you in words of one syllable or less?"

"Cut the jawing and give us all the damn ballots, will you," Masters sighed, "before it's time to break for lunch."

O'Farrell passed them around and everybody scribbled, each of us looking around furtively as we did. Then we all gave the folded sheets to the City News kid to lock in his drawer, seeing as how none of us completely trusted any of the others, and with reason.

For the record, I put down October 28, which was four months to the day before the primaries. I still think it was a good guess, but of course, we will never know.

Chapter 5

Wet snow flurries floated down on the city that February Tuesday, which slowed the morning rush hour traffic, including the streetcars, and which also made me ten minutes late getting to the pressroom at 11th and State. Normally, my coming in at 9:10 was not a cause for concern but, as I was about to learn, this day would be far from normal.

"Damn it, Snap, where have you been?" Nick Corcoran, sweat beading on his upper lip and in twin arcs above his overgrown black eyebrows, pounced on me as I entered the room, which was unusually crowded and noisy. Nick was our overnight man, a 35-year *Trib* veteran who liked the graveyard shift because he didn't have to work too hard and had almost nothing to do with any level of management back in the Tower. He was terrified of anyone or anything that smelled of management.

"Jesus Christ, Snap, all hell's breaking loose, didn't ya hear about it on the radio or anything?" Nick rasped over the din made by the other reporters and, as I now noticed, photographers as well, including two of our own picture jockeys, McGee and Langley.

"I didn't turn on the radio this morning. What was I supposed to hear, for God's sake?"

"Martindale," Nick sputtered, starting to hyperventilate. "Martindale. Lloyd Martindale. Got shot clean through the pump. Body found a few minutes after 6:00 this morning by a newsie who happened by."

"Where?"

"Lying near his car in a parking lot on Broadway about a block north of Diversey, close to a restaurant where he'd been addressing some sort of 'citizens against crime' group. He left the place alone a few minutes after 11 last night, so he probably caught it just a little later."

"I'll be damned. You filed, of course?"

Nick nodded. "Yeah, about ten graphs, with a couple of fairly good quotes from Fahey about how it looks like–surprise–a mob hit. Of course it's a mob hit. I was too late to make the three-star, though. The city desk's been hollering for you since quarter to nine. And the commissioner's holding a press conference in his office here at 10:00. Prob'ly wants to beat Courtney to the punch. I was afraid you wasn't gonna make it."

"I'm sure you were. I'll call in right now and calm down all the generals in the tower. Can you stick around and give me a hand at the press conference?"

Nick nodded grimly. He usually tore out the door of the pressroom the instant I came through it, sometimes with barely a hello. Today, he might actually have to earn his salary.

Police Commissioner James P. Allman had two offices, one next door to the mayor's suite in City Hall down on LaSalle Street in the Loop and the other at Police Headquarters. Years ago some mayor, very likely Big Bill Thompson, had wanted the top cop under his nose downtown so he could have more control over the Police Department. And even now, Allman spent the majority of his time in his City Hall digs. But today, he chose 11th and State for his press conference because, as Anson Masters observed, "he figures he'll get better treatment from us than from the City Hall press boys. Besides, here he's the top dog, the star. Down at the Hall, he's just another department head."

The carpeted reception area outside Allman's Headquarters office was jammed with newspaper and radio reporters and photographers. A scarred mahogany rostrum had been hauled out, and four of the local radio stations had clamped their microphones to it. Nick Corcoran was right; Allman wanted to have his say before the Cook County State's Attorney, Tom Courtney, waded in with his own press conference, which he surely would hold sometime before noon at the County Building, which adjoined City Hall. Courtney himself was a likely challenger for mayor in the Democratic primaries, and he wasn't about to lose the opportunity to take his whacks at the mayor, the police, and what he would doubtless call "general lawlessness" in a city governed by the Honorable Edward J. Kelly.

At precisely 10 by my watch, the door to Allman's office swung open, and the commissioner, lips pursed and jaw set, strode purposefully into the overcrowded, overheated room, followed by an equally grim-faced Chief of Detectives Fergus S. Fahey.

"Gentlemen, thank you for rearranging what I appreciate are busy schedules," Allman intoned after clearing his throat and striking a pose as flashguns popped. He had no notes. "As all of you are aware, a shocking crime took place last night. One of this city's most outstanding and exemplary citizens, Lloyd Martindale, age forty-seven, was shot dead after having been the guest speaker at a dinner meeting of the North Side Citizens Against Crime organization in the back room of a street-level restaurant in the 2900 block of North Broadway. Mr. Martindale's body was found at 6:03 this morning lying in a parking lot twenty-two feet from his car, a '35 Lincoln Le Baron roadster, by a newsstand operator who was passing by on foot en route to his stand, which is located at the intersection of Broadway and Diversey."

"Commissioner, can you—"

"Let me continue, and then there will be ample time for questions," Allman snapped at a radio reporter, clearly upset that the rhythm of his oratory had been broken. "Mr. Martindale was shot once, through the heart, probably with a .32 caliber bullet—it's still in the body. Death was virtually instantaneous, according to the coroner's office, and the shooting probably occurred before midnight.

"Robbery does not appear to have been a motive, as the victim's billfold was still on his person and contained $48.55. Also, a gold pocket watch worth several times that amount was in his vest pocket. We have no suspects at this time, but then, the case is barely hours old. I can assure you that the vast resources of this department are being marshaled, and I have every confidence that the perpetrator will swiftly be brought to justice. I know that Chief of Detectives Fahey here"–Allman gestured to his right–"is prepared to use extraordinary measures to ferret out the killer or killers." Fahey, looking uncomfortable, nodded.

"Now, are there questions?" Allman asked.

"Yes, Commissioner." It was Anson Masters, who started by clearing his throat. "Do you attach any significance to the fact, the very interesting fact, that Mr. Martindale was killed on Saint Valentine's Day? Exactly nine years after the massacre?"

"That apparent coincidence has not been lost upon us, Mr. Masters," Allman responded coldly, turning again to Fahey. "Chief, would you care to comment at this time?" Fahey stepped to the rostrum, scowling. "It seems probable that Lloyd Martindale has been the victim of the crime syndicate or one of its number. It has not been widely revealed until now, but Mr. Martindale had received–and duly reported the fact to us–several telephone threats within the last year."

"What kind of threats?" I asked.

"Threats on his life. The caller or callers told him, in essence, to stop his crusading against prostitution, handbooks, numbers, etcetera."

"But we keep hearing official word that none of these vices still even exist within the city," Packy Farmer said with a smirk as several members of the media chuckled.

Fahey's always ruddy face got a few shades redder. "I'm not going to dignify that with a comment," he growled.

"Was Martindale getting any kind of official protection?" one of the radio guys asked.

"He wouldn't take any," Fahey said. "Told us he didn't want to be perceived as hiding behind the shield of the Police Department. We have, however, maintained 'round-the-clock patrols in the immediate vicinity of the Lake Shore Drive apartment building where he had lived for the last eight months. Our men never saw anyone suspicious in all that time."

"Martindale has also been pretty hard on the police department," another radio reporter put in.

Allman aimed an Arctic glare in the questioner's direction. "Meaning?"

"Just an observation."

The commissioner blinked once, then looked away. "Any other pertinent questions?"

Indeed, more questions followed, none of which added to the apparently scant information about Martindale's murder. As the noisy group shuffled out of the police commissioner's anteroom and headed back to the pressroom to phone in their stories on the conference, Packy Farmer sidled up and gave my arm a tug. "Snap, you're going to see Fahey now, aren't you?" he asked *sotto voce*.

"Well, he sure as hell wouldn't want to talk to *you* after that smart-ass comment you tossed his way," I said. "But before I do anything else, I'm going to phone in a piece. Aren't you?"

"Oh, yeah, yeah, I'll call in something now, mainly to hold space for the later editions. But our first deadline's a damn sight earlier than yours. We need some good stuff from him."

"Could be that whatever he gives me, he'll stipulate that I can share it with everybody but you."

"Aw, come on, Snap. Don't be that way."

I felt like telling Packy to go and dig something up himself, but he had fed my vanity with his suggestion that I "owned" Fahey.

In fact, I'm not stretching the truth when I say that I was in thick with the chief of detectives. That Sunday feature I'd done on him hadn't hurt any, to be sure, but our relationship went deeper than that single article. Whatever his reasons, the grizzled old police dick seemed to like me, or at least put up with me.

Maybe part of it was that he was reasonably sure that he could trust me—as sure as a copper ever can be about a reporter. When he talked off the record, I honored that, because I knew

I'd eventually get the story from him, and usually get it all, when he was ready to unload. And he didn't use the off-the-record dodge often, maybe because he figured I could find ways to make life hot for him in the pages of the *Trib* if I thought he was giving me the runaround. He was right.

And yes, Packy Farmer would get some of Fahey's quotes for the next edition of the *American*, all right, but I'd make sure he would sweat a little first. If I had to share, I'd have a little fun first.

Back in the pressroom, I called the city desk and dictated a few graphs to a rewrite man on the press conference for our outstate edition, even though the deadline was nowhere close. Packy watched me all the while, drumming his fingers on his desk and rolling another one of his ugly little smokes. I never understood how a guy who had been making his own cigarettes for all of his adult years couldn't do a better job of it.

After I hung up with rewrite, I leaned back, feet on the desk, and lit up myself–a real cigarette, a Lucky–closing my eyes and struggling to keep from laughing. The *Daily News*, also a p.m. paper, had roughly the same schedule of editions as Packy's *American*, but Anson Masters always seemed unconcerned until minutes before deadline. So while Packy fumed about my inactivity, Anson pored over the Ely Culbertson bridge column in his own paper from the day before, trying to figure out how a guy in a tournament someplace in Europe managed to take all the tricks in a deal even though he and his partner were missing an ace and two kings.

Elsie Dugo looked up from her typewriter, blinked once, and gave me a toothy grin as I eased into her six-foot-square alcove, which guarded the inner sanctum of the chief of detectives. "That grand old fellow on the premises?" I asked, returning her smile.

She nodded, pressing a button and pronouncing my name into a box on her desk. "You know the way, big boy," Elsie chirped after getting what was to me an unintelligible squawk out of the box. "Be warned, however, that he's not in the best of tempers."

"Thanks for the heads up on his frame of mind. Knowing him as I do, I never would have guessed it."

To call Fergus Fahey's office dingy would be to pay it a compliment. It did have a carpet all right, albeit edging toward threadbare and of a shade somewhere between dirty brown and dirty gray. And there were two padded, semi-comfortable but unmatched chairs, each of which had arms. These were the only concessions to refinement in a room that looked like a Trappist monk had decorated it. Banks of gray filing cabinets lined two gray, pictureless walls, and on the wall behind Fahey's desk, a single window that hadn't been washed since Coolidge first took the oath of office looked out on the Elevated tracks.

The man himself slouched behind a battered, brown wooden desk that seemed to function primarily as support for stacks of paperwork. He dipped his chin almost imperceptibly in acknowledgment of my presence.

"Well, and a nice warm hello to you, too," I said, sliding into one of the guest chairs.

"Got a Lucky?" he snorted, knowing I always did.

"Yeah. Got coffee?" I responded, knowing he always did. This was a ritual we had fallen into sometime back. The coffee in his office, brewed by Elsie in her anteroom, was the best in the building. Fahey hit the intercom buzzer three times–the coffee signal–as I handed my pack of smokes across and he pulled two out. He never took just one.

Elsie clicked in on her high heels carrying a steaming mug of caffeine juice and set it on the corner of the desk, one of the few spots not covered with stacks of papers.

"I'm pretty sure I love you," I said, hoisting the cup to her in salute and getting a dimpled smile in response before she stuck out her tongue at me.

"You two could do a lot worse than each other," the chief observed dryly, looking from her to me and back again. "Elsie, what did I tell you when I came back from that damned press conference?"

"You said that Snap–Mr. Malek–would show up here at 10:25."

"What time is it now?"

She looked at the clock on the wall behind Fahey and grinned in my direction. "It's 10:27."

"And how long has our Mr. Malek been here?"

"Two minutes?" It was a question, but tentatively posed.

"Right!   I'm just trying to confirm patterns of predictability.   Thank you, Elsie." She did a graceful about-face and left the room, which instantly reverted to its drab state.

I drank coffee and crossed one leg over the other. "Okay, now that you have flushed all that bile out of your system, want to talk about Lloyd Martindale?" I asked.

"Not particularly."

"Force yourself, open up. What's your opinion? Off the record this time. I'm feeling generous."

Fahey lit up and leaned back, blowing smoke and running a hand over the gray fringe of hair that formed a semicircle around that ruddy scalp of his. "Christ, what do *you* think, Snap? If I was in the syndicate, I'd be looking for ways to get rid of the guy, too. Off the record, of course."

"Of course. No question it was them?"

"Or one of them. Or somebody in their hire."

"Why?"

"Oh, come on, you know the answer to that question as well as I do, probably better," the chief sighed, taking a long drag on his cigarette. "He looked like he was headed for the mayor's office."

"You really think he would have won?"

He shrugged. "Don't know for sure–maybe not. But the possibility was definitely there, which may have been enough to scare the boys. Things are fairly comfortable for them as long as Kelly sits in the big office with Pat Nash's power backing him up. But Martindale figured to turn the town on its ear, even if he was a pompous, posturing, publicity-hungry ass. He would have made life miserable for a lot of people who don't like being uncomfortable."

"And you really figure that they'd kill him rather than risk his getting into the Hall?"

The chief shrugged again and threw his arms up. "You know as well as I do that they've done it for a lot smaller stakes."

"So now what happens?"

Fahey furiously ground out his butt in a ceramic ashtray bearing the name of a Wabash Avenue steak house. "You know the answer to that one, too. What happens, of course, is that the heat is on the department, which is to say, yours truly, thank you. Altman had his 'we'll-leave-no-stone-unturned' speech a little while ago, as you heard. At 11:00, Courtney gets his chance to chest-thump down at the County Building about this horrible crime and how the city desperately needs new leadership, which–though he won't say so outright–is none other than himself, of course. And what are you willing to wager that by 3:00 this afternoon, Hizzoner the Mayor, with puppet master Pat Nash nodding soberly at his side, holds his own press conference in which he'll rail about how he doesn't get enough support in his ongoing, unrelenting war on organized crime."

"What war on organized crime?"

Fahey actually started to grin before catching himself. "Just so. But he'll make it sound good, damn good, and some newspapermen are dumb enough, or gullible enough, to take the bait. Present company excluded, of course."

"Of course. You sound a touch on the acid side," I chided.

"More than a touch, Snap. And what really pisses me off is that Martindale will come out of this looking like a goddamn martyr. Hellfire, the last couple of years, he's been all over the department about our inability to nail any of the post-Capone syndicate biggies. Never mind that he had no specific suggestions on how to do it. What a pain in the ass he got to be, for all of us. If I wasn't so sure who was behind his killing, I'd guess it was somebody high up in the Department who got sick of hearing him carp. But I never said that, did I?"

"Nah. And I never heard it. Although I noticed at the press conference that the good commissioner is a little thin-skinned on that particular subject. Okay, I need some quotes that I–and all the other clowns in the pressroom–can use."

"That's right, you're here as usual representing that syndicate of your own, right? Including that jackass Farmer; tell him to go–oh, the hell with it. Okay, pull out your notebook and your pack of Luckies and I'll buzz Elsie to bring more coffee. This could take a while."

Chapter 6

Nothing sells like murder or sex, and the papers all saw the Martindale murder as a newsstand bonanza as they spit out extras and changed their banners for each edition. Among them were MOB GUNS DOWN REFORMER in the *Herald and Examiner*; MARTINDALE MARTYRED in the *Times*; and THE SYNDICATE STRIKES AGAIN in the *American*, while the *Trib* and the *Daily News* were less strident with CRUSADER'S LIFE SNUFFED OUT and KELLY VOWS ALL-OUT WAR ON CRIME, respectively.

In my interview with Fahey, which everyone else in the pressroom borrowed freely from or paraphrased, the chief said: "There is no question that this was an underworld hit" and "As long as the residents of this city continue to patronize the prostitutes and the policy wheels and the bookmakers and the slots, organized crime will continue to brazenly flaunt its power and wreak its terror, regardless of the best efforts of local and federal law enforcement agencies. We will continue to be unflagging in our efforts to fight the underworld but, plain and simple, we need more cooperation and more outrage from the citizenry."

That set off the Chicago Crime Commission, a civic watchdog group whose president blasted Fahey in a press conference on the sidewalk in front of the LaSalle Street entrance to City Hall—not so coincidentally the identical spot where the late Lloyd Martindale had unleashed his own tirade against organized crime on New Year's Eve.

The CCC head assailed the chief's comments as "typical of the defeatist attitude the Chicago Police Department has adopted for years with respect to the crime syndicate. They wring their hands and shrug in helplessness. In their defense, the pathetic reality is that, to at least some degree, the police *are* indeed helpless. Why? In part because of the lack of support they receive from a city administration that is either corrupt or apathetic, or both."

The Crime Commission was by no means alone in its outcry. The papers all rose up in a state of high dudgeon, each of them running editorials that blasted various elements of local government–Mayor, City Council, State's Attorney's office, Police Department–for their ineffectiveness in coping with the crime syndicate and its activities.

"In the days of Capone, the very word 'Chicago' became synonymous around the world with lawlessness and gangsterism and violence," wrote the *American* in a rare front-page editorial, which Packy Farmer insisted on reading aloud in the pressroom. He continued: "Some among us were naïve enough to believe that with this pariah safely behind bars, all of that would change. It has not, and the callous murder of a reform-minded public figure has once again underscored the sorry state of law enforcement and good government in this mighty metropolis. Once again, we are sorry to report, Chicago stands unchallenged as a global symbol of organized crime and government ineffectiveness. Mr. Mayor, we at this newspaper offer a humble suggestion for the design of a new city flag: a smoking black Tommy gun silhouetted against a blood-red background."

"Hah, that's givin' it to the bastards!" Packy chortled, flipping his paper onto the desk and leaning back with a smirk. "Don't even need to guess who wrote that. Had to be Motherwell, that old cuss. Nobody spits vitriol like him. Bet he cackled all the time he was batting it out with two fingers on his Underwood."

"It's heartening to see you exhibit so much pride in your publication, Cyril," Anson Masters said. "But don't you think Mr. Motherwell's writing is just a shade on the florid side?"

"Ah, go screw yourself, Antsy," Farmer sneered. "Your damn rag is so prissy in its editorials that you can't even tell who they're mad at, or even if they *are* mad. Don't those guys in your ivory tower over at Madison and Canal have any balls at all?"

"Hey, how 'bout we work up a pool on when the cops make an arrest," Eddie Metz put in.

"My guess is, oh…August the 8th, 1943," Dirk O'Farrell offered, clearly pleased by the laughter that followed.

"Seriously, do all of you think it really was a mob killing?" the City News kid asked, straight-faced and wide-eyed as ever.

It was clear from O'Farrell's expression that he was struggling against making a sarcastic retort. He, like the rest of us, had become fond of the kid, despite–or maybe because of–his innocence.

"I can't speak for these reprobates here," Dirk said, making a sweeping gesture with his arm. "But how the hell else are you going to read it? Martindale, windbag that he admittedly is, starts making noise, lots of noise, about cleaning up all the vice around town, and whaddya know, he begins to draw a following.

"Pretty soon, a couple of the papers, including of course that good gray Madonna, the *Daily News*"–he tilted his head in Masters' direction–"start praising the guy in editorials. It begins to look like Saint Martindale just might land the Republican nomination for mayor. And–although I admit it's a long shot–he might also just push Hizzoner Edward J. and his Svengali, Pat Nash, right out of City Hall and onto LaSalle Street on the seat of their overstuffed pants."

"Long shot is right!" Masters retorted.

"Okay, but even those long odds figured to make the syndicate boys edgy," O'Farrell countered. "Life is jim dandy for them now, but if Martindale was rattling around City Hall out of control, which would have been the case, he'd have ended up cramping their style."

"Yeah, but was it really worth killing him?" the City Press kid asked plaintively.

O'Farrell shrugged. "Where's the risk? Damn, they've been knocking people off for twenty years now, and that includes a few reformers, but do they ever get caught? You honestly think that Chicago's Best, and I use that term loosely, will ever nail the trigger man?"

The kid shook his head, not in answer to the question, but rather in what looked like bewilderment. "I just don't figure Lloyd Martindale was a real threat to organized crime."

"I'm inclined to agree," I put in.

"So you really think somebody other than the Organization erased Sir Galahad, eh, Snap?" O'Farrell said with what I would describe as a sneer.

"Well, no…I can't imagine who else it could have been. I was just concurring with the opinion of this man," I said, gesturing toward the junior member of the pressroom. "I can't see Martindale as a real threat to these guys."

The Martindale murder got successively less play in the papers with each day, as February gave way to March. A couple of psychopaths, one of them recently released from the Dunning mental asylum on the Northwest Side of the city, confessed to the murder.

This sort of thing often happens in a headline crime, and, not surprising, each of their stories had more holes than the South Shore Country Club, so they were none too gently sent on their way by the police. There had been no real leads, although the cops hauled in three or four minor-league hoodlums and grilled them for hours, just to show they were on the job.

As usual, I made my daily trips to Fahey's office, but after the requisite questioning about whether there was any progress in the case, his textbook answer was, "We continue to give this investigation top priority at all levels of the department." Our conversation turned to such subjects as the Cubs' chances for the pennant in '38 and speculation as to who the Republicans would run against Kelly in '39.

I saw Peter every Saturday, and sometimes he'd stay in the apartment with me until Sunday afternoon. We'd go to the coal mine at the Museum of Science and Industry or to the Planetarium or to a movie. Most recently I had suggested

"Snow White and the Seven Dwarfs," in part because I wanted to see it myself after all the laudatory reviews I'd read about the Walt Disney animation, but that got a frown and an "Aw, Dad," from Peter, who lobbied for "Submarine D-1" with Pat O'Brien and George Brent. We ended up going to the submarine film, which I was forced to admit wasn't bad.

Another time, at his urging, we spent almost a whole day riding Elevated trains. We rode all the way north through Uptown and Rogers Park to Evanston and then back down on the Howard line and then out to Oak Park on the Lake Street train and back downtown and over to the Stock Yards on that branch, and he never got tired of it.

"I must have fallen asleep a half dozen times today on those old rattlers," I told Norma after I dropped Peter off following our El marathon. He had gone to his room and we were standing in the living room. "I've never seen the roofs of so damn many apartment buildings and houses in my life. Or so many back porches with long johns hanging on their clotheslines."

She laughed sympathetically. "Well, it's clear from his face that he had a wonderful day. That was awfully nice of you to do."

"Yeah, well I owe him a lot more days like that. There were too many times…" I didn't have to finish the sentence, and she didn't respond. "I'm trying to do better," I said.

"I know you are," she replied softly. "And he appreciates it; he looks forward to your times together, and he talks about them for days afterward."

"I'm glad to hear that. Do you appreciate it, too?"

"Well, of course I do, Steve. I want to see him happy, and I think it's terribly important that he have a close relationship with you."

"So do I. Say, how about you and I have dinner one of these days, Norma? Maybe next weekend?"

"Um, I don't think so…not right now, anyway," she said, her voice still soft, maybe to keep Peter from hearing.

"Oh? Why not?"

"Well, I just don't think it would be a very good idea right now, Steve."

"You're seeing someone?"

She nodded, looking away. "I'm sure Peter has probably said something about him."

"He has, just a little. You like him quite a bit?"

"Yes, quite a bit."

It was awkward, being in the living room of what used to be my home. I had never felt less like I belonged than at that moment.

On a Wednesday evening in mid-March, I swung off the Clark Street car and into a battering downpour, opened my umbrella, and paused on the sidewalk, wondering whether to go up to my apartment and fix dinner or stop first at Kilkenny's for a beer or two. I decided on the Killer's and turned north on Clark, angling the umbrella into the wind and the almost horizontal sheets of rain.

I didn't notice the long car that was idling at the curb until I'd pulled even with it and a disembodied voice came from the rolled-down back seat window. "Hey, Mr. Malek."

"Huh?" I turned to look and as I did, someone grabbed my arm from behind and moved me effortlessly toward the sedan.

"What the hell–"

"Easy there, Mac." It was a second voice, this one belonging to whoever was doing the shoving. "Just get in and everything will be jake." He grabbed my umbrella and pushed my head down, forcing me into the back seat, all in one fluid motion.

I found myself inside a large sedan, probably a Cadillac or its slightly smaller sibling, a LaSalle. On my left, his face partially obscured by a fedora and the darkness, was the one who had called my name. On my right, the shover, also wearing a fedora. And in the front seat was a third fedora, on the head of the figure behind the wheel.

"Mr. Malek, we need to talk to you," said the man on my

left, his voice scratchy and high-pitched, like he'd been shouting a lot. "Mel, drive around for awhile."

"Just what is it that we're talking about?" I asked in the toughest tone I could muster as the car eased from the curb and moved into the flow of traffic north on Clark.

"We talk, you listen," Mr. Left said firmly, but with no trace of hostility. "Mr. Capone wanted us to see you. It's about the unfortunate death of Mr. Lloyd Martindale."

"What to you mean, Capone? He's out in–"

I was cut short by a hard jab in the ribs on my right. "Shaddup and listen," gruffed Mr. Right.

"Don't have to get rough with him," Mr. Left remonstrated with his partner as the car turned west on Addison at the Wrigley Field corner. "Now, as I started to tell you, Mr. Capone requested we talk to you. He has a message: It is that the organization had nothing to do with the Martindale death, no matter what the papers and the cops and the politicians say."

I was breathing a little easier now, but still trying hard not to let my fear show.

"How can Capone–*ugh*!" I was cut short again by another painful jab to my right side.

"That's enough, Monk!" Mr. Left said sharply. "Let him talk. Go on, Mr. Malek."

I dropped my right arm, protecting my rib cage. "How can Capone know who killed Martindale? He's been holed up out there at Alcatraz for almost four years now."

My answer came from the left. "Listen good, Mr. Malek. He knows everything that happens on the outside."

"All right, then. Why did Capone want to tell *me*, of all people, that Martindale wasn't a…mob hit? And how do I even know that you really are messengers on this? And third, if this wasn't a mob hit, just who did it?"

"You ask a lot of questions, just like Mr. Capone said you would. First, the reason he wanted you to know was that he says you're a straight-shooter and you're fair. Second, he said to remind you that when you talked to him down in Atlanta, you were wearing a light gray suit and a red-and-blue striped tie, and that you both ate beef and boiled potatoes and peas and apple pie. And that when he asked you how the Cubs were going to do that year, you said no better than third, that the Giants and the Cardinals were just too good for them. You remember?"

"Yes-s-s."

"Good. Okay, and third, he doesn't *know* who got Martindale, nobody does…yet. And he's mad as hell that we– that the wrong people–are getting the blame on this."

"So, what's the purpose in telling *me*?" I asked as the driver wheeled back south on Ashland.

Mr. Left made a growling noise, down deep in his throat. "He says you're a damned good reporter. Me, I wouldn't know, because I think you're all a bunch of wise-assed shits, and not very frigging smart on top of it. But he figured maybe you could find out who did the job."

And in the process clear the "good name" of the mob, I thought but had the sense not to mouth. I took a safer tack: "So you've got no clues as to where I should start?"

"We got nothing. But now you're ahead of the pack, because you know who *didn't* do the job."

Maybe, I thought. Or maybe I was being fed a line of bull, although if that were the case, I didn't see the point of it. "I understand Alphonse is a pretty sick boy," I said, recalling a piece that I'd read a few weeks back in the *Trib* about how Capone was diagnosed with an advanced case of syphilis out at Alcatraz. That earned me another jab in the ribs on my right ride, and this time Mr. Left didn't voice an objection.

"Mr. Capone is just fine," he snarled. "Just fine. Don't believe everything you read in the newspapers, including your own rag."

As we were having our stimulating conversation, the driver had turned east on Fullerton and then north on Clark. When we got to the spot where I'd been picked up, the car slid to the curb. "Mr. Malek, this meeting never happened, did it?" Mr. Left asked.

"It never happened," I repeated. Mr. Right, who I now

knew to be Monk, got out and handed me my umbrella, grunting something unintelligible. I didn't respond, figuring anything I said might earn me yet another whack in the ribs. As the car sped away, I peered at the license plate but could see nothing. The light bulb above it was out.

The rain had almost stopped, although I put up the umbrella anyway, with shaking hands. I rubbed my sore right side through my trench coat and took a step toward my apartment building, but checked myself again and set a course for Kilkenny's. Now I really needed that beer.

Three Strikes You're Dead

Chapter 7

Kilkenny's was nearly deserted–nobody in the booths and only two guys I didn't recognize down at the far end of the long bar eating T-bones. Killer had a first-rate kitchen and a deserved reputation for serving some of the best steaks on the North Side.

"Aha, Snap, a buffeted and bedraggled orphan of the storm, come to seek refuge in my humble dram shop," the Killer intoned, savoring each word. "Indulging in the usual, I trust?" I nodded, wincing slightly as I settled myself on a barstool well removed from the other two customers and wondering if Monk had been jabbing me with his knuckles or with the barrel of a pistol. Either way, the dull ache was spreading through my right side.

"Killer, since you're not exactly overwhelmed with business at the moment, got a few minutes to chin?"

"When did I not, even *when* busy, my scrivener *compadre*?" he responded, placing a frosted stein of Schlitz on a coaster on the scarred cherrywood surface. He leaned on burly elbows and his round face seemed to get rounder as he broke into a benevolent smile. "What be the subject of our interlocution?"

I lowered my voice. "If I was to tell you that there may be a good chance Lloyd Martindale was *not* killed by or because of the crime syndicate, what would your reaction be?"

He crinkled his eyes and ran a hand through thick, chalk-white hair that he parted down the middle. "Hmmm. Surprise, for starters. And then, after I'd chewed on it for awhile, downright shock, I suppose. And after that, my native curiosity would of course kick in, and I would commence to pose questions. Such as: If the mob or one of its duly chosen

77

representatives did not pull the trigger on Mr. Martindale, who did?"

I took a long, welcome drink and set my mug down, licking my lips. "Precisely my question to you, innkeeper. Tell me where your mind would take you next."

"Hmm. How about maybe *cherchez la femme*? As in perhaps a cuckolded husband?"

I shook my head. "Not according to your countryman, Chief of Detectives Fergus Sean Fahey. He says they've looked at that angle, and apparently Martindale was the ideal family man, a paragon of domestic virtues. His wife, his friends, his neighbors, they all say he was right out of the movies: faithful and loyal and true and all those other Boy Scout virtues."

"Well then, what of a gambling debt so big that he couldn't pay it, even being as prosperous as he was said to be? With the result that he gets eradicated by whomever was holding his markers?"

"You've got a great mind, Killer, because it works just like mine. That was my second query to Fahey, and he knocked it down, too. Said that Martindale never–quote *never*–gambled. The guy apparently was without sin."

"And no doubt dull, too," the barkeep observed as he looked down and traced circles on the bar top with a thick finger. "Ah, Snap my friend, I don't like what I'm thinking."

"Try me."

His head came up slowly. "All right, the syndicate didn't do it, at least so you're telling me, and apparently there wasn't a jealous husband or an angry boyfriend. And no bookmaker who Martindale had welshed on."

"You've listened well."

"I always listen well. Snap, you see before you a staunch Democrat; have been for twenty-five years and then some, but I wonder…"

I gave the Killer time to finish the sentence, and when he didn't, I finished it for him. "You wonder if somebody in the party, or somebody who was hired by somebody in the party, did the job."

He held up a hand. "Now I'm not saying that's what happened, mind you, but it's just a thought–off the record, of course–not that anything I'd say would be of interest to the newspaper-buying masses. Getting back to the subject: Do I think Mr. Martindale could have won an election against Edward J. Kelly? Ah…probably not. But it might have been close, and maybe, just maybe, one of the faithful–nobody high up or important, mind you, but someone terrified by the idea that this reformer could win–endeavored to do something about it." The Killer took a deep breath and shook his head as if to erase the almost-sacrilegious thought of a Democrat committing a capital crime. "Now I must concede that is a long shot, Snap–at least I devoutly hope it's a long shot."

"I'd have to agree, but it's worth considering. Question is, where do I find a loyal Democrat who can do some poking around for me? Or maybe more to the point–is there *anyone* in the party who'd be willing to help me poke around?"

Kilkenny screwed up his map-of-Ireland face. "Most of the party regulars I know in this neighborhood are small-timers–ward and precinct bosses, that sort of thing. Two-bit stuff. But back in Bridgeport on the South Side, there's a fellow named Mike Daley, a sheet metal worker, a noble man. In fact, we came from the very same slice of the Old Sod, County Wexford it was, and I even knew him back then, only just slightly mind you, when we were lads. But over here, Mike and yours truly got to be pretty good friends, although I don't see much of him now. He really ragged me about moving up this way when I bought the saloon after Repeal. 'Ah, goin' North Side high-hat on us, are you now, Seamus?' he said. 'And to think, you, a good Sox fan, buyin' a pub within an outfielder's toss of that Wrigley Field place. The shame of it, the shame.' And Mike, he was only half jollying, if that. And in truth, he has never come through that door, although I've invited him more than once."

"So you see this Mike as a possible contact within the party? Somebody I can talk to?"

"No, no," the Killer said. "Oh, Mike is one-hundred-percent Democrat, always has been and always will be; but it wasn't him I was thinking of; it's his son, who's a comer. He's down in Springfield now, sitting in the Legislature. Lord, I've known Dick since he was crawling on the living room floor of their flat over on Lowe, corner of 36th. He was always a good lad, an only child, too. And both his parents doted on him, but I wouldn't call him spoiled, not at all. Well-cared-for, indeed, but not spoiled. His mother, Lillian...now there was a pistol, let me tell you. She fought for women getting the vote–even used to take the little fellow along on those suffragette marches of hers. Damndest thing. And Dick himself, he's been toiling for the party since he was maybe twelve or so, ringing doorbells, passing out handbills, and the like."

"If I were to approach this guy, the son that is, think he'd be willing to do some digging around?"

The Killer folded his arms across his chest and contemplated. "I would vote for the direct approach. He is as honest as they come. At least that is my humble conviction."

"I'll be damned, Killer. I was just thinking that all the times I've been in here, I never knew your first name was Seamus. And I guess I should have figured it out, but I also never knew you were born in Ireland. How'd you get rid of your accent? You sound like you've lived in Chicago forever."

"A fair question from a fair man. Do you know the phrase 'Irish need not apply'?"

"Sure. When I was a kid growing up in Pilsen, I saw signs saying that in the windows of shops that were hiring. Haven't seen one in years, though."

"There was a veritable plethora of them when I came over with my folks and my sisters in '97, you can believe it. I was but seventeen then, and we were church-mouse poor. My father, rest his noble soul, got a job working nights in the Stock Yards, and he was happy as a leprechaun to have it. And I had to go to work, too–school was beyond the question. So I hit the pavement all around the South Side looking for work, and when these butchers and tailors and other shopkeepers heard my brogue, that was it." He snapped his fingers. "I was out the door without so much as a fare-thee-well.

"Now Snap, as the good Lord is my witness, it's fair to say I'm as proud of being Irish as the next chap, indeed maybe a shade more so. But we needed money badly, even with my fine father's salary, so I got rid of the brogue and forced myself to speak 'American.' There you are." He spread his arms.

I nodded. "I remember my mother telling me that my father's Bohemian accent hurt him early on, too. But he's still got the accent, and somehow he persisted and finally landed with the streetcar company, our good old Chicago Surface Lines, where he's been ever since."

"Good for him," the Killer said. "I don't mean to disparage him or the fine Bohemians, but I honestly don't believe anybody had it as bad as the Irish. There was a lot of hatred back then–worse than it is today, I feel. But we were talking about Dick Daley."

"Sorry, I get sidetracked easily. So you think the young Daley's pretty well wired into the Kelly-Nash machine?"

The Killer flipped a hand over. "I didn't say that–what I said was, Dick is honest. But yes, although he's pretty young– probably just about your age, I'd say–he's already had a good lot of experience, and from what little I know, he knows a multitude of well-placed people in the party."

"Would you give him a call for me?"

"Why not, given that you're such a loyal patron of this establishment. I can get his number from his folks. Pray tell, what am I supposed to say?"

"Ask him if he'd be willing to talk to me. You don't have to say what it's about, or he might get spooked, but tell him I'm prepared to go down to Springfield to talk to him–the Legislature's in session now. And Killer, make sure he knows that even though I work for the *Trib*, I vote Democratic. Which happens to be true. By the way, straight ticket in '36."

Kilkenny said he'd make the call. And he did. Two days later, he phoned me at home. "Snap, I just got off the line with young Richard in Springfield–and you owe me for that call, by the way. He was a mite suspicious about why some *Tribune* reporter would want to go and see him, especially when your paper already has a fellow down there covering the State House. That threw me for a second, but I told him you were on a confidential assignment. And I also said you were honest, trustworthy, and a passel of other fine adjectives. You wouldn't go and make a liar out of me now, would you?"

"Killer, I'll be on my best behavior. And I owe you. Feed me that Springfield number."

Three days later, Friday afternoon, I hoofed it the three blocks east from Police Headquarters over to the Illinois Central Station at 12th and Michigan with my small suitcase. I had gotten our evening man, Ellis, to relieve me early so I could catch the 4:45 to Springfield. He couldn't very well gripe about it, given all the times I'd hung around the pressroom waiting for him to drag in anywhere from ten minutes to a half hour late.

I bought a round trip ticket in the dreary, drafty old waiting room of the depot and went down the stairway to my track. What greeted me looked unlike any train I'd ever seen; it was low and tubular and green, sort of an elongated earthworm with windows, and it had a grille on the front end that must have been copied straight from a '34 Chrysler Airflow sedan.

"Is this thing safe?" I asked the portly conductor, who stood on the platform whistling "Camptown Races" off-key.

"Safe? Darn tootin' right it's safe, son," he grunted, peering at me over half-glasses. "You mean to say you haven't seen the Green Diamond before–pride of the Illinois Central line? You been off hibernatin' someplace like ol' Rip Van Winkle? The Diamond's been running better'n two years now."

He shook his head, as if pitying my ignorance. "Hellfire, son, this is the last word, the smoothest thing on the rails. Rides like you're floating on air. Is this safe? Huh!"

I felt like I should say something after that spirited defense of the Green Diamond, but I didn't know what the etiquette is about apologizing to a train, so I grinned sheepishly and climbed aboard. I settled into a window seat and had to admit to myself that I couldn't even tell when we began to move.

The earthworm picked up speed quickly as we headed south, with Lake Michigan off to the left and apartment buildings on the right. At one place two or three miles south of the station, we were so close to the windows of the flats that I could see a baby bouncing in his playpen on a sun porch and grinning toothlessly as we flew past. He reminded me of the way Peter welcomed me home from work by jumping up and down in his own little barred enclosure when he was a tyke. That had been only ten years ago, but it seemed like a lifetime had passed, and in a sense, it had.

When I had phoned Dick Daley, he wanted to know what I needed to see him about. After I told him I'd rather discuss it in person, he sounded dubious but told me to come ahead, that he'd meet me in the lobby of the St. Nicholas Hotel at nine o'clock, which was fifty minutes after the train was due to arrive in Springfield.

And the earthworm arrived exactly on time. "Told you it rode smooth, didn't I, son?" the conductor said as I swung off onto the platform.

"You did, and you were right. In fact, I enjoyed it so much that I'll even ride it back to Chicago tomorrow," I answered.

He chuckled as I headed off in the direction of the St. Nicholas a few blocks away, enjoying a spring warmth that hadn't yet arrived farther north. I checked in and splashed water on my face in my room, which was plain but clean. At 5 before 9:00, I went down to the lobby and saw a guy with a well-fitting suit and slicked-down hair standing near the front door. He had clean-cut written all over him.

"Richard Daley?" I asked.

He nodded somberly. "You're Mr. Malek?"

"Steve Malek," I said, sticking out a hand, which he gripped firmly. "Thanks for taking the time to see me tonight."

"Time is something I got right now," he said in a slightly husky Chicago voice. "I try to get home weekends, but I got a special committee meeting tomorrow, so I'm stuck here until the end of next week."

"Can I buy you a drink someplace?"

"I'd rather just take a walk," he answered. "I walk a lot nights when I'm down here."

I said that was fine with me, and we stepped out into the mild evening air. It was refreshing being without a topcoat. I let Daley set the course, which took us through the streets of downtown Springfield and over into the area around the domed State Capitol.

"You know, I've lived in Chicago all my life," I told him, "and I've never been here before. We were supposed to come down on a class trip when I was in school, but there was a scarlet fever epidemic, so it got canceled."

"I enjoy it," Daley said off-handedly. "When I walk around at night, the streets are quiet, peaceful, and I think it must have been a lot like this when Lincoln was here himself, before he went to Washington. He walked these same streets, past some of these same houses."

"A great president."

"For a Republican," Daley said, his smooth face creased by a slight smile. "I've gotten interested in him since being here the last couple of years. There's something Lincoln said about this town that I like so much I memorized it: 'I believe that a man should be proud of the city in which he lives, and he will so live that his city will be proud that he lives in it.' That's how I feel about Chicago."

"I guess I do too," I agreed, figuring his comment begged a response, "although I've never thought about it."

"Where'd you grow up?" he asked.

"Pilsen."

"What parish? I'm Nativity of Our Lord–always have been. That's in Bridgeport."

"St. Agnes," I said without missing a beat, although my parents had stopped being active Catholics years before, and I hadn't been inside a church since a year or so after Norma and I were married.

"Mm, 26th Street, isn't it?"

"You know the city well–26th and Lawndale." I didn't bother to tell him I'd moved up north, because he'd surely ask what my parish was now. And unless I had misread this man, he gauged others at least in part by their involvement in the church, specifically of the Catholic variety. It was not an area where I could stand much scrutiny, and at the moment I felt it was important to have Daley's good opinion.

We walked for the next few minutes in silence through residential streets before Daley spoke. "You wanted to talk to me. About what?"

I drew in air and let in out slowly, choosing my words with care. "You've been following the coverage of the Martindale murder?"

"Of course I've read about it, just about everywhere I've turned. You can't avoid it. So?"

"Well…I've got sources–maybe because I've been in the news business so long–and they tell me it wasn't a mob hit."

Daley's full face registered surprise. "Who would have done it then?"

"That's the question. There are several theories floating around," I improvised. "Now I want to stress that that's all they are–theories. And…"

"But the police think it was the syndicate, don't they? That's what I've been reading in all the papers, including yours."

"The cops publicly say it's the syndicate because they've got no other leads and it seems like a logical explanation. When in doubt, blame the organization; who's going to contradict you?"

Daley sniffed dismissively. "When in doubt, when somebody gets gunned down the way Martindale was, it usually *is* the organization. What's all this got to do with me?"

"Nothing, really, except I need your help."

"Yeah, how so?" He tossed a suspicious look in my direction but kept up his brisk pace.

"One theory is that somebody in the Democratic organization hired a gun to–"

"That is totally ridiculous!" Dick Daley snapped in a voice that was just below a shout. He stopped in the middle of a residential block and pivoted to face me, chin out. "I should have expected this from the *Tribune*. Your paper will do anything to smear us."

I held up a hand. "This isn't the *Tribune*, honest. This is me. Nobody on the paper even knows that I'm down here."

"Huh! I'm supposed to believe that?"

"Look, I'm a Democrat myself, always have been. There's lots of us at the *Trib*," I said, even though only two or maybe three reporters I was aware of consistently voted Democratic.

"If you're one of us, how can you stand to work for that damned Colonel?" Daley demanded, hands on hips and head tilted aggressively.

I lifted my shoulders and let them drop. "It's a living. They pay on time, and they don't tell me how to write, or what to write, no matter what you hear around town. And remember, the *Tribune* did endorse Kelly for mayor in '35."

"Well, sure, but they couldn't very well come out for that Wetten guy the Republicans were running," Daley said. "That would have been a joke. Besides, the Colonel and Kelly are cronies, so that endorsement wasn't politics as much as it was the buddy system working."

"Maybe so, but the *Trib* also endorsed Brady for city clerk, and the last time I looked, he was a one hundred percent Democrat," I persisted. "Now I'm not saying somebody from the party is behind the murder, but it is one possibility."

Daley dismissed that with the sweep of a hand. "Bull! In the first place, people on opposite sides of politics may not like each other, but they don't go around knocking one another off. And second, nobody I know or have talked to in the party considered Martindale a threat to Kelly next year. Ed would've squashed him like a bug. In fact, regulars I know who have been around forever said they *hoped* Martindale would be the Republican candidate because they figured he'd be easier to beat than Green or even old Thompson."

"What do you think?"

"That's an easy one. Kelly will win against anybody, and win big. Let the Republicans run whoever they want to, it's not gonna matter. Hey, why are you even talking to me about this? I'm small potatoes–way down the line in the party."

"Seamus Kilkenney said you were a comer, someone to watch."

Another wave of the hand, this one not dismissive. "Well, Mr. K's a friend of my folks, a wonderful guy. He'd say things like that."

"Maybe, but I know him pretty well, and he only says what he means. I want a favor from you."

We were under a streetlamp at a corner, facing each other in its cheery circle of light. Daley looked down at his well-polished shoes, then at me. "After Mr. K called me the other day and said you wanted to see me, I phoned my father. He doesn't know you–never met you, but he says you bailed Mr. K out once."

"People help their friends."

"Sure. This was a big one though…the way I hear it; they were going to put him out of business."

He was referring to the time just after I'd moved to Clark Street that a district police lieutenant had been shaking down the Killer for big bucks–so big that, as Daley said, he was close to shutting down.

"That greedy bastard," I said. "One of the slimiest cops this town's ever known, and that takes in a lot of territory. He was bleeding businesses all over his district. Somebody had to do something."

"And it was you." A hint of respect had crept into Daley's tone.

"Being a reporter has its ups and downs. One of the downs is the wages, which are okay at the *Trib*–I'm not griping, mind you–but it's still not the kind of money that'll ever get me a house in Winnetka or Park Ridge or Elmhurst. One of the ups is that you get to know people–famous people, interesting people, strange people, and sometimes disgusting, dishonest, disreputable people–it comes with the job. And because I happen to work at Police Headquarters, I know cops–*lots* of cops. And I was damned if I was going to let some greasy-palmed stooge with brass on his uniform shutter my new favorite saloon because its owner wouldn't help finance that stooge's cottage at Lake Geneva and the swivel-hipped floozie he kept in some Drake Towers duplex."

"So you got the cop tossed out on his ear, and off the force."

"You could put it that way."

"I just did. You saved Mr. K and his bar."

"Sort of."

"Not 'sort of.' You did."

"All right, I did. But being with the paper helped. Brass on the force listened to what I had to say. If I had just been Joe Blow, who knows whether I'd have gotten anywhere."

Daley nodded. "You said you want a favor."

"Yeah."

Another nod. The shadows thrown across his face by the streetlamp made him seem older and more careworn than earlier. "All right, I'll hear you out, as long as it doesn't involve anything illegal."

"Thanks, it doesn't. I need to know if somebody–anybody–in the Democratic Party was in any way involved in Martindale's killing."

Daley jammed his hands into his pants pockets. He was working to control what I later learned was a high-octane temper. After two deep breaths, he responded. "I can tell you now that I'm not going to find anything." The words were spaced, and uttered with a quiet intensity.

"But you'll make an honest effort?"

His body tensed under the well-fitting, pin-striped suit. "Mr. Malek, that is the only kind of effort I ever make," he said, and coming from him, somehow those words didn't sound stuffy.

"Thanks again. And at the risk of pushing my luck, I have one more favor to ask you–but this one's really of your father."

"Huh?"

"The Killer–Mr. K, that is…most of his customers called him the Killer–keeps hoping that maybe sometime your father will stop by his watering hole. If maybe you could say something…"

This time, Daley's nod was accompanied by a full-fledged smile, which looked good on him. He should try it more often.

Chapter 8

A week passed, then another, and more, with no word from State Representative Daley. Not that I really expected to hear anything; I figured the guy had tolerated me–even humored me–down in Springfield because of my role in helping the Killer sweep that larcenous police lieutenant out of his life. But I was far too much of a realist to have illusions that Daley would do any serious poking around inside his own party in search of the murderer of a potential Republican mayoral candidate.

The calendar now claimed we were in April, although a snowstorm the first week made it feel more like February. Interest in the Martindale murder, both in the Police Headquarters pressroom and around town, had dwindled so that it ranked somewhere between curling and field hockey. The prevailing opinion was that the syndicate had been responsible, which meant by logical extension that the case was effectively closed–or permanently open if you viewed it from the Police Department's perspective, based on their past successes at solving mob rub-outs.

The Crime Commission made periodic grumblings, but that was hardly news. And I was still intrigued myself, in large measure because of my enforced joyride with Monk and Mel and the hoarse-voiced hood who seemed to be their leader. But there was plenty else keeping me occupied, both on the job and in the world at large.

Like for instance the pissing contest between the Police Department and the State's Attorney's office. It started when two detectives from the Town Hall station house on the North Side gave a pair of suspects a "pass"–let them go free in the holdup of a driver of a horse-race handbook–because, as the dicks later claimed, "we didn't believe they were guilty."

Courtney, the State's Attorney, blew his stack because he had to learn about this in the papers, not from the police. He countered by subpoenaing four of the city's top cops, including John Prendergast, chief of the uniformed force, and Commissioner Allman himself, to explain why they allowed bookies to operate freely.

Courtney, already angling to take on Ed Kelly in the Democratic mayoral primary in '39, wasn't about to stop there. To further embarrass the Police Department, he got his own force to raid downtown handbooks. Among his catch were John "Chew Tobacco" Ryan and Hymie "Loud Mouth" Levin, the latter a long-time hood who'd been one of Capone's bagmen before Al got sent off on his federally funded vacations in Georgia and California.

All this, plus Allman's limp denial that the police frequently gave passes to suspects, kept the pressroom crew at Headquarters busy filing stories that more often than not ended up on the front pages of our respective papers–sometimes as the headline story. But that kind of play was soon to end, courtesy of one Adolph Hitler.

The Fuehrer's troops had marched into Austria, seized Vienna, "annexed" (Hitler's word) that land to Germany, and begun the Nazi harassment of Austrian Jews in what later was recognized as the de facto beginning of World War II. And, although nobody knew it at the time, that invasion–along with the Spanish Civil War and Japan's takeover of China–marked the rise of international news to the extent that local stories, particularly those about police and crime, would never again command the headlines and dominate the front pages as they had over the previous two decades.

But to those of us who covered the police, the courts, and other areas of city government, such faraway events seemed as inessential and transitory as they appeared in the grainy newsreel footage on Movietone News preceding the feature films in the theaters.

"Hell, this'll all blow over now that Hitler's got Austria,"

Anson Masters pronounced, dismissively tapping the front page of his own newspaper, which shrilled the invasion in three-inch capital letters. "That tin-pot Napoleon just wants all the heinie-talkers together in one country. Seems reasonable enough."

"Following that line of reasoning, he'll also be wanting chunks of Switzerland and Czechoslovakia–they've got German-speaking regions, too," said the City News kid, who as the weeks passed had grown bolder and had started challenging the wisdom and the pronouncements of his elders.

Masters waved the comment aside. "Not likely, my young friend. The guy may love uniforms and parades and be power-hungry, but he's not stupid. He knows when to stop pushing."

I wondered if the kid wasn't right, however. I'd read an article somewhere, maybe in *Time* magazine, about Hitler's interest in Czechoslovakia. The writer suggested that his intentions went well beyond that little country's Sudeten German population. The Fuehrer was said to covet the Czech industrial might, not all of which lay in what was being termed Sudetenland. I thought about my father's sister over there, Aunt Hana, who he wrote to every month and whose sepia bridal photograph from the '20s or earlier was framed in oval on the mahogany table next to the Tiffany lamp in the living room of my parents' Pilsen apartment. And there were my mother's cousins and nephews and nieces in Brno to whom she sent money and candy every Easter and Christmas.

But to be honest, I didn't think long about them. To me, what was going on over in Europe was only mildly troubling, like reading about an earthquake in Japan or a revolution in Central America. I was swept up in my own life–seeing Peter on weekends, trying to figure out whether there was any way to get back together with Norma, and taking my enjoyment where I could find it, which more often than not was on a barstool at the Killer's.

One Friday, Leo Cahill from the *Trib* sports copy desk rang me at headquarters to say that he had an extra Annie Oakley in the fourth row for the heavyweight title fight at the

Chicago Stadium between the new champ, Joe Louis, and some pug from Minnesota named Harry Thomas.

I'd never been much interested in boxing, but there was a lot of excitement centering on Louis–the "Brown Bomber" as the sportswriters had tagged him–and what a fighting machine he was. Plus I'd never seen a championship bout, so I shoveled down a fast supper at a Pixley & Ehlers cafeteria in the Loop after work and met Cahill at one of the Stadium gates.

Leo and I were a long way from being close friends–if he had any close friends, I wasn't aware of it. He was a needler, always looking for ways to rile people, particularly Cub fans (like me), Republicans (unlike me), suburbanites, and Protestants. He was that relative rarity, an Irish teetotaler, a member of a group that called itself the "Pioneers"–Irishmen who had taken the pledge. Leo knew about my own drinking history; nothing about private lives on a newspaper ever stays confidential for more than forty-eight hours. And he found frequent occasion to bring up what he liked to call my "little Achilles heel," always in a patronizing manner laced with pity and overly solicitous sympathy.

Maybe that's why the moment we were settled into our seats at the Stadium, I ordered a Schlitz from a vendor and winked at Leo. "Coke man'll be along in a minute," I told him. "I'll treat." He didn't smile.

The big barn looked to be less than half-filled, with almost nobody up in the rafter levels. The next day's papers reported the crowd at ten-grand-plus, but they had to be counting the Andy Frain ushers, vendors, janitors, and cockroaches–none of whom saw much of a fight.

From the opening bell, it was clear even to my uneducated pugilistic eye that the champion was in total charge. He pounded Thomas all over the ring, knocking him down a half dozen times, four of them in the fourth round alone, before finally putting the poor outclassed lug away at the end of the fifth.

"Louis was carrying him," I told Leo on the way out of the Stadium, doing a little jabbing of my own. "He must've been

94

told that the fight had to go five."

He wheeled on me. "You're full of garbage," he spat, causing heads to turn. "There was no fix–Louis is straight as they come. Snap, your problem is that you just don't like Negroes."

"Now it's you who's full of garbage," I fired back in genuine anger. "Boxing's been filled with white bums for years, like that Primo Carnera guy. Hell, I got no beef with Louis, he's the best around, by far. I'm just saying that the fight could have been over in the first round, and you damn well know it. Be interesting to know why it lasted as long as it did."

Surprisingly, Leo had no comeback, only a shake of the head, and I went home with the satisfaction of having out-needled the needler. I should have known, though, that he'd find a way to counterpunch. A couple of weeks later, my phone rang on a Sunday morning around 8:00. I rolled over in bed, groaning and reaching for it on the nightstand. My effort was rewarded with Leo's voice.

"Hey, Snap, seen today's Final?"

"Not yet, why?" I croaked irritably.

He chuckled. "I tried to call you last night, but got no answer. I suppose you were out on the town, eh?"

"Dammit, Leo, quit beating around the bush. You got me up, now what do you want?"

Another laugh. "It's a fine, fine day, Snap. I been up for two hours, been to Mass, and had a good breakfast. Now I'm just rereading the sports section and thinking I ought to call my old Cub fan buddy Snap Malek and see what he thinks about his team's latest batty move."

"What in the hell are you talking about?"

"Snap, guess who the Cubs traded for yesterday. Go on, guess."

"Leo, I'm not in the mood for guessing games."

"Go on, just take a guess."

"Leo, I got no idea. Mel Ott maybe?"

This time he roared. "Now *that* would have been smart, but the Cubs aren't smart, are they? Or any good, either, for that matter."

"They beat your South Side warriors ten out of sixteen out in California this spring," I reminded him.

"Sure, but that's just exhibition stuff and you know it. Wait till they play in the City Series this fall, when it really counts for something; it'll be the same old script–Sox in five games, six at most. Now, got another guess on who your boys picked up off the scrap heap?"

"No, tell me before I pass out from the suspense."

"The once-great Dizzy Dean, believe it or not, my poor misguided friend. And you know what they gave up to get that tattered, battered arm of his? Davis, Shoun, and Stainback, that's who. Plus close to a hunnert thou. Just about the biggest deal in baseball history, and by far the stupidest."

"For the Cardinals, that is," I put in gamely, still stunned by what I had just heard.

"Poor old Snap, ever the optimist in the face of disaster," Leo clucked. "If Diz had been any good, Branch Rickey woulda never peddled him. He won't win five games this year– hell, he'll be lucky if he even *pitches* in five games. Care to make a small wager on where your Wrigleys finish this season?"

I drew in air, letting it out slowly and working to keep my voice even. "Sure, Leo, I've got fifty bucks that says they'll win the pennant," I told him, listening to my own words as if someone else were mouthing them.

That shut him up for two heartbeats. "Snap, I don't want to take advantage of, well…that Achilles' heel of yours."

"Stuff it, Leo. You're the one who was so hot to make a bet. As they say on the street, put up or shut up."

"What kind of odds you want?"

"Who said anything about odds?"

"Even up? You're kidding!"

"Try me, Leo."

"Geez, Snap, that's a lot of jack," he said, lowering his voice, probably so Marie couldn't hear him.

"I'm surprised. I figured that you'd jump at such easy

money," I pressed on. "After all, we both know that ol' Diz is through, right?"

"You're on, but as the Good Lord is my witness, you're givin' cash away," Leo replied stiffly. For a few seconds after we hung up, I felt a surge of exhilaration, but it dissolved when the rational part of my brain reminded me that I had just laid out more than a week's gross pay on a nag–make that a team– that might just finish out of the money, behind the Giants, Cards, Pirates, and maybe even the Reds.

I felt a little more confident about the bet a few days later, though, when Dean was the winning pitcher against Cincinnati in the second game of the season, although he gave up four runs. And I felt a whole lot better about it the next Sunday. I was one of 35,000–a large turnout for a gray day in April–at Wrigley Field to see Dizzy go the distance and throw a four-hit shutout against the Cardinals–the very bunch whose uniform he'd worn just nine days earlier. The fastball I remember from his St. Louis glory days was gone, as the whole league had begun to realize last season. But his slow stuff–and it was really slow–seemed to fool his former mates, which had to delight him. And by the late innings, chants of "Diz...Diz...Diz" were breaking out all over the park. That must have spurred Dean on, because he retired the last nine Cardinal batters.

After walking back along Clark Street to my apartment from the game, I suppressed the urge to call Leo and gloat, and I'm glad I did. I might have been on the line and missed the call from State Representative Daley.

Chapter 9

I had been back in the apartment for less than three minutes when the phone rang. I didn't recognize Daley's voice until he identified himself.

"Be damned. I figured I wasn't going to hear from you," I said.

"You figured wrong," he answered without hostility or any other emotion as far as I could tell. "I've been calling all afternoon. Do you plan to be at work tomorrow?"

"It's a Monday, so I figure to, unless I was canned over the weekend and haven't gotten the word."

Daley let my attempt at drollery pass without comment. "I'm up here for a couple of days," he said. "There's a little restaurant about a block and a half north of Police Headquarters on the west side of State, and I assume your bosses give you time off for lunch. Can you meet me there at noon tomorrow?"

"On the condition that I pick up the lunch tab."

"I won't fight you for it," Daley answered.

The café, barely a sharp knife's cut above being a greasy spoon, was nonetheless always crowded with uniformed cops, dicks, lawyers, reporters, judges, bondsmen, bailiffs, bookmakers, pimps, prostitutes, and assorted other players in the cavalcade that moved through the law enforcement nerve center of the country's second-largest city.

I got there at 5 to 12:00 and settled into a booth near the back. Dick Daley arrived two minutes later, and I hailed him as he breezed confidently through the front door, dapper in a brown double-breasted suit, starched white shirt, and brown-and-yellow tie. He stopped twice on his way back, once to pump the paw of a white-haired uniformed sergeant at the counter, and then to lean down and exchange apparently friendly words with a guy in a booth who was the only person in the place better dressed than he.

"How y'been?" he asked as we shook hands mechanically and he slid in opposite me.

"Makin' it. You?"

He nodded. "All right. I gather you're still interested in that Martindale business, right?"

"Of course."

"I figured you would be." Daley threw a glance over one shoulder, not that anyone, even in the next booth, could hear us above the din, and leaned forward, riveting me with his light blue eyes. "Lloyd Martindale was not a nice man," the legislator pronounced, giving each word equal emphasis.

"Because he was a Republican?"

Daley shook his head vigorously. "Hey, I don't judge people by their party." He grinned for an instant. "Not most of them, anyway. But on this I'm dead serious. It's got nothing to do with party."

"You have my full attention," I answered. He started in, but was interrupted by the arrival of a waitress reeking of cologne. We each ordered corned beef on rye and coffee.

"All right," Daley continued, leaning forward again as if he were letting me in on a secret. "I did some checking with a source, who–"

"Care to name the source?"

He set his jaw. "I do not. Listen, Mr. Malek, I'll lay my cards down. I was bothered by what you said when we met in Springfield last month. You seemed more or less convinced, for whatever reasons, that Martindale was not a mob hit, and I have to take you on faith about that, especially knowing that as a newspaperman you must have good sources. Now I want you to know that I never, not for one minute, truly believed he was killed for political reasons. But–"

"But you wanted to be sure?"

Daley gave a slow, reluctant nod as the coffee was poured. "I need your word that this conversation is confidential." He threw a glance over his shoulder again, and I noticed that beads of perspiration had formed on his upper lip.

"You've got my word. And you can check again with Kilkenny about whether that word is good."

"Oh, I've done that. Now, my source had already…my source did some checking and learned among other things that Mr. Martindale was not the sterling individual that he–and some members of the press–led people to believe he was."

"And I gather that your source also put your mind to rest regarding any machine or party role in the killing, right?"

Another nod, this one not reluctant.

"All right, time to summarize," I said as the corned beef sandwiches (with pickle) were plunked down unceremoniously in front of us, along with the check, which I scooped up. "Now I am, as I said, more or less convinced that the crime syndicate is clean on Martindale. You apparently are positive that the Democratic Party is clean as well, but you also suggest that Lloyd Martindale himself was *not* so clean. You're not going to tell me that he had ties with the mob, are you? Because I'm not as gullible as I may look."

Daley took a healthy bite of his sandwich and held up a palm for silence while he chewed. "No, I am not going to tell you that. Mr. Malek, Lloyd Martindale was a pervert."

That sent my eyebrows shooting halfway up my forehead. "We are talking here about 'Model Citizen' Martindale, aren't we?"

"We are." Richard Daley was grim-faced. "Twenty-five years or so ago, when Martindale was a young man in his early twenties, he was accused–more than once–of molesting children. Young kids, both boys and girls."

I almost choked on the last bite of my sandwich. "My God. As far as I know, nothing about that ever made it into the papers."

"Yeah, and for good reason," Daley growled. "His father, the grand and rich steel tycoon Edgar Martindale, used his connections at City Hall and with the police and God only knows where else to get the business hushed up tight, really tight. Apparently, no charges were ever made."

"If this is true, your source, or sources, impress me. Do you have any specifics?"

Daley shook his head and finished his sandwich.

"Okay, let's back up a step. You haven't said why you're so sure Martindale's murder was not committed or ordered by the Democratic Party or the machine."

"I can assure you that my sources checked out this aspect very, very thoroughly."

"All right, that being the case, then do you, or your sources, know who the murderer was?"

"No, but based on what was learned, I have to wonder–and this is only speculation–I have to wonder if someone was getting revenge for…what I mentioned before."

"The molestings. But you said that those were–what–about twenty-five years ago?"

"People have long memories about certain things," Daley observed somberly.

"Granted. Especially something like this. I'd like to do some checking on those charges. You must have gotten some specifics, like the year, or the name, or the location."

His expression remained grim. "There were at least two, and they happened in Chicago. And I can tell you this much for sure…Lloyd Martindale's name never even made it onto the police blotter, his old man saw to that." Daley's tone reflected his disgust. "That is all I know, and even that is more than I care to know."

I finished the watery coffee in my cup (refills free). "Mr. Daley, do you know what I think? I think your source is some sort of private investigator, and maybe an off-duty cop, who is either on the party payroll or on retainer. Or possibly there's more than one of them. My guess is that he, or they, had already begun poking around into Martindale's past when it looked like the guy had a damned good chance to be the Republican candidate for mayor in the next election."

Daley's broad face reddened slightly, but he said nothing, so I ploughed on. "The digging apparently hit the jackpot, at least from a Democratic point of view. And I have no doubt–I don't expect you to comment on this–that if Martindale *had* been the candidate, his long-hidden past would have become public, and very quickly."

"You're right about one thing that you said–I won't comment," Daley replied curtly.

"So now that Martindale has gone to his final reward, wherever that may be, the information is of no value to the party, and it dies with the man, right?"

He shrugged and looked at his watch. "As I told you, I won't comment, except to say that some things are better off left alone, Mr. Malek. I found out what you asked me to and now, if you'll excuse me, I'm due at a meeting in the Loop in less than half an hour. Thank you very much for lunch."

"My pleasure," I said half-heartedly, rising with him. We shook hands, even more formally than at the beginning of the meal, and State Representative Richard J. Daley left the noisy café with the self-assured stride of a man who knew precisely who he was and where he was going.

Three Strikes You're Dead

Chapter 10

By the time my frustration at Daley's reticence had abated, I was back at my desk in the Headquarters pressroom. After exchanging jibes with Eddie Metz and staring at the peeling paint on the ceiling, I put in a call to Ruby Ryan, who had worked the switchboard at the City News Bureau since sometime back in the '20s.

"Stevie, how you doin'?" she effused. It had been a decade since I left City News for the *Trib*, yet she still remembered me. But then, it was said that Ruby Ryan remembered everybody who's passed through City News, which meant most of the reporters on the Chicago dailies, plus scores of others on papers from Savannah to Sioux Falls to Sacramento.

"I'm one step ahead of my creditors and a half-step ahead of the law," I cracked. "Ruby, is 'Steel Trap' Bascomb still among us?"

"Well, yes, but not in very good shape nowadays," she said in a stage whisper. Ruby liked sounding conspiratorial. "He's slipped a lot the last couple of years, so I hear tell. His Sylvia died three, maybe four years back now, but he still lives in the same house he always has, out in Oak Park. His daughter's moved in with him–she's divorced–and she looks after him. She's swell, a real peach."

"Got the number?" I asked, knowing the answer. Ruby was a repository for hundreds of phone numbers–many of them in her head.

"Of course, Stevie," she said, reeling it off without pause. "But be prepared; I'm told that Lemuel's gotten pretty senile, poor guy." I thanked her and promised that I would drop by the office sometime soon and say hello, which both of us knew was unlikely.

Lem "Steel Trap" Bascomb was a top-drawer reporter who had covered the Criminal Courts for City News from around the turn of the century until his retirement a half dozen years ago, and we'd worked together for several months in the early '30s when I filled in for the *Trib's* man on that beat. Steel Trap had been tagged with that moniker because of his remarkable ability to remember names, cases, and exact dates. How much of that once-fabled memory was left I now intended to discover.

The voice on the other end of the line was soft, almost childlike. I told her who I was, that I had known her father years before, and that I wanted to stop by for a visit with him.

"Daddy's...well, not always too lucid," she said apologetically. "He has his days, but also days that aren't so good, and it's hard to know how you'll find him if you do come. What did you want to see him about?"

"I'm working on a story that has its origins in a case that happened a number of years ago. I think he might remember me, I hope he does. But even more, I was hoping he might be able to recall some of the details."

"Well, I realize Daddy was known for his great memory, but I'm afraid you may be disappointed. However, today he's been quite clear-headed."

"Well, would it be convenient if I came by tonight?"

A pause. "Yes, I guess that would be fine. You're welcome to have dinner with us, although it's nothing fancy– just franks and beans. We usually eat about 5:30."

"Thanks for the kind offer, but I couldn't get there that soon from work, and I don't want to upset your schedule, so I'd better pass on dinner. Would it be all right if I came at about 6:30?" She said it would and gave me the address.

I rode the Lake Street El west to beyond where the tracks drop down onto street level and got off at the Ridgeland Avenue station. Other than the day-long El ride Peter and I had taken, I'd only been in Oak Park once before, years ago, but I had a good map. I walked several blocks south along quiet, shaded streets lined with solid and substantial two-story houses of frame or stucco that were set well back from the sidewalk on neat, narrow lots.

My destination turned out to be one of the stucco numbers, white and fronted by an enclosed porch that ran the width of the house and had four lace-curtained windows on each side of its front door. I pushed the buzzer and heard nothing from within, but after a half-minute, the door opened inward to reveal a petite, auburn-haired woman of perhaps thirty-five with an oval face, brown eyes, ivory complexion, and a shy, tentative smile.

"Mr. Malek? Please come in," she said, gracefully stepping aside.

I thanked her and mumbled something about not having asked her name when we were on the phone.

"Oh, don't apologize," she said with a pleasant laugh. "I should have introduced myself when you called; it's my fault. I'm Catherine–Catherine Reed. I told Daddy you were coming, and it seemed to me that he showed some recognition of your name, although honestly, I couldn't be sure."

"It wouldn't surprise me if he didn't remember. We did only work together for a few months," I said, following the small woman into the house and admiring her trim figure, which was modestly displayed in a blue, belted dress. We passed through a beamed-ceiling living room with dark walls, dark furniture, landscape paintings, and a brick fireplace, then turned left into an airy, cheerful little sitting room with yellow, flowered wallpaper.

In an easy chair next to a window with Venetian blinds sat a wizened, prow-jawed, and hollow-eyed man in bedroom slippers, baggy slacks, and a red flannel shirt buttoned at the top. He bore little more resemblance to the Steel Trap Bascomb of my memory than I did to Franklin Roosevelt.

"Daddy, here is Mr. Malek, from the *Tribune*," Catherine said cheerfully. "He's come here all the way from the city just to see you."

Bascomb raised a gnarled hand and said something that

sounded like "Hey" as I dropped into a straight-backed chair opposite him.

"You're looking good, Steel Trap," I lied. "It's been a lot of years since I've seen you."

"Yeah, lotta years, lotta years." He ran a hand through sparse and unkempt dust-colored hair and raised the hand again, then let it drop limply into his lap.

"Mr. Malek, can I get you a cup of coffee?" Catherine asked from the doorway. "Daddy's already had his."

I said thanks, told her I took it black, and turned back to her father, who was looking straight ahead, unblinking. "Do you keep up with the news these days?" I asked.

That brought a nod. "News…lotsa news. See the papers. *Trib…Examiner…Times*…all of 'em."

"Glad to hear it. You were always a better reporter than anybody on any of the dailies."

He chuckled hoarsely, slapping a leg. "Damn right. Lazy sumbitches."

"Did you read about Lloyd Martindale's murder in February?"

"Marn'dale…yeah. Plugged in the pump."

"Did you know him?"

He turned to me, squinting and cocking his head. "Rich father. Buncha steel mills."

"That's right," I said, mildly encouraged by his recall. Catherine tiptoed in and set a cup of coffee on the small lamp table at my elbow. "Edgar Martindale was one of the richest men in town, maybe in the whole country," I went on. "Do you remember whether his son was ever in any sort of trouble? A long time ago, that is?"

Steel Trap Bascomb screwed up his face and made clicking noises with his tongue. "*Mmm*…trouble…" He hunched his shoulders, closed his eyes, and formed a steeple with his hands.

"Daddy always does that when he's trying to remember something," Catherine murmured from the hallway, where she had remained standing. "It's good for him to have someone ask him specifics–it forces him to make his mind work."

I gave her a smile and drank coffee while Bascomb kept struggling to recapture some shard of recollection. "Ask him again," Catherine prompted.

"Steel Trap, do you remember if Lloyd Martindale was ever arrested?"

He opened his eyes and his head jerked up and down, which I took to be a nod. "Sumbitch. Messed with kids…damn…with kids."

My heart beat faster. "You mean that Lloyd Martindale was a child molester? Is that what you're saying?" Catherine, still at the door, drew in air sharply, but I kept myself fixated on the old man.

"Sumbitch…bastard."

I leaned forward, elbows on knees. "And was he charged, Steel Trap? Did Lloyd Martindale get charged for what he did?"

He tried to laugh, but it came out a rasp. "Oh, nossir, no siree. Father's money, lotsa money…no stories…no stories. No siree."

"Do you know who any of these were–" now I was the one stumbling for words "any of these children were that he hurt?"

"Next door. Right…"

Steel Trap's angular chin dipped and nudged his chest. He had run down like a music box at the end of its tune, and I didn't have the key to wind him up again.

Neither, apparently, did Catherine. When I turned to her, she gave a shake of the head and beckoned me with an index finger.

I followed her into the living room, where we sat side by side on a davenport. "Mr. Malek, you won't get any more from Daddy tonight, I'm afraid. As it is, you did very well–and I'll say again what I said before: This was good for him, too."

"You really believe that?"

"Absolutely. I know it probably didn't seem that way to you, but I'm here with Daddy almost all the time, when I'm not at work, and he seemed very animated tonight, compared to the usual. Some days, he doesn't speak ten words from morning till he goes to bed, just reads the papers–at least I guess he's reading them–and stares at the walls or listens to the radio. Also, he loved being called 'Steel Trap' again–I could tell. You brought back some of his favorite times, back in the days when he felt he was somebody."

"Well, he *was* somebody, maybe the best beat reporter this town's ever seen, even though he wasn't with one of the dailies. And to think that I almost didn't use his old nickname because I felt I might be getting too familiar with him."

She smiled. "Well, I'm awfully glad you did. And–oh!–that sounds terrible about Lloyd Martindale and what he did. I hope you don't mind that I was eavesdropping."

"Not at all, Mrs. Reed. Do you think your father might remember any more, later on?"

"You're one step ahead of me," Mr. Malek. "I was about to say that, if you have no objections, I'll bring the subject up with Daddy again when I think the moment is right. His memory fades in and out, like that radio next to his chair."

"I have no objection to anything except you calling me Mr. Malek. I answer to Steve."

"And I am Catherine," she responded, folding her hands in her lap in a gesture of finality.

"But not Cathy?"

She shook her head. "For some reason, I never liked Cathy, maybe because a fifth-grade teacher I couldn't stand used to call me that. Mr.–Steve, if I can get Daddy talking about Lloyd Martindale again, what specifically do you want to know?"

"Names, of course–any names he can recall, either victims or police who might have been part of the investigations. And dates, or at least years, although I don't expect your father to dredge those up from the recesses of his memory. Remember, all this probably happened well before we got into the World War."

Catherine appeared thoughtful, her wide brown eyes casting around the room as if she were seeking inspiration.

"When I read about the murder, I suppose I automatically assumed that Lloyd Martindale was killed by the crime syndicate. And the papers, your *Tribune* among them, certainly led us to think so, judging by what they wrote. But you truly believe it might have had something to do with some perversions, don't you?"

"The thought has occurred to me. I probably shouldn't object to the syndicate taking the rap here–God knows they've pulled off enough in the last twenty years that they didn't get tagged with. But…"

"But your newspaperman's curiosity gets in the way of that kind of thinking, doesn't it?"

"Hey, spoken like the daughter of a reporter," I told her.

That drew an almost gleeful laugh as Catherine clapped her hands. "Oh, when Mama was alive and I was in school, how both of us used to tease Daddy about how seriously he always took his work." She became suddenly serious. "But it was a respectful sort of teasing…we really admired the way he dug into stories and ferreted out information."

"With good reason…he was a bulldog," I replied. "Is it true, as I've heard other reporters say, that he would come home after work, have a quick dinner, and then start calling police and other sources?"

She nodded. "Yes, it's true; right here in this house. It used to drive my mother crazy that he'd stay on our telephone some nights until midnight or even later. Once he called the police commissioner at home and wouldn't get off the line until he–the commissioner–gave Daddy some piece of information, I have no idea what it even was. Are you like that, Steve? Do you drive your family crazy, too? By always being on the job?" she asked good-naturedly.

"No, and no. First, I live alone–I'm divorced. So there's nobody to drive crazy except myself. Second, I'm afraid I don't have that same late-night zeal for the job that your father did."

"Oh, I am sorry," Catherine said, putting fingers to her lips. "I didn't mean to be nosy–about your private life, I mean. First I eavesdrop, then I pry."

"No offense of any kind taken," I laughed. "Honestly."

"Thank you." She laughed, too, self-consciously. "I guess I just don't get enough practice with conversation these days. I'm divorced, too, by the way. I work four mornings a week at the Oak Park Public Library, where nobody–including the staff–says much. And when they do, it's of course in whispers, or close to it. The rest of the time, I'm mostly here with Daddy, and you can see how hard it is to carry on an extended dialogue with him, poor dear."

"True enough. Say, you can answer a question for me, Catherine. I've often wondered why your father always stayed with City News. He must have gotten offers from the dailies."

"Oh, he did, yes he did!" she said, eyes now sparkling. "Several times. I remember Mama saying that the *Examiner* tried to hire him at least once, and so did the *Evening Post,* long gone now. And your *Tribune* did, too. He had actually worked on a paper, the *Inter-Ocean*, for a short time way back in the '90s, I think, but he disliked one of the editors so much that he vowed he'd never work on another paper again. Said there was just too much office politics and favoritism, plus pressure from the advertising department to keep stories out of the paper that might reflect poorly on certain companies that advertised."

"He may have a point there," I said. "I didn't really know your father all that well–as I alluded to earlier, we only worked out of the same pressroom at the Criminal Courts Building for a few months once, fairly near the end of his career–but I can tell you that he was respected, almost revered, really, by guys on every paper in this town, to say nothing of police and judges and lawyers. Nobody ever even referred to him by name–he was just Steel Trap. I doubt if most of them even knew his first name."

"That means a lot coming from another newspaperman; thank you," she said softly. I thought I saw a tear forming in a corner of her eye, so I looked away, concentrating on brushing nonexistent lint from a trouser leg.

After a pause, she went on. "I promise I'll keep asking

Daddy about Martindale. And Steve?"

"Yes?"

"Will you come to dinner soon? We can make it a little later to suit your schedule. I know that Daddy would really enjoy it."

I said I would as I rose to leave. And I suppose I hoped it wasn't only her father who would enjoy having me at the table.

Three Strikes You're Dead

Chapter 11

As the Lake Street El rattled and swayed eastward from Oak Park through the spring darkness toward the twinkling lights of the Loop skyscrapers, I took stock of the Martindale situation.

Scenario Number One (the Police and Newspaper Theory): The crime syndicate had Lloyd Martindale killed to eliminate him from the mayoral picture, fearing that if elected, he would mount a drive to shut down every form of vice racier than church bingo. The major flaw in this theory was that even in the unlikely event that Martindale had got himself elected, he would never have been able to slice through enough layers of institutionalized corruption–including police, aldermen, ward heelers, and Satan knows who else–to accomplish much, if anything. To me a second although less-compelling flaw was Al Capone's insistence, relayed to me from Alcatraz none too gently by his presumed loyalists, that the mob was clean on the Martindale hit. When I had seen him in Atlanta, Capone had told me the same thing about the Lingle killing, and I didn't buy that for an instant; but in this situation, Capone seemed to have little to gain by lying. And as far as I could tell, the syndicate also had little to gain from Martindale's death. In fact, if anything, increased attention and public outcry were being aimed at them because of the murder. And the last thing the businesslike Frank Nitti wanted for the organization he now ruled was the klieg light of notoriety.

Scenario Number Two (the erstwhile Malek Theory): The Democratic Party was behind the murder. Other than Kilkenny's praise for him and my own instincts, I didn't know enough about Dick Daley to trust him completely, but Steel Trap Bascomb already had begun to confirm Daley's information regarding Martindale and his apparent sexual penchant for children.

Okay, I was never really strong on my theory, anyway. Like the syndicate, the Democrats didn't have a lot to gain by knocking Martindale off. They figured to win City Hall again in '39, and by killing the reformer they would run the risk of turning him into a martyr, not to mention possibly stampeding an outraged electorate toward the eventual Republican candidate.

Scenario Number Three (the New Malek Theory, with an assist by Dick Daley): Martindale's past sins had come home to roost, with fatal results. The more I thought about this one, the more it made sense, although…where to begin? Daley had told me that no arrest records existed on Martindale, and therefore no victims' names, no dates, no places. I was ready to take that on faith, given that the Democrats' investigator in all likelihood had researched it thoroughly. And what little I'd seen of State Representative Daley was enough to persuade me that I'd never get him to reveal the investigator's identity.

I briefly toyed with going to Fergus Fahey to see what he could–or would–dredge up from contacts within the department, but I nixed the idea as fast as I'd gotten it. For one thing, some twenty-five years ago the elder Martindale apparently bought off some number of police, among others. And Fahey, although essentially honest, was above all loyal to the force and would never feed me anything that would reflect badly on it. Also, this was shaping up as my story and nobody else's, and I didn't want to risk letting other reporters get their long noses under the tent, which might well happen if word got around to the current crop of reporters that Martindale had a sordid past.

As my train clattered above the Loop streets and I rose to exit and change for a northbound car on Clark Street, I was forced to conclude that at least now I would have to bide my time and hope that, with prodding from his daughter, Steel Trap Bascomb's memory would revive. That happened sooner than I expected.

Three days after my visit to Oak Park, I was in the Headquarters pressroom firing up a Lucky just after lunch when I got a call from Catherine Reed.

"Steve?" She pronounced the name as though still unsure that she should be so familiar.

"Hello, Catherine," I replied, placing the conversation solidly on a first-name basis. "How's your father?"

"Well…that's why I'm phoning. The last couple of days, I've been asking him things about…what we discussed the other night. And he's remembered some more, quite a bit more, in fact."

"I'm glad to hear that," I answered, keeping my voice low and cupping the mouthpiece.

"Yes. I thought you would be. I also thought you might like to come to dinner. You can either talk to Daddy about it when you come or…if he's having one of his bad times, I've, well, I've been taking some notes."

"That's a very nice offer. When did you have in mind?"

She paused, and I could hear her inhale. "Well, I know that you're probably very busy, but I was thinking that maybe tonight…that is, if…"

"Catherine, it just so happens that tonight would suit me fine, if you don't mind eating until after 6:30, which as you know is the earliest I could probably get there, although I'll shoot for 6:15."

The three of us sat at the thick-legged mahogany dining room table tying into Catherine's Yankee pot roast. Steel Trap's mind might have slipped, but it was nice to see that his appetite hadn't, and there was nothing wrong with his table manners either. At Catherine's whispered suggestion when I arrived, I held off asking the old reporter any questions until after we'd finished dinner.

"He doesn't like to talk while he's eating nowadays," she said as she hung my raincoat in the hall closet, "and yet in the old days, he'd chatter about work all the way through dinner, practically nonstop. Now it's as if there isn't room in his mind to do both at once."

I handed her the small bouquet of carnations that I had picked up at a florist in the Loop and told her I liked her dress, a pink number that looked to be the same style as the blue one she had worn on my earlier visit. She lowered her eyes, thanking me softly for both the flowers and the compliment as I pondered whether she was coquettish or just shy. I settled on the latter, maybe because that's the way I wanted it to be.

Steel Trap had acknowledged me with a muttered "Howyadoin?" and a vague wave as we began eating. Catherine was right about her father's table conversation–it was nonexistent. She held up her end though, asking me about current news stories in Chicago, including the kidnapping of a car full of socialites in front of the Drake Towers, where they were robbed of money and jewelry and released unharmed, and of the fistfight between two drunken police sergeants in a North Side precinct house that spilled out into the street and drew a crowd of cheering neighbors (formal investigation pending).

I put color and detail into my commentary about these and a couple of other newsy, crime-related events, and although Steel Trap made no comments, he nodded several times as he ate and seemed to follow the conversation with interest.

I got gladder by the minute that Catherine had been taking notes on her father's recollections the last few days, as I now despaired of getting anything substantial from the man face-to-face. But he fooled me.

After dinner, we retired to the sitting room, with Steel Trap dropping into the stuffed chair he had occupied when I saw him three days ago. Also as before, I drew up the chair opposite as Catherine came in with coffee for each of us. She then nodded in my direction, which I took to be a cue to start in on him.

"Well, Steel Trap," I said after taking a sip, "have you been thinking about Lloyd Martindale?"

He made a sort of snorting noise and threw up his arms, almost knocking his coffee cup off the end table. "Goddamn pervert!"

"Sure sounds like it," I said as Catherine rose from her chair and slipped around behind me to move the endangered cup farther from his elbow. "Did you ever report on what he did?"

Another snort, or whatever it was. "Huh! Tried, but that rich prick father put the lid on. Payoffs, payoffs, all over."

"Did the Martindales try to buy you off?"

That drew a wheezing laugh. "Nah, didn't hafta, f'Chrissake. Got to the bosses."

"Your bosses?"

"Everybody's bosses. Cops…editors…everybody. Lotsa dough. Lots. Spread around."

"Uh-huh. Do you know how many children Martindale messed around with?"

The tongue clicking began. He drank coffee, set the cup down deliberately, and sat back, lacing his hands over his stomach. "Ask him again," Catherine prompted.

"Steel Trap, stay with me on this. Do you know how many children Martindale did things to?"

More clicking as he came forward in his chair. "Two, maybe more. Two, yeah, two."

"Do you know who they were?"

"Two, 'least two." He leaned back again, nodding slowly.

"Boy or girls, Steel Trap?" I persisted.

"Both. Yeah, both."

I turned to Catherine. "Am I losing him?" I asked.

"I think you should keep trying," she urged. "Actually, you're doing at least as well as I did over more than two days. He responds to you."

If this was what she called responding, I began to realize just how difficult her life with the old guy must be. "Do you remember who those children were?" I asked him, spacing the words and giving each equal stress, as though I were talking to a four-year-old.

"Girl nex' door," he slurred. "Little girl."

"Next door to Martindale?"

He nodded–at least it seemed like a nod–and drank more

coffee. "Nex' door. Bastard."

"Do you remember the girl's name?"

He shook his head and closed his eyes.

"And was there a boy?"

Steel Trap kept his eyes closed but started making that clicking noise again with his tongue. "Yeah, a boy. Older'n the girl."

"Was he a neighbor, too?" I prompted. His eyes stayed closed, but there was no more tongue noise, just deep, slow breathing. "What do you think now?" I asked Catherine, who had risen silently and was standing next to my chair.

"He's tired. But all in all you caught him at a good time. For some reason, he talks more after dinner than at any other time of the day–if he's not listening to the radio, that is. I know it probably didn't seem like much to you, but for him, this is talkative, believe me. If you want to go into the front room, I can give you what Daddy has said to me the last few days."

We carried our coffee cups into the living room, leaving Steel Trap with whatever dreams he was able to enjoy in a mind that was all but used up.

"All right," Catherine said, clearing her throat as she sat next to me on the davenport and opened a small spiral notebook. "Daddy mentioned the little girl to me, too, and he told me she lived next door to the Martindales, which you also just heard. I asked what her name was, and he said something like 'Kiki;' he repeated it two or three times. But he couldn't remember, or didn't know, a last name."

"Did he recall who the boy was?"

She nodded, studying a page in her notebook. "It was 'Chess' or something like that, but again, no last name."

"Did he say where Martindale lived in those days?"

"No. I asked him that, too, but got no response at all from him. I tried three or four times."

"That's okay. Seems like I read in his obit that he grew up down in Beverly Hills, which would figure, given that it's the nicest area out south, and his father had that big mill down in South Chicago. Anyway, I can find that out easily enough."

"Steve, I'm truly amazed that Daddy could remember all that he did about an event that so many people were trying to hush up."

"I'm not amazed at all. From everything I know or have heard about him, your father was one hell of a reporter, one hell of a digger. And he had great sources all over town: cops at every level, from patrolmen right on up to the commissioner, as well as probably aldermen, judges, bailiffs, bondsmen, and so on. In a situation like Martindale's, no matter how much his old man tried to keep the lid on, there were bound to be more leaks than a rusty bucket–and your father likely would have found them all. Although he probably paid for a few drinks now and then and laid on a few bucks in the right places to help those leaks get bigger."

"Do you really mean Daddy would have done that–pay people, I mean?" She looked doubtful.

I raised my shoulders and let them drop. "Just about everybody else did, and just about everybody still does. Why not?"

Now it was Catherine's turn to shrug. "I don't know. I just suppose I always thought all you reporters were somehow…"

"Above greasing a few palms or maybe wetting a few whistles to get some information?"

She colored slightly. "Well, Daddy never mentioned anything like that. I guess I just never realized how things really worked in his world."

"He probably *wouldn't* have mentioned it," I said gently. "It's not something any of us like to go around bragging about. But on occasion, it's the only way to loosen tongues and get the story."

"Oh, I know you're right," she sighed, closing the notebook and resting a palm on it. "I didn't mean to go sounding like some sort of prude. It's just that I've always sort of idealized Daddy."

"And with good reason, Catherine. To repeat what I told you when I came here the other night, from all I've heard and

121

from what little I've seen first-hand, your father was the classic reporter–tough, fair, honest, and accurate to a fault." I might have been laying it on a little thick, but there was enough truth in what I said about Steel Trap Bascomb to keep me from feeling like a liar.

"And look at him now, poor man," she whispered, inclining her head in the direction of the sitting room. "He can barely speak a complete sentence, let alone remember what happened yesterday. Or even an hour ago."

"Has he had a stroke?"

"No, Steve, not according to the doctors. They've told me there's nothing very physically wrong with him, other than old age and its usual ailments. Daddy's seventy-one, which isn't young, but they say his heart's still strong, and his other organs seem to be in good shape, too. And he was never that much of a drinker, unlike a lot of the men he worked with. For him, it was just a bootleg beer now and then."

"Well, he sure hasn't lost his appetite," I observed.

"Oh, no, he eats as much as he ever did. And we take a walk together around the neighborhood most days, which really isn't difficult for him–he enjoys it. It's just that he's senile, and the doctors say there's nothing that can be done about that." She put her palms to her mouth and shook her head in a gesture of helplessness.

"Well, it's good that he's got you to look after him."

"I really don't mind it," she said, sitting up straight. "Are you terribly disappointed that you didn't learn more from him tonight?"

Now I did lie. "Not at all, no. I've got a few things to go on now–it's a real good start," I said with a confidence I didn't feel.

"Steve, I realize that I don't know you very well, so maybe I'm being presumptuous, but I want to ask you something."

"You don't strike me as the presumptuous type. By all means, ask."

She sucked on her lower lip and did the looking-around-the-room routine. "You seem to be very sure that Lloyd

Martindale was not murdered by the crime syndicate, aren't you?"

"Yes, I am. I'm more than sure, I'm positive. But I think you already knew that, didn't you?"

"I guess I did, but that's not really my question," she said. "What I wonder is, why are you so intent on finding out who really *did* kill Martindale? Why not just let it go? What's the harm in letting the world think that the syndicate really was behind the murder? Heaven knows, they've committed enough others that they've gotten away with."

I leaned forward and gently laid a hand on her arm. "This could be a big story. So far, it's *my* story, nobody else's, and I intend to keep it that way. Catherine, these last few years have not been all that good for me, either in my personal life or on the job. That's a tale I won't bore you with, other than to say that I'm the cause of most of my own problems. But now, I may have a chance to come back in a big way."

"At whose expense?"

"How do you mean?"

"You think one of those children–of course they wouldn't be children any more–that Martindale messed with may have killed him, don't you?"

"Well…I believe there's a good chance."

Now she squeezed my arm. "Assuming that's true, don't you think that he, or maybe she, has suffered enough through the years?"

"Murder is murder," I said, realizing as soon as the words were out just how pompous I must have sounded.

"Once something…something like that…happens to a person, it changes everything about how they think and feel…and, well, almost everything about them," she said haltingly, her eyes down. "I know."

"Catherine, what are you telling me?"

She wouldn't look at me. "Right here…in this house."

"My God. You mean…" I gestured toward the sitting room, where Steel Trap presumably slumbered.

"Oh, no Steve, no! Not Daddy. Don't think that for a

123

moment. It was my uncle, Daddy's older brother, who…" She proceeded to haltingly tell me how, when she was in grade school and her parents took camping trips to Wisconsin, her bachelor uncle would move into the house to watch after her. Except that what he did was far more than watch after her.

"Did you ever tell your parents?" I asked after she had stumbled through her tale of horror.

"Lord, no, I couldn't have! Daddy and Mother both thought Uncle Paul was a wonderful person. It would have broken their hearts."

"To say nothing of what it did to you. How long did this go on? Or would you rather not say any more?"

She took two deep breaths. "No–it's all right. It was years before I got over it, if I ever really have. I never told my husband, of course, but he knew that something was wrong with me because I was never very good at…you know what I mean."

"I think so."

"That was a big part of why our marriage went to pieces in such a short time, less than three years."

"And what about Uncle Paul?"

"Oh–yes. He was killed in an automobile accident out near Rock Island when I was eleven. His car stalled on a railroad crossing and was hit by a train. And I was glad, really glad–almost deliriously happy, as awful as that sounds."

"No, it sounds like a perfectly normal reaction to me."

"I appreciate your saying that, Steve. Not everybody would–the principle of Christian forgiveness and all. I'll never forget the funeral. I couldn't bear to even look at him in the casket. My mother kept saying, 'Oh, Catherine, your poor uncle. Dying so young. He was so fond of you, he loved you so much.' It was all I could do to keep from running screaming from the mortuary."

"And your parents never knew?"

"Never, ever. And neither did anybody else until now. Except a priest. And do you know what he said to me back then? He said 'To forgive is divine.' That's all–nothing else.

'To forgive is divine.' How I detest that phrase. Well, I didn't forgive, Steve. I couldn't. And I can't even today."

"Why should you have to? From my point of view, some things are beyond forgiveness, no matter what any church says. And what happened to you was one of those things."

"And do you know something else?" she said, anger evident for the first time in her voice. "If my uncle had lived much longer, I truly believe I might have killed him. What do you think would have happened to me then?"

I had no answer.

Chapter 12

On the first Saturday of May, just as I was leaving the apartment to pick up Peter for a trip to the Riverview amusement park, the phone rang.

"Snap, ol' pal, how's everything goin'?" Leo Cahill bubbled. Whenever Leo calls me "ol' pal," I want to check my pocket for my billfold.

"I'm just fine, Leo. Or at least I was until you called. To what do I owe the supposed pleasure?"

"Hey, what kind of attitude is that?" he said, voice still sounding jovial. "I just wondered if you'd heard the latest about Dizzy Dean?"

"I do read those sports pages of yours occasionally, you know."

"Then you must know that good ol' Diz is on the shelf–for at least a month, so they say–with that torn muscle in his pitching wing. A damn shame."

"Yeah, I can tell that you're all broken up about it."

"Well, Snap, after all, I did warn you that the old buzzard wouldn't win five games this year, remember?"

"How could I forget–you bring it up enough. But he's already won three and we're not even a month into the season," I growled. "And he hasn't lost any. Seems to me that's hard to improve on."

Leo chuckled. "Always an optimist, aren't 'cha? Shoot, I guess a Cub fan has to be, though. But you know as well as I do that Diz is through, finished, done. He'll never pitch another game, so I hear from my sources. And Snap, I've got good sources, damn good sources. I just figured that I'd be a good guy and let you off the hook on the little wager of ours."

"Getting cold feet, are you, Leo?"

"Hey, not me. I…"

"I figured you'd eventually want to back out, not that I blame you. I just didn't think it would be this soon."

"Listen, Snap, here I'm tryin' to do you a good turn, and this is the kind of thanks I get."

"Leo, let me spell it out for you: I'm real happy with the bet, exactly as it stands. And as I recall, the whole thing was your idea. But if you want to call it off, I can understand why. You figured that the Cubs weren't going to be so hot, and so far they–and Dean–have fooled you.   As an old friend, I'm prepared to do *you* a good turn, but with this condition: I'll let you out of the bet, but you'll have to write me a note that says it's you, not me, who wants out. And be sure to sign it. And date it."

"Dammit, Snap, you're throwing good money away," he spat angrily.

"Well, if you feel that's what I'm doing, be ready to catch it," I told him. I started to say something else, but the line went dead.

I climbed the front steps of the two-flat in Logan Square a little past nine, and when I got buzzed in, I discovered that Peter was home alone.

"Your Mama's not here?" I asked, surprised.

"No, gone to work." He grinned, slipping on his jacket. "Hey, Dad, she lets me stay alone now, since you talked to her about it. Thanks."

"Aha! No more Mrs. 'What's-Her-Name' with the body odor, eh?"

"Mrs. McAfee. Nope. No sitter anymore."

"Glad to hear it. Let's get out of here and celebrate your new freedom."

Two streetcar rides later, we were at the elaborate arched wooden entrance to Riverview Park, at Western and Belmont on the Northwest side, which had just opened for the season. It billed itself as the world's largest amusement park, and for all I know, it might have been. I'd been going there myself since the ninth grade, when my father deemed that I was old enough to ride the streetcars with just my friends, no adults. Last summer, I introduced Peter to the place briefly–we only had time for two or three rides–and ever since the weather started warming up this spring, he'd been asking when he could go back.

"I want to ride all the roller coasters this year, Dad," he announced after we were inside. "There's six of 'em, aren't there?"

"That sounds about right. You even want to go on the Bobs?" I asked, referring to the fastest, scariest, most famous of them all.

"Sure, even the Bobs."

"Well, you're going to have to do that one by yourself," I told him. "My stomach isn't what it used to be. What about the Parachute Jump?" I pointed to the twenty-story girdered tower that loomed over the park like a gaunt, skeletal dinosaur rearing up on its hind legs. Riders got strapped onto open, backless seats and were hoisted slowly to the top, then they plummeted earthward on cables in a free fall until their parachutes opened, about halfway down.

"Uh, maybe not that," he said, eyeing the tower with respect. "Did you ever go on it?"

"It's only been open since last year. And for me, it's in the same category as the Bobs; watching it is excitement enough. It really does look a lot like that tower you built at home with the Erector set, doesn't it?"

Peter agreed, but he clearly had no interest in riding the thing; his heart belonged to the roller coasters. And I did manage to survive three of them with him, along with the Chutes, a relatively tame water slide. As we walked under newly leafed trees on the park grounds with frankfurters and Cokes, we passed a row of metal cages called the "African Dip," where Negroes were perched precariously on boards above tanks of water. For a nickel, or maybe a dime, you got to throw three baseballs at a target, and if you hit it, the board would drop, dunking its occupant into the water tank.

"Want to try?" I asked Peter, gesturing toward the cages,

where the colored men good-naturedly and loudly heckled potential pitchers.

He wrinkled his nose and shook his head vigorously. "That's really dumb. Why would they want to do that?"

"They get paid," I said. "And jobs are hard to come by these days, especially if you're a Negro."

"Really dumb," he repeated, looking over his shoulder at them as we headed off in the direction of the fabled Bobs.

Before work on Monday, I stopped in at Tribune Tower and paid a visit to the morgue–or reference room, as some of its staff insist on referring to it.

"Well, by God, if it isn't old Snap. What brings you inside the holiest of the holies? Haven't seen you around here for a couple of years. Been called on the carpet for insubordination?"

It was "Popeye" Petrucci, so named because he sported a black patch over his left eye. Stories varied as to its origin–among them that he was beaned in a minor-league baseball game in Louisiana about 1905, partially blinding him; that he lost his eye in a barroom brawl on the Marseilles waterfront just after the Armistice; or that he was stabbed in the face by a holdup man while guarding a shipment of gold on a train going through the Canadian Rockies, date unknown. Popeye wouldn't confirm any of the versions, although I always suspected he generated all of them himself.

"Believe it or not, I'm here in search of information, although given the quality of this so-called archive, that may be a fool's errand."

"Them thar's real fightin' words, padnuh," Popeye cracked, doing a middling Walter Brennan imitation. "This here dollar says that we got what you're looking for. Even money."

"Put your cash away, you old fraud of a trail hand. Actually, my request is simplicity itself; I'm after a Chicago phone directory, circa 1910."

"Duck soup! Goddamit, Snap, I thought you was really gonna give me a challenge. I could use a real challenge." Popeye limped back into the rows of shoulder-high filing cabinets and returned two minutes later with a mildewed, dog-eared directory. "You ask for 1910, you get 1910," he proclaimed as he slapped the big book down on the table, raising so much dust we both coughed.

Normally, the overly nosy Popeye would have asked why I wanted something as abstruse as a twenty-eight-year-old Chicago directory, but today I was spared an inquisition. The phone jangled at that moment, and he was the only one on duty in the morgue.

As he shuffled off to answer the rings, I flipped the directory open, gently turning its brittle pages to the M's. Edgar Martindale was listed on Longwood Drive, all right, which I vaguely knew to be in the expensive Beverly Hills district on the Far South Side of the city.

Next, I went to the reference shelf and pulled down the current city directory, or "criss-cross," as reporters refer to it. As thick as the phone directory, this volume lists residences and businesses by street address, rather than alphabetically by name. I paged to Longwood Drive and found a listing for "Mrs. E. Martindale" at the same address as the one in the 1910 directory. I recalled that in Lloyd Martindale's obituary, his mother was mentioned as one of the survivors, and she had been described as something like "long active in both social and charitable circles."

I wrote down the addresses of a half-dozen names on the Martindale block of Longwood and returned to the ancient phone directory to see how many had lived in the neighborhood almost three decades earlier. The answer was two, surnamed Warburton and Cook, both on the opposite side of the street from the Martindale address. The Warburton name in the earlier book was Harold, with the current listing being Mrs. Harold, presumably his widow. The Cook entry had remained unchanged: Lewis J.

Popeye was off the phone. "Find what you want, Snap?"

"Pretty much. Thanks."

"Don't get a lot of requests for old directories," he observed pointedly, eyebrow raised in anticipation of an explanation.

"I'm sure that's true, Popeye. Good to see you again; sorry, I've got to run or I'll be late getting down to 11th and State."

The next weekend, Peter was staying overnight with a friend from school, and although I enjoyed and valued my time with him, I was glad for the freedom and I planned to make effective use of it. On Saturday morning, I climbed onto a sooty Rock Island Line commuter local at the LaSalle Street Station and rode south to Beverly Hills, a trip of a half-hour. It was hard to conceive that I was still well inside Chicago's city limits as I stepped off the train at 103rd Street. The cozy little business district that clustered around the depot had the feel of a small village or a distant suburb with its block of groceries, meat markets, barber shop, and the like, and at the far end, a church spire poking above the trees.

Once again referring to my ratty pocket map, I walked west one block to Longwood Drive, which parallels the railroad tracks, and here I got another surprise: hills! I haven't traveled extensively, but from what I've seen of other places across the U.S., Chicago is about the flattest city around. Yet here, only a dozen miles or so south of the Loop, the streets actually climbed uphill west from Longwood. Okay, I grant that these slopes would not be impressive to somebody from San Francisco, but for me, at least, they were a local novelty.

I guessed it was the Martindale house even before I got close enough to read the address. Stone-and-brick Victorian, it was three stories and had even higher round turrets topped by dunce-cap roofs on two of the corners. I counted six brick chimneys, although there could have been even more on the back side, hidden by the steep slate roof. With its front entrance framed by a bulky stone archway, the house loomed on a grassy, elm-shaded hill well above the street. A flight of brick steps that rose from the sidewalk had been cut into the embankment. At the top of the rise, the steps leveled off to a brick walk leading to the front door. A brick driveway also scaled the grade and curved around behind the big house, presumably to the garage or coach house.

But the Martindale manse was not my destination, not now, anyway. On the opposite side of Longwood, the east side, the homes were at street level, which despite their sizes and elegant styles made them seem less impressive than the higher-altitude neighbors that looked down on them. I passed in front of a two-story graystone house with a flat roof and a porte-cochere on the right side and checked its address against my notebook.

This was the residence of Edna Warburton, with whom I had an appointment. To back up a bit: Of the two long-time dwellers on the block other than the Martindales themselves, I had decided to try Mrs. Warburton on the theory that elderly women (I assumed her to be elderly), particularly widows, tend to be garrulous and to enjoy talking about their neighborhoods and the people in them. I telephoned her, identifying myself as a *Tribune* writer (I didn't specify what kind of writer) and saying that I was thinking of doing a story on Beverly Hills and its history. I also told her that I heard, I couldn't remember from whom, that she was a long-time resident of the area.

"Well, Mr....Malek, is it? I don't know that I qualify as any sort of expert on the history of our fine little community," she had responded in a quavering though friendly voice. "But I would be happy to talk to you, and perhaps direct you to some other folks who might be more helpful than I." I told her that I was perfectly happy to take my chances on her as a source, at least for starters, and we made the date.

A Negro maid in a starched white uniform answered my ring of the Warburton chimes. I took off my hat and introduced myself.

"Oh, yes, Miz Warburton's expecting you," she said in a cultured tone when I gave her my name. "Please come in, sir."

The oval-shaped foyer was twice the size of my bedroom, with a vaulted, coffered ceiling and a chandelier that would have held its own in the grand ballroom of the Drake Hotel. A staircase with an elaborate white balustrade swept gracefully upward, hugging the contour of the foyer's back wall. Looking down on the flight of white-carpeted steps was an oil painting of a standing woman in a long, lavender gown, her delicate face framed by russet hair and dominated by intense blue eyes.

I followed the maid through a parlor that looked like a set piece from an English drawing-room comedy and then along an unlit, wood-paneled corridor. Just as my eyes were adapting to the dark, we burst into the startling brilliance of a solarium. A forest of ferns and leafy plants, some of them taller than me, fought a losing battle for attention with splashes of red, yellow, and purple flowers that were highlighted by the rays of the morning sun pouring through the glass walls and roof.

"It's quite a sight, isn't it? I do so enjoy receiving people in here." The voice came from the far corner, giving me a start. All but enveloped by the greenery and flowers, she sat in a white wicker chair with a wool blanket covering her lap, despite the room's warmth. Her face, now framed by well-coiffed white hair, was still dominated by the intense blue eyes of the foyer portrait.

"I'm Edna Warburton. Please sit down, Mr. Malek," she said in a voice that showed no hint of the quaver I had heard when we spoke on the phone. She gestured me to a twin wicker chair separated from her own by a small table, also wicker. "Armantha has gone to get coffee. Or would you prefer tea? That's what I'm having."

Only then did I realize that the maid was no longer in the room. "Coffee is fine," I answered, ducking under a branch and easing into the chair, which proved to be more comfortable than it looked.

She nodded. "Every man I have ever known–every *American* man that is–has preferred coffee over tea." As she adjusted her blanket, I studied Edna Warburton. She was about seventy-five, I guessed, although her skin was remarkably smooth, and even her small and well-tended hands were wrinkle-free. Maybe that had something to do with the climate in this room.

"Well, what can I tell you about Beverly Hills?" she

asked. "As I said when you called, there are others who know far more than I about the community, although I *have* been here a long time, over forty years now."

I looked duly impressed. "This is a beautiful neighborhood," I said, pulling a notebook from my pocket because I would be expected to write things down.

"Prettiest section of Chicago," she stated as if daring contradiction. "And, I might add, more civilized and genteel than that *other* Beverly Hills." She made a vague gesture toward the west with a delicate hand and sniffed disparagingly. "Warburton and I traveled to California by Pullman back in the '20s to visit friends in Los Angeles, and they drove us through their Beverly Hills. Ostentatious, that's what it was, Mr. Malek. Motion picture stars with no taste living in garish houses that only proved that they had no taste."

It was time to redirect the conversation. "So, you've been here for forty years, four decades; you've probably seen a lot of changes."

"And not all for the good. Your surname sounds very European. Are you a Catholic, Mr. Malek?" Her tone made it clear that she was not.

"Lapsed," I said with what I hoped she would interpret as a self-deprecating shrug.

Her nod seemed to signal approval of my religious status. "Well, I have nothing against their church–live and let live, I always say. But when a few move into a neighborhood, all of a sudden it seems like they bring others, and pretty soon that's all you have. And that is just what's happened here, Mr. Malek." She paused for breath as Armantha entered carrying a silver tray with matching coffee and teapots and china cups. The maid poured for both of us and slipped out noiselessly.

"So this area is heavily Catholic now?"

"More so every day," she conceded, shaking her head. "When Warburton and I built this house a few years after the fair–the '93 fair, that is–our neighbors were mostly Episcopalians and Methodists and a few Presbyterians. We were among our own, you might say. We're Episcopal. But the Catholics bought land and planned to build a church–right here on Longwood, would you believe! Well, that didn't work, because a group in the neighborhood got that piece of land condemned for a park. But eventually, *they* built a church in the neighborhood anyway, and now they've built a second one here, up at 93rd and Hamilton."

I scribbled some notes on my pad, feeling only marginally deceitful. "Has all this caused neighborhood problems or tensions?"

She sipped tea and set her cup in its saucer gingerly. "I'll just say that most of these newcomers are Irish, that should answer your question. Now, more than ever, it's a good thing we don't allow saloons around here, by law."

I nodded, thinking of Kilkenny's description of growing up Irish in another South Side neighborhood almost two generations ago. Possibly, attitudes had not changed as much as I thought.

"And of course they're all Democrats, every last one of them," Edna Warburton went on with feeling. "It seems like the whole country is Democratic now, what with that man in the White House and all of his socialist scheming. Every day I thank the Lord for your *Tribune* and your fine Colonel McCormick," she said, reaching across the table and patting my arm. "A voice of sanity and reason crying out in the wilderness. We've always gotten the *Tribune*–Warburton wouldn't have any other paper in the house." She apparently never used her husband's first name.

"Mr. Warburton, is he…?" I let my question trail off.

"Oh, I guess I didn't tell you, did I? He died a little over five years ago; heart attack, the doctor said. But I can tell you what really finished him; it was that man getting elected."

"Roosevelt?"

"That turncoat Episcopal! I never saw Warburton so angry as he was right after the election. And he died six weeks later. Six weeks, mind you. Heart attack–hah! He was killed by Franklin Damn Roosevelt." Her hand trembled slightly as she picked up her cup.

I waited the requisite moment and then plunged back in. "That's an impressive house across the street from you."

She nodded absently. "*Mmm*. The Martindale place."

"Oh! Would that be *the* Martindales?"

"It would," she said somberly. "Of course Lloyd hadn't lived there for years. He and his wife–she's a Catholic–lived up on Lake Shore Drive in one of those big apartment buildings along the Gold Coast. What a tragedy. He would have made a fine mayor, unlike that Irish hooligan we have now. From what I read in your newspaper, they say that the crime syndicate had Lloyd murdered. But do you know what I think?" She fastened her blue eyes on me, waiting for a prompting.

"What?"

"I think it was those Democrats who murdered Lloyd, that vile Kelly-Nash crowd. What do you think, Mr. Malek?"

"You might very well be right," I responded, eager to keep steering the conversation. "Have the Martindales lived here a long time?"

"Oh my, yes. Longer even than we have."

"Do you ever see Mrs. Martindale?"

She straightened up and folded her hands primly in her lap. "Years ago, when her Edgar and Warburton were both alive, we used to get together to play bridge once in awhile, or cocktails. In fact, back then there was a lot of socializing all along this block of Longwood, parties and dinners and such, wonderful festive parties. Anyway, as time has passed, Beatrice–that's Mrs. Martindale–has become more and more, well, reclusive is the word, yes. Doesn't leave the house often, doesn't have visitors. Just lately I did see her, of course, at Lloyd's funeral, and said my regrets. And although I have talked to her on the telephone very occasionally, that was the first time I'd laid eyes on her or spoken to her face-to-face since my own Warburton's funeral five years ago. And my, how she had aged, although I grant you that a tragedy can do that to you. Beatrice must be, oh, probably close to eighty by now. But it was more than just being older; she seemed...*harder* somehow, as if she had frozen people out. She barely acknowledged me–and the same was true regarding others in the neighborhood that she has known for years and years. Some of them remarked on it to me."

"Maybe it really is her age," I ventured.

Edna Warburton looked doubtful. "She didn't show any particular signs of senility, and she certainly wasn't doddering, no cane or anything like that to support her. No sir, I think her personality has changed. Now I realize that I only saw her for a few minutes, and I only talked to her for one or two, but she's changed, yes she has. I saw her long enough to be sure of that much."

"*Hmm.* I'm sorry to hear that she doesn't see people. I thought I might call on her sometime and ask her about her own recollections of this neighborhood. What do you think?"

"Well…she certainly should have many recollections, I'll grant you that. I would be glad to telephone her by way of introducing you, but I can't promise that she would be receptive."

"Thank you. I might ask you to do that. I noticed walking here from the station that there were some other big houses on either side of the Martindales'. Are they long-time residents as well?"

She shook her head emphatically. "The one on the left is an Irish family, I forget the name. Reilly, or some such," she said dismissively. "And the house on the right is for sale. It used to be the Peabodys', but they've been gone for years now, and there have been two or three owners since they moved to Florida for Arthur Peabody's health. I haven't known any of those people."

I began to zero in. "Over the years, were there ever a lot of children on this block?"

"Well, yes, quite a few. Warburton and I never had any ourselves, so we really did not become involved in activities regarding children, such as the schools and such. But let's see, there was Lloyd, of course, he was a toddler when we moved in, and his sister was maybe five. Next door to us to the south, the MacGregors, rest their souls, had two boys, fine boys, Duncan and Malcolm. They're both lawyers on LaSalle Street now in their father's old firm and live somewhere out in the suburbs. And for all I know, they may be grandparents–they'd be old enough. Back across the street, next door to the Martindales, the Stovers had two children, a boy and a girl."

"You've got a wonderful memory, Mrs. Warburton. I'm impressed. Do you remember the names of the Stover kids?" I asked in a casual tone.

"The boy was Chester, I believe, and the girl was Nicolette." She looked thoughtful. "My, but that was a long time ago, because the Stovers have been gone for…well, since 1912."

I took note that these must be the children Steel Trap had talked about, then grinned at her and shook my head in wonderment. "Just out of curiosity, how do you happen to know the *exact year*?"

"With good reason!" she replied. "That was the year of the Titanic, and some folks that lived down the block, the Fergusons, were supposed to be on that maiden trip it made from England to New York."

"The trip it never completed."

She nodded somberly. "Yes, when we heard that the ship had gone down, everyone on Longwood and the surrounding streets was despondent–the Fergusons were such fine, upstanding people. But then imagine our great joy when we learned they were not on board! They had had an automobile accident in Scotland–Mr. Ferguson, Howard, forgot to drive on the left-hand side of the road and was in a collision. Fortunately, they were not badly hurt, only scratches, but they couldn't make their way down to the port, Southampton, I think it was, in time for the sailing. Well sir, we threw a big party for them when they finally did arrive home; we had it right here in this very house. We invited people from blocks around. I think it may have been the biggest party we ever had. It was a joyous celebration."

"And the Stovers?"

"Oh, yes. That was the strange thing. We tried to invite them, too, of course, but they were gone."

"Gone?"

"Moved out, practically overnight. Nobody seemed to know why, and they never said good-bye to anyone so far as I know. The house didn't even go on the market until after they'd gone, it all happened so quickly. And they had always seemed like such a friendly couple, too."

"Interesting. Ever learn where they went?"

"Yes. Sometime later we heard, I forget from whom now, that they were living down in Flossmoor, supposedly in a much bigger house than they had here, although their house across the way, as you can see yourself, is very nice. As to why they moved so quickly, no one ever knew. We sent them Christmas cards for a few years, but never received one, so we finally stopped."

"That's quite a story," I remarked. "Was Lloyd Martindale still living in his parents' house at the time the Stovers left?"

"Oh, my, Mr. Malek, you *are* putting my memory to some tests now, aren't you? Well, let's see...yes, I think Lloyd probably was in college then–it was Harvard, you know–but he was of course home summers and holidays."

"And another question, just to test you. How old were the Stover children when the family moved?"

She looked at me and moved her head slowly from side to side in puzzlement. "I don't know what all this has to do with our neighborhood history, but I realize that you newspaper people have your methods. Oh, I suppose that the boy, Chester, was about twelve or so, and the girl was probably a few years younger–maybe eight or nine."

"What did Mr. Stover do for a living?"

"He was an accountant of some sort up in the Loop, probably a CPA."

"Wealthy?"

She wrinkled her nose. "Not at all. I always suspected they were mortgaged to the hilt, and so did Warburton. A nice couple, I'll grant, but if you ask me, I think they were living beyond their means. Which made it even more surprising to us that they moved to a larger house in a wealthy suburb. It has always been puzzling to me how they could have afforded it."

"Uh-huh. That does sound quite puzzling. You said their daughter was named Nicolette–I had a girl friend by that name once," I improvised. "People used to call her Nikki."

"Well, I believe that's what Tom and Wilma–those were the Stovers–called their girl, too. Cute little blonde she was, head full of curls. Or…no, I think perhaps they called her Kiki," she said, rubbing her cheek with her hand. "Oh, well, what does it matter? That was a long time ago."

"Yes it was," I agreed, making sure to dodge the branch as I rose. "And I've been here for a long time, too. I really must be leaving. Thank you so much for your hospitality; you've been very helpful."

"Oh, I'm so sorry that you have to leave," she said, tilting her head to one side in a gesture that probably set male hearts aflutter in the Chicago society of a half-century earlier. "But I'm afraid I really haven't been all that much help. We hardly got into the history of Beverly Hills at all."

"Oh, but I feel it was a very good start, and I may stop back and see you again, with your permission, of course." She told me to come back any time, and when I leaned down and took her hand in parting, Armantha magically materialized to show me out. As I left the solarium, I turned back and smiled. Edna Warburton waved vaguely and returned the smile, nestled among her flowers and foliage and memories.

Chapter 13

As I waited at the 103rd Street station in Beverly Hills for a train back to the Loop, I stuck my head into the pay telephone booth on the platform and, to my surprise, found not only a Chicago directory chained to the shelf, but also a far thinner one for a cluster of southern suburbs, Flossmoor among them.

That small community had a single Stover listing–Thomas R. I scribbled the address and telephone number in my notebook and began forming a plan for the next day.

I now felt like a seasoned rail commuter. First had been the Lake Street elevated rides out to Oak Park, then the Rock Island to Beverly Hills, and now, early on a cloudless Sunday afternoon, I rode a near-empty Illinois Central electric train south to the village of Flossmoor, some twenty miles out from the Loop.

The Stover house was four blocks from the little depot and sat on a serene and self-satisfied avenue lined with elms and poplars. The homes on the block, though newer than those I had seen in Beverly Hills, were every bit as imposing in their own way, set well back from the street and fronted by lawns as big as football fields. The architectural styles varied from English Tudor to French to Georgian to Colonial, and the biggest house of all, the Stover residence, was a Spanish-style palazzo of maize-colored stucco with a red tile roof and an arched doorway with ornamental iron gates. This hacienda, looking like a transplant from Edna Warburton's "other" Beverly Hills, cried out for some sort of tropical trees–palms, perhaps–rather than the elms that graced its stately grounds.

Crushing the remains of a Lucky Strike with my heel and adjusting the tilt of my hat from jaunty to businesslike, I tucked my clipboard under one arm and strode up the pebbled, serpentine sidewalk. When I got to the iron gates, I found they opened into a small walled courtyard with a bed of red and yellow tulips proclaiming the season and a working fountain that gurgled discreetly.

The gates were unlocked, so I passed through the courtyard on another pebbled sidewalk leading to the front door, which appeared to be oak and had six recessed panels with carved leaves in them. When I pushed the brass button, a four-note chime sounded within.

After a few beats, the door opened just far enough to reveal a woman of perhaps fifty-five. She had a pleasant face framed by sandy hair tinged with gray and pulled back in a bun.

"Yes?" she said, raising her eyebrows.

"Mrs. Stover?"

"I'm Wilma Stover. Can I help you?"

"I hope so," I said in a cheerful tone, tipping my hat. "My name is Charles J. Melrose, and I represent the U.S. Bureau of Census, which of course is an arm of our federal government. I handed her a calling card proclaiming this identity in raised lettering and garnished with the Great Seal of the United States.

"As you know, Mrs. Stover, there will be a nationwide census in just two years, as of course there is every ten years at the turn of the decade. However, it is now the practice of the Bureau, as you may be aware, to undertake 'pre-census' surveys. A small percentage of the United States population is selected at random for brief interviews. The purpose of these is to help us–the Bureau, that is–to develop a questionnaire that better reflects the diversity of the American populace as a whole. We are always striving to improve the accuracy and depth of our information, and this is just another example of that ongoing program. Might I take just a few minutes of your time and your husband's? I promise it will be brief."

"Well...Tom is out golfing right now. It's been a long winter, and when a nice day like this comes along, well..." She smiled. "However, I'd be happy to talk to you, or do you need to see both people in a house?"

"Oh, no, no, this will be just fine," I said, trying to keep from sounding pleased. I had hoped I might talk to one of them alone, preferably the wife. I followed Wilma Stover through a dark entrance hall and into a living room with a beamed, cathedral ceiling, stucco walls, and what I took to be Spanish furnishings, including a multicolored, striped, and fringed tapestry that hung on one wall. A balcony with an ornate carved iron railing looked down on us from the upper floor, and an honest-to-goodness suit of armor stood sentinel in one corner, complete with a mace in one of its metal hands.

"This is a very impressive room," I told her as she gestured me to a bulky sofa and took a big-backed, dark wood chair at right angles to it.

"Thank you very much," she said, obviously pleased. "Both Tom and I love Mexico, and this room–this whole house, really–helps to remind us of the pleasant times we have had there over the years. I'm quite surprised that census people like yourself are making calls on a Sunday." Her tone was serious and questioning, but fell well short of disapproval.

I cleared my throat. "Well, yes, that is something of a departure from our past practices, I must concede. But the Bureau felt it was easier to find people at home at this time. Having said that, however, we have strict instructions to ask people if they feel we are infringing on their day of rest or on their religious practices by our presence on a Sunday. If this is a concern of yours, I will of course depart immediately."

"Oh, no, please don't worry about that," she said, waving a hand lightly. "I just found it unusual. But as I said before, I'm most willing to help."

"Thank you, Mrs. Stover," I said, poising a sharpened No. 2 yellow pencil over a sheet of paper on my clipboard. "I have a series of questions to run through, and I'll try to be as brief as possible."

She nodded and I started in, using the most-businesslike tone I could muster. I learned that the family had indeed moved to Flossmoor from Chicago in 1912, which squared with what Edna Warburton had told me, and that they had moved three blocks from that first house in the suburb to this one in 1928. I also learned that Thomas Stover was a partner in a Loop accounting firm.

"Do you have offspring?" I asked.

She nodded, expressionless. "A daughter–grown, of course."

"I see. Does she live here with you and Mr. Stover?"

Still no expression. "Oh, no. She's in the city, has been for years."

"Married?"

Eyes glazed over, she shook her head. This was like pulling teeth, and I felt guilty pushing on. But I did.

"Might I ask her occupation?"

"Nicolette works as an assistant manager at one of the Harding's restaurants downtown," she answered mechanically.

"Ah, yes, nice places, good value for the price," I said, scribbling on my clipboard for effect. "Would it be the one on West Van Buren by any chance? I go there often…when I'm working in the district office, of course."

"No…she's in one on Wabash, it's in the block between Madison and Monroe, east side of the street. Under those noisy El tracks."

"Oh, of course, I know exactly where it is, and I've been to that one, too. Is she your only offspring?"

Wilma Stover picked at a cuticle, then looked up slowly, her eyes focusing at a spot somewhere beyond me on the far wall. "We had a son, but we lost him to influenza in 1918."

"I'm sorry. That was a terrible epidemic."

"Yes it was, tragic. Chester was a junior in high school at the time. Two of his classmates also died."

I reacted with what I hoped was a sympathetic nod, trying to think whether I could learn any more about Nicolette Stover from her mother. But I decided further questions that might bring useful answers were too far afield for a census taker to be asking.

"Now, we also have a few questions relating to your dwelling," I went on, spacing my words as if reading from a script. "Do you own this beautiful home?"

"Oh, yes, yes we do, outright. No mortgage," she said, the pride coming through in her voice.

"That is always satisfying to hear, especially in these hard times," I said. "I believe you said this is your second home in this fine community?"

"Yes. As I mentioned earlier, our first house in Flossmoor was just a few blocks from here."

"Very good. When people find a community they like, they should try to remain there. And that first home of yours in Flossmoor…I assume that when you purchased it, you had a mortgage?"

She shifted in her chair. "Well…no, we didn't. We were fortunate enough to be able to…buy that house outright, also."

"You were indeed fortunate, for a couple so young," I observed, making it clear in both my tone and my expression that I was impressed.

"Yes, well, Tom–my husband–has done very well," she said, clearly not wanting to prolong the topic of discussion.

I spent the next five minutes posing innocuous queries, then thanked her and rose to leave. "I appreciate your time, Mrs. Stover."

"You are most welcome," she replied as she stood, returning to a semblance of the graciousness with which she had welcomed me. "Will you be visiting others along our block?"

"I don't believe so," I told her as I made a show of consulting my clipboard. "No, my next call is two streets away."

In fact, my next stop, selected on the spur of the moment, was only two *doors* away, just far enough from the Stover house–and on the other side of a high hedge–that I would be blocked from Mrs. Stover's view if by chance she happened to be watching me from within her hacienda.

A squat, balding man gnawing on a cigar and gripping a section of the Sunday *Tribune* answered my ring at the English Tudor. "We don't allow salesmen here," he snapped, starting to close the door.

"Wait–I'm not selling anything," I blurted, holding up a calling card. "Credit check on one of your neighbors."

He took the card and squinted at it, reading aloud: "Rodney Gilchrist, Zephyr Credit Bureau, 410 W. Madison St., Chicago. Huh! And you're Gilchrist?"

"Yes, sir, I am," I told him, handing over an ID card encased in plastic that identified me as Rodney Gilchrist, a credit investigator licensed by Cook County.

"Who d'ya wanna know about?"

"The Stovers two doors down. It's just routine information that I'm after, but it's necessary."

"Awright, come on in," he said grudgingly. "But you'll hafta talk to the wife. I'm on the road a lot, so I'm not around enough to know any of the neighbors. Hey Lorraine, there's a guy here who needs to speak with you," he said in a near bellow as he led the way through an entrance hall and into a living room dominated by American Colonial furnishings. Why didn't they live in an American Colonial home, I wondered. Surely there were several of them in the area.

A woman at least two inches under five feet scooted into the room wearing a maroon housedress and a worried look. "Yes, what is it?" she asked breathlessly.

"He needs to see you about the Stovers," her husband gruffed, gesturing toward me with a thick thumb. "I'm going into the den to finish reading my paper." He lumbered out and Lorraine smiled nervously, bidding me to sit on a davenport as she eased into a chair.

"What do you need to know, Mr…?"

"Gilchrist, Rodney Gilchrist," I said, offering another of the calling cards that Larry's Quality Printing ("The Best in Job Printing–Fast & Friendly Service") had done up for me. Courtesy of Larry, over the years I had also been a building inspector, a lawyer, a private detective, and a gas company meter reader. And of course an employee of the Bureau of Census. "And you are?"

"Lorraine Hokinson." She moved her head up and down

several times, as if to underscore to me that she really *was* Lorraine Hokinson. Her small, triangular face doubtless had been pretty once, but a road map of deeply etched worry lines now detracted from the light gray eyes, well-formed cheekbones, and small, straight nose. And she probably was not over forty-five.

"Well, Mrs. Hokinson, as your husband said, we are making some confidential inquiries about your neighbors, the Stover family. Nothing of a serious nature, you understand; just routine credit checking, very routine. We do this sort of thing all the time, as requested by various companies and vendors."

She studied my card and started in on the nodding again. "Oh, are they purchasing something big?"

I shrugged and turned my palms upward. "I'm not allowed to be specific, as I am sure you can understand."

"Of...of course, of course; I didn't mean to be nosy." She seemed as jumpy as a kid on a pogo stick, which I suspected was a permanent condition.

"Not at all, Mrs. Hokinson," I said soothingly. "Have you known the Stovers for a long time?"

"*Mmm*...as long as they've lived on this block, which is, oh...probably about ten years or so."

"I gather that Mr. Stover is quite successful."

Her eyes widened. "Oh, my, yes indeed. Orville–that's my husband–says he must be to afford that house of theirs. It's the biggest on the block by far, and one of the biggest in the whole of our little Flossmoor."

"Uh-huh. I understand he's an accountant."

"Well, yes. Actually, I do believe that Tom *owns* the firm, a very large firm," she said with awe.

"What about children?"

Lorraine Hokinson's expression changed from serious to stern. "They lost a boy to that awful influenza epidemic during the World War, long before we knew them. They lived a few streets over in those days."

"A terrible thing. I remember it like it was yesterday," I

said. "Was he an only child?"

Now she was shaking her head and pursing her small, pinched lips. "No, no, there's a daughter, too, but, well…"

"Yes? Remember, this is confidential."

She seemed unsure she should continue, but after fiddling with a pearl necklace and drawing in air, she spoke again, her words preceded by more head shaking. "The daughter, Nicolette–Kiki, they used to call her–well, I don't mean to sound cruel or anything of that sort, but I don't think that she's quite right."

"How so?"

She leaned forward and lowered her voice. "It's a little hard to explain, Mr. Gilchrist, and I probably shouldn't be talking this way, but she's been, well…*put away* at least once."

"In an asylum?"

That brought a single nod. "Up at Dunning," she said. "Wilma, the poor dear, didn't tell me that–I certainly wouldn't have expected her to–but, well…others did. It was all I could do to keep from comforting her when I learned about her daughter, but I couldn't very well, could I? After all, I was told about Nicolette in confidence."

"I take it you mean the Dunning mental asylum in Chicago?"

"Yes, that's the place. Now I can't say that Orville or I knew her very well, Mr. Gilchrist. When the Stovers moved onto the block, Nicolette was already living up in the city–working in some restaurant, I believe. But we've met her a few times at Christmas and other holidays when she came to stay with her parents for a day or two, and she always seemed like a nice woman–very quiet, but nice. And truly rather pretty, in a plain sort of way, if you know what I mean."

"I think so. Do you happen to know if she has ever been married?"

"No, I don't, although Wilma has never talked very much about her, at least not to me. But I think I'd probably know if she had ever been–married, that is."

"Do you happen to know if her parents are supporting

their daughter financially, Mrs. Hokinson? Or at least helping to support her?" I figured that those were the kind of questions someone doing a credit check ought to be asking, even if I wasn't much interested myself in the answers.

"I honestly don't," she said. "As I mentioned, her mother has never talked much about her–maybe for good reason."

I asked if she knew anything about the nature of Nicolette Stover's mental problems, but she couldn't even speculate. "Her parents are such wonderful people–and so very successful," she said, the awe again showing. "I can't imagine what would have gone wrong with the girl. It's the sort of thing that makes me almost glad that Orville and I couldn't have any children. They can just break your heart, can't they?" She sighed and looked toward the doorway through which her husband had exited with his newspaper and stogie, the smell of which lingered in the room like a guest who didn't know when to leave.

I mouthed my agreement and told her how much I appreciated her time, assuring her that everything she told me would be held in the strictest confidence.

"They can't be buying a new house, can they?" Lorraine Hokinson asked plaintively as she walked me to the front door. "They're such nice neighbors. Why would they want to leave that beautiful home of theirs? But then, why else would you be here asking these questions?"

"Credit checks are made for many, many different reasons," I replied as I stepped out into the spring sunshine and put on my hat. "As I told you earlier, we are not allowed to talk about specifics, but I do think that it's permissible for me to tell you that the Stovers are indeed happy with their present home."

For the first time since I had arrived, Lorraine Hokinson broke into a smile. "I appreciate your telling me that, Mr. Gilchrist," she said, holding out a hand. I took it and returned the smile, inexplicably pleased that something I said had made her happy.

Chapter 14

"So it's been three goddamn months now since Martindale got himself popped, and what do our illustrious gendarmes have to show for all their investigations? Nothin', that's what. Naught, nil, zero." Dirk O'Farrell scowled and formed an "O" with his forefinger and thumb as he leaned back at his desk in the pressroom on a gray and gusty Monday morning. We all were still on our initial cups of coffee, and for the first time in several weeks, the topic on the floor was the Martindale murder.

"Aw, keep your britches on, Dirk," Packy Farmer drawled as he rolled a cigarette. "You didn't really think they were ever gonna get the trigger man, did you? The outfit's boys ain't that sloppy, y'know."

O'Farrell lifted his lean shoulders and let them drop. "Maybe not, but I figured by this time the dicks would find some poor bastard they could hang the rap on. The way both Tom Courtney and the Crime Commission have been hammering on the department, seems like that would've been the logical move."

"Interesting you should say that," Anson Masters observed. "This very weekend, a tipster I've known for years strongly suggested to me that the police are in the process of doing exactly what you suggest."

"You mean they've gone and got themselves a stooge?" O'Farrell demanded.

Masters nodded. "Or close to it."

"Well, why the hell haven't you followed up on it?" Farmer accused, waving his newly minted cigarette like a dwarf baton.

"Easy there, Cyril," Masters tweaked. "As a matter of

fact, I was about to bring the subject up. And I was also going to suggest that since our very own Mr. Malek here is a confidante of one Fergus Fahey, he would be an ideal choice to beard the noble chief in his den."

"Heaven forbid that you should initiate any activity yourself, Anson," Farmer said, swiveling to face me. "Well, what about it, Snap?"

"Yeah, Malek, what about it? Chop chop," Eddie Metz put in, as usual the last one to enter the fray.

"Well, hellfire, I've been propping you lads up for so long anyway that it's become a habit. I might as well stay in character. And who knows, I might even let you in on some of Fahey's pearls of wisdom," I muttered after stifling a stage yawn. "Anybody want to come along and keep me honest?"

"Nah, we trust ya, Snap old boy," Farmer said, doing a yawn of his own. "How 'bout some good quotes this time around, though, huh?"

"Even if I have to make them up myself," I said over my shoulder as I headed out the door in the direction of Fergus Fahey's office.

"Morning, you vision of ecstasy," I whispered to Elsie Dugo as I ambled into her anteroom. "The grand poohbah receiving visitors today, or has he taken a sabbatical?"

"Good morning yourself, you silver-tongued knave. Last I knew, he was in there, unless he stepped out his window and flipped onto a passing El," she sassed. "Let me announce you. Are you Snap today, or Mr. Malek?"

"Let's try the formal approach. Maybe he'll develop a new appreciation for my importance."

"Anything is possible," she said. She spoke into the intercom and got what must have been a positive squawk, because she gestured toward the closed door. A haggard Fahey was seated behind his desk signing papers. He didn't look up, so I gently laid two Lucky Strikes on the only open acreage on his blotter.

"Suppose you expect coffee in return," he grunted, still concentrating on the papers.

"Well, isn't this the deal we struck yea these many years ago? I scratch your back and you scratch mine?"

Another grunt, as he reached for one of the smokes and lit it up. "Okay, what brings you sniffing around?"

"I'm hurt, Fergus, I truly am. Can't a fellow just casually drop by and say hello to an old friend every so often?"

"So you're here just to say hello, are you? Okay, then my name is Valentino, that's Rudolph Valentino, and I'm masquerading as a weather-beaten old homicide dick just hanging on until his pension kicks in," he rasped, glancing up from the disarray in front of him and eyeing me dubiously. He looked like he hadn't slept in days.

"Bad example. Valentino's been pushing up posies for years now, and at last report you're still alive and very possibly weather-beaten although by no means old," I responded as Elsie brought in a steaming cup of coffee and set it in front of me. I nodded my thanks, winking and getting a wink in return as she swept out saucily and closed the door behind her.

Fahey took a long drag on his cigarette and leaned back, cupping his hands behind his head. "All right, now that you've gotten your requisite flirting with Elsie and the witty repartee out of your system, what's on your mind, Snap? As you can see, I'm buried here."

I sipped from the cup, smiling my approval. "What's new on the Martindale case?" I asked matter-of-factly.

"Huh! I wish I had an answer. You tell me."

"All right, I'll make a stab at it, Fergus. How about this: The police have an alleged suspect in custody, but they're keeping him under wraps–way under wraps, at least for now. There's some doubt as to whether said suspect actually plugged Lloyd the Laudable, but even if he didn't, well…he may end up choosing to confess anyway."

"Meaning?" Fahey's voice took on a hard edge.

"Meaning whatever you interpret it to mean," I said lightly.

Face the color of an eggplant, the chief came forward in his chair, sticking out his chin. "And you claim to be a friend, suggesting something like that," he snarled through clenched teeth.

"But I'm also a newspaperman, Fergus, remember? We have a reputation for being curious. And that's just what I'm doing now–being curious. About an interesting story that's been floating around."

"Sounds to me like you're doing a little fishing," Fahey snorted.

"Care to comment on the story?"

"I do not," he snapped, rising slowly. "Now if you'll excuse me, I have work to do, unlike certain members of the press."

"Don't bother to show me out; I know the way," I said over my shoulder, keeping my tone light.

That afternoon about 5:30, I hopped a northbound El train at the Roosevelt Road station a block from headquarters and got off at Wabash and Madison in the Loop a half-dozen minutes later. The Harding's restaurant on Wabash was similar to the others in the chain: clean, well-lit, inexpensive, unadorned, and with moderately good food.

The eatery was about three-quarters full with suppertime diners, couples, and singles. The hostess ushered me to a table for two that hugged a mirrored wall near the back. When a waitress with a script-lettered "Betty" stitched on her uniform pocket came over with a menu and a glass of water, I asked if the assistant manager, Nicolette Stover, was on duty.

"She's on duty, all right, but what's this assistant manager stuff? Somebody steered you wrong, Mac," Betty said in a nasal tone that I took to be Downstate Illinois, or maybe Indiana. "She's over there–second-shift cashier, same as always. We don't even have an assistant manager. For that matter, we don't have much of a manager, either, damn his cheap hide. But I never said that, did I?"

"Didn't hear a word," I said, returning her smile and looking in the direction Betty indicated. I saw a sallow-faced, expressionless woman who could have been anywhere from thirty to forty-five perched behind the cash register counter at the front of the restaurant, the bustle of Wabash Avenue forming a backdrop through the plate glass window.

After I ordered, I studied Nicolette Stover in profile. It would have been a stretch to term the woman pretty, as Lorraine Hokinson had, although Nicolette wasn't giving herself much help in that department. Her hair, which I would have called oatmeal-colored, looked like it had been hacked with shears, and (assuming she did it herself) without benefit of a mirror. From where I sat, she appeared to wear no makeup or lipstick, and she never moved a facial muscle as she rang up customers' checks and then, robot-like, gave them change.

After settling on how I was going to approach the woman, I tied into my roast pork and sauerkraut (passable but hardly first-rate) and replayed the day's meeting with Fergus Fahey. The chief's out-of-character behavior made it seem all but certain that Anson Masters' informer was onto something.

Police have been beating confessions out of suspects since the birth of law enforcement, whenever that was, making it easy to believe they were doing it again now, especially given the high profile of the Martindale murder. My hunch was that an ill-starred mob lackey, probably usually employed as a bagman or a driver, was getting worked over methodically by the police someplace far removed–possibly even outside the city. And after he finally spit out a confession, he'd be given time for the bruises to heal and then be trotted out for arraignment.

I'd been covering the homicide operation and Fergus Fahey long enough to know that despite his hard-boiled demeanor, he was basically an all-right cop who was uneasy with this ham-handed approach to crime-solving, particularly when the subject of such "interrogation" was innocent of said crime. But I also was aware of the intense pressure being applied to the force in general and the commissioner and his chief of detectives in particular by the massed array of the mayor, the State's Attorney, the Crime Commission, the press, and public opinion–all clamoring for a Barabbas to send to his death. Fahey was torn, all right; I had seen it in sharp relief etched on his face this morning, and in his manner as well. He couldn't bear to admit to what was happening, or so I reasoned.

Such is the lot of a high-ranking cop who also happens to come with a bona fide conscience, I told myself, finishing the sauerkraut and draining what was left of my coffee. But, I argued, he went into this line of work with his eyes open, right? Granted, but should he then be put in a position where his professional future, his entire career, hinges on condoning coercion to get a confession? Maybe not, but isn't he paid to make hard decisions? Yes, however…at this point, I ended the internal debate and brought my focus back to Nicolette Stover.

All during dinner, I watched her at her post and had yet to see even a trace of animation. Now, as the crowd in the restaurant gradually thinned, I lingered until I was confident that none of the few remaining diners were about to pay their tab. Then I left a quarter tip, rose, and walked to the cashier.

"The roast pork was excellent tonight, absolutely superb," I pronounced as I handed over my check and two singles to Nicolette.

"Uh-huh. S'nice," she responded in a wooden tone, her surprisingly dark eyes never leaving the cash register as her fingers danced over its keys.

"Nicolette Stover?" I lowered my voice an octave, watching her for a reaction. "Huh?" She jerked upright and tensed as if she'd just stuck her finger into an electric light socket.

"Bob McNeil of the *American*," I said *sotto voce*, placing another of my collection of calling cards on the scarred glass top on the counter in front of her. "I'm writing a Sunday feature on Lloyd Martindale and I understand you once lived next door to him down in Beverly Hills."

"Who told you that?" she spat, her body rigid and her face at last showing some emotion–I would have termed it terror.

"Just a source," I replied nonchalantly. "Anyway, I'd like a few minutes of your time when you get off work. It won't take long at all; I'm just looking for some reminiscences."

"I didn't say I knew him," she fired back in a hoarse

whisper, her eyes darting around the dining room either in search of rescue or hoping that we were unobserved and unheard. "Here's your change–thank you!" She said it more loudly than necessary, turning quickly away from me and busying herself by thumbing through a stack of dinner checks. I stood watching her for what seemed like a minute but may have been less than half that time. When it was clear that she wasn't about to look up and acknowledge me further, I gave her a crisp, polite "thank you" and spun out through the revolving door.

I didn't spin far, though–just to the opposite side of Wabash Avenue. I took up a position leaning against an Elevated pillar, where I had an unobstructed view of Nicolette through the restaurant window. Dusk yielded to darkness as the trains pounded overhead every few minutes, shaking my pillar as well as the street itself. I lit up a Lucky, then another, and another, until I lost count of the butts on the sidewalk at my feet. Auto and pedestrian traffic gradually dropped off, and diners filed out of Harding's in ones and twos, with almost no one replacing them.

At a couple of minutes past 8:00 by my watch–which meant I had been supporting that pillar for better than an hour–a short, pot-bellied man in a coat and tie, presumably the manager, joined Nicolette at the counter. They talked briefly, and then she slipped on a raincoat and emerged onto the sidewalk, walking north. I crossed Wabash behind her and closed the gap until we were side-by-side at Madison, waiting for the light to change.

"Hi, remember me? Can we talk now?" I said, giving her my most sincere smile.

Nicolette pivoted toward me, the fright back in her eyes. "No! Leave me alone!"

"Hey, I just want to ask you a few questions," I told her as she started across Madison on the green.

"Get away! Get away from me!" she keened, speeding her gait. I started to pick up my own pace when I was spun around by a beefy hand on my shoulder. "You heard what the lady said–leave her alone, chum," growled a flat-nosed, whiskey-reeking mountain wearing a checked sports coat two sizes to small for him.

"Mind your own damn business, *chum*," I growled back, pushing his hand away and starting after Nicolette, now almost a half block away on Wabash's nearly deserted sidewalk.

I didn't see the punch, which caught me on the left cheek and knocked me to my knees. "I told you to leave the lady alone," the big galoot mouthed, looming over me with his fists clenched at his sides as an El train thundered above us.

"All right, all right, no need for you to go and get hostile, Buddy," I said, rising slowly, brushing off my pants and holding up a palm in mock surrender.

He unclenched his big fists, and as he did, I used all the force I had and drove a right to his stomach, which as I suspected–and hoped–was as soft and unresistant as a goosedown pillow. With a sound like a balloon deflating, he doubled over, holding his oversized gut with both paws.

The next noise I heard was his retching, but I didn't hang around to watch. I sprinted after Nicolette Stover, who by now had crossed Washington Boulevard. She looked over her shoulder at me and started running herself. I was halted at the Washington corner by a red light and a squadron of taxis, and by the time I made it to the other side of the street, she was a full block ahead of me, climbing into a northbound Checker Cab at Randolph.

I briefly considered flagging a hack of my own and giving chase, but my cheek was starting to throb where I had taken the punch, both of my knees felt like they had been massaged with steel wool, and I had to work to get my breath back. I turned around and looked in the direction of my erstwhile sparring partner, saw that he was on his feet and walking unsteadily in the opposite direction, and decided that I had had enough excitement for one evening.

Unfortunately, others felt differently.

Chapter 15

During the slow ride north on the Clark Street car, I held a handkerchief against my slightly bloodied and now swollen cheek, cursing Nicolette Stover and muttering that we would meet again. When I got back to my apartment, I would look her up in the telephone directory, and–assuming she was listed–pay her a visit at home, and soon. If she was not in the book, my plan was to wait for her outside Harding's again and tail her home.

My knees barking their complaint, I eased off the red car at the usual stop and gingerly edged across Clark, giving a careening Yellow Cab plenty of leeway. As I neared the door of my building, an all-too-familiar form materialized from the darkness.

"Getting home from work kind of late now, aren't you, Mr. Malek?" It was Monk, the long-faced rib-jabber from several weeks back who had pushed me into a car–probably the same car that he now was herding me toward.

"If it's all the same to you, I'm really not up to a ride tonight," I said over my shoulder, getting–what else?–a jab in the side.

Monk shoved me into the back seat, were I once again found myself beside the "Mr. Left" from our earlier meeting. "All right, Mel, move it," he pronounced to the driver in that high-pitched voice of his. The car drew away from the curb with Monk settled in on my right, also as before.

"So, we meet again," Mr. Left said. "What can you tell us?"

"About what?" I deadpanned.

"Come, come, don't play games like that, Mr. Malek. They only waste everyone's time. What have you learned about Lloyd Martindale?"

"Not a lot," I told him honestly. "I have been talking to a number of people who knew him over the years, but so far...nothing."

He made a grunting sound. "A good friend of ours, and a particular favorite of Mr. Capone's and of Mr. Nitti's, is being held. By the police." He clearly expected a response.

I put on my interested and concerned face. "Yeah? On a murder charge?"

His scratchy laugh contained no mirth whatever. "You should know they don't bother with charges, Mr. Malek. But they're trying to...persuade him to confess. And they know how to persuade."

"Does he have a lawyer?"

"You ask a lot of questions," Mr. Left said, the hawk-like features beneath his gray fedora accentuated in silhouette by the passing streetlights.

I chuckled nervously, feeling the perspiration build under my arms. "An occupational trait."

"Yeah, I'm sure. The man we are talking about has not been allowed to see an attorney–far from it. He's strong, but also isolated and at least for now beyond our help. And there are many ways to break a man."

Sure, and you've used every one of them at one time or another, I thought before speaking. "Like I said, I've made almost no progress. And as you know, I do happen to have a job that takes a substantial portion of my time. Do you have any ideas or suggestions?"

"Mr. Malek, we should ask you that. Your job doesn't seem to have prevented you from riding a number of trains recently."

"Maybe so."

"Not maybe." His voice had an ominous edge. "And tonight, your face is bruised."

"I mixed it up with a guy in a bar earlier–I think you could term it a minor disagreement over a woman. He looks a lot worse than I do. And that's why I was a little late getting home," I improvised.

"Be careful where you buy your drinks," he cautioned. "What did you find out in your train rides from the LaSalle and Randolph Street Stations?"

"Almost nothing, dammit," I said with feeling, trying to hide the surprise that I had been tailed at least as far as the downtown stations. "I was working on a couple of long shots, and they didn't pan out for me."

"That's too bad, but there are other days, other times, Mr. Malek. And when you do learn something, which of course you will, we don't want to read it first in your newspaper."

"All right, then how am I supposed to get in touch with you if I do have some information?"

"There is a club not far from here–on Diversey, one block west of Clark on the south side of the street. It's the Centurion." I had heard of it, of course; a notorious syndicate joint that was said to be a bar that fronted for one of the biggest brothels in town.

I nodded. "Yeah, I've been by the place, but never stopped in."

"Sit at the end of the bar nearest the door after 8:00 on any night and tell the bartender that you want to see the Brother."

"Who's that?"

"Just ask for the Brother, that's all. You will not have to wait long."

"Anything else?"

Mr. Left–a.k.a. the Brother?–wheezed an exhale. "Only that it would be smart of you to keep us informed about what you learn. From what we know, you are good at getting what your business calls scoops."

"Shit, you're giving me way too much credit. I haven't had one of those in a long time."

He looked out of the window and nodded deliberately as Mel eased the car to the curb at the same spot where I'd been picked up. "Here we are, Mr. Malek. And take care of that cheek, or you might have a permanent bruise. And remember: Mr. Capone likes you." His tone suggested that I would be wise to keep it that way.

As the long black car–it was indeed a Cadillac–joined the northbound traffic flow on Clark, I watched the taillights fade into the night and I started to stack up questions: Was I being shadowed constantly? The comment about my boarding trains at downtown stations suggested that was the case. I hadn't sensed a tail at any time, but then, I hadn't been looking for one. They must have followed me only as far as the stations, which posed another question: Why didn't Mr. Left mention my trips to Steel Trap Bascomb in Oak Park or my visit tonight to Harding's? Was it because I made those directly from work, while on the Beverly Hills and Flossmoor jaunts I left from home? That would indicate the tail was posted outside my apartment, but not at 11th and State. Was it possible that the outfit, as brazen as it was, didn't want to lurk in the neighborhood of Police Headquarters?

Also, why hadn't my tail followed me as I rode those trains, I asked myself. I figured it was because he really *would* be easy to spot when we got off, unlike in the crowds of the city.

More questions occurred to me: Did the mob, perceived so often by so many, often including the press, as omniscient, truly have no information or no clues as to who killed Martindale? I found that hard to digest. It seemed strange that they would have to rely on someone like me–a rank amateur investigator at best operating alone–as a major source of information. Did they really not know the location where their man, purportedly a favorite of Capone, was being questioned? And who was the Brother the brother *of*–if anyone?

Also, on the subject of Al Capone, were these people indeed still in close contact with him? And was he still really calling the shots, or at least some of them, when it came to the syndicate's operations in Chicago? My own answers to the last two queries leaned strongly toward the negative–one, given the supposed tightness of security at Alcatraz, and two, the apparently secure position of Frank Nitti as kingpin of the Chicago organization. My semi-educated guess was that whatever positive reputation I had with the syndicate had been passed along by Capone, and now Nitti, in his efforts to rehabilitate the mob's reputation, was prepared to turn to any source, me included, for help.

Yet another question–actually a series of them: Why did the mob want me to tell them who I suspected of Lloyd Martindale's murder, assuming I was able to find out? The quick answer would be that they planned to kill that individual. But what would that accomplish? Wasn't it their goal to make it known that they didn't murder Martindale? And if they indeed commissioned the actual killer, how could they ever argue that they were clean on the Martindale death?

Then there was the ultimate question: Where to go next? Tonight's blessedly brief ride with the Three Stooges convinced me more than ever that a mob hit man had not killed Martindale. Assuming–which I was not yet prepared to do– that Nicolette Stover had pulled the trigger on her former neighbor (and apparent molester), she had to rank near the top of the list. But assuming that Martindale had messed around with Nicolette (and her long-dead brother), likely there were other kids he'd done things with as well, and maybe one of them had extracted long-delayed revenge. I now found myself with a headache from all the surmising, among other reasons.

Once in the apartment, I went directly to the bathroom mirror where I grimaced at what was looking back at me. My cheek was swollen and red, and I had the beginnings of a shiner. More than ever, I hoped that beer-bellied palooka had tossed his cookies on the Wabash Avenue sidewalk.

After peeling off my clothes and assessing the damage to my knees, both of them scraped and sore but neither one bleeding, I was at least comforted to note that there were no rips in the legs of my suit trousers–probably the only positive aspect of an evening that had been too filled with adventure.

The Chicago phone book listed "Stover, Nicolette" at an address in the 1900 block of Grace Street, less than a mile north of my apartment. I momentarily toyed with the idea of calling her, but outvoted myself, figuring that I'd just get hung up on. There was time enough for the skittish Miss Stover.

I took the expected razzing about the condition of my face in the pressroom the next morning. "Hey, Snap, did some raging and irate husband finally catch up with you?" Packy Farmer chortled as I eased into my chair.

"I guess you'd know about irate husbands, now, wouldn't you, Pack?" Dirk O'Farrell sniped. "How many have run you off their property, be it either real estate or spousal, over the years?"

"Yeah, Packy, how many, huh? How many?" Eddie Metz put in as the City Press kid looked on with his normal mixture of puzzlement and dismay.

"Now that's enough raillery, lads," Anson Masters intoned with mock solemnity. "Let us now hear how our Mr. Malek got his physiognomy rearranged. Snap, you have the floor."

"Physiognomy, eh, Antsie? So that's what it is," I replied in an amiable tone, passing a hand over my tender cheek. "All right, fellow knights, sit back with your piping of cups o'java while your ol' Uncle Snap relates an inspiring tale of bravado and honor."

O'Farrell flashed his lopsided grin. "Be it bullshit or not, I think I like it already."

I cleared my throat and paused for effect. "Last evening, I find myself seized with a great thirst as I traverse the byways of our throbbing and exciting Loop, see. At that very moment, as Dame Fortune would have it, I happen by a public house– saloon to you vulgarians–and decide to partake of a sampling of their nectar."

"As in Schlitz?" Farmer jibed.

"The brand, Sir, is irrelevant," I sniffed, dismissing Packy's interjection with a raised eyebrow. "I settle myself upon a stool and enter into a spirited dialogue with the publican, a learned chap equally at ease conversing about Plato or the Pittsburgh Pirates. Well, we are in deep discussions on myriad topics when a comely lass enters the premises–alone."

"Yeah, yeah," Metz nodded.

"Said lass, tall, raven-haired, and with more curves than a

mountain road, takes a seat at the far end of the bar, of course attracting the attention of every red-blooded man on said premises."

"Including you," O'Farrell put in.

"Indeed including me. She's been seated maybe ten minutes with a bourbon highball when a large, ugly specimen lumbers in, goes straight over to this doll, and starts shouting that she'd walked out on him. Using words she never learned in Sunday School back in Muncie, Indiana, the doll tells him to hit the road, and he grabs her by the arm and starts to drag her off the stool.

"With that, a slope-shouldered guy about five-seven gets up and takes a swing at the galoot, who blocks the punch like it was a slap on the wrist and proceeds to cold-cock the poor bastard with a right cross. So this would-be hero is flat on the floor hearing sparrows chirping.

"Now the big guy's wrapped his arms around the doll's waist and is truly dragging her out of the place, her feet not even touching the floor, and all the while she's screaming like a banshee, got it? Okay, I know I'm giving away–what–sixty pounds? But I figure the galoot's distracted now. So I block his way and he gives me a shove with a paw the size of Delaware while he's holding the doll in his other arm. I pop him with a left jab, which knocks him back a little, but he counters with a right, and you can see where that landed." I patted my cheek.

"His punch staggers me, and he relaxes for an instant–big mistake for him, good fortune for me. I drive a right into his overstuffed gut, and damned if the lummox doesn't fold up like a pup tent when you pull out the support poles. Once he hits the floor, a couple of guys all of a sudden get brave, kick him and punch him and drag him to the door, leaving him lying out on the sidewalk groaning. He didn't come back in."

"That's all very interesting, Snap," Masters said, "but I fail to detect any bruises on your knuckles."

"Ah, Anson, your keen powers of observation are among those things that make you stand out as a reporter. I wrapped my belt around my fist before I started swinging, like any good street fighter does, see?" I shot back without hesitation. "It's second nature, Anson. And besides, how many bruises you likely to get from punching flab? So anyway, after this man-mountain gets dragged outside to lick his wounds, the doll sidles over and cozies up to me, cooing about how wonderful I am, which of course is true. She gets a cold, damp cloth from the barkeep and holds it on my face. And then she wants to buy me a drink–the best whiskey in the place."

"Which of course you quickly accepted," Eddie Metz said between slurps of coffee.

"Nah. I tell her that when I go into a bar, it's because I'm looking for peace and quiet and maybe some stimulating conversation to boot, but not brawling, and that this place is too damn violent for me. Then I kiss her on the cheek, tell her to be more careful when she picks a companion, and walk out of the joint without so much as a backward glance."

"Geez," the City News kid murmured.

"God damn, Snap, you really had me following along until that last part," O'Farrell announced, shaking his head. "You really are a master of bullshit, but here's where your story falls apart: You just ain't the type to turn your back on a warm honey and a cold drink. Try to deny that. Go ahead."

The City News kid turned to me with a disillusioned expression on an unlined puss that had yet to meet a razor. "Well then, so how did you *really* get banged up?" he asked.

"You heard my story, son. And when you get yourself a good story, always stick with it. If these jaded old geezers don't choose to believe me, hell, that's their lookout."

I didn't get any more comments about my face from the pressroom crew after that, so my story accomplished its intent. And after all, there really were a few small nuggets of truth sprinkled through the tale.

The next morning at 8:00, when I stepped from the foyer of my building into the dazzling spring sunlight on Clark Street, I scanned the block in both directions, almost overlooking an innocuous gray Studebaker sedan at the curb several doors to the north. It was the only parked car in sight with anyone inside–a pair of heads in the front seat, much too far away to identify and both wearing fedoras that covered their brows. I wondered how many mornings they had waited there for my emergence. I also wondered if either of them had been among the trio in the Cadillac during my night rides.

Turning away quickly and striking what I hoped was a nonchalant pose, I lit up a Lucky, flipped the match aside, and strolled to the next corner south, where I waited three minutes for a southbound Clark car. I took a seat near the back of the streetcar and looked out of its open rear window at the Studie, which had pulled away from the curb and made a squealing U-turn, heading north. As they must have every day lately, the car's occupants probably figured I was on my way to work, which meant they didn't have anything to gain by tailing me.

They figured right.

Chapter 16

From that day forward, I was on guard. Every morning as I stepped out onto the street, I would spot a sedan, sometimes the Studebaker, occasionally a Ford, and once or twice a Hudson, parked somewhere along my block on Clark with two fedora-topped silhouettes inside. Subtle they weren't. And each time I climbed aboard the southbound streetcar, they immediately lost interest in me.

One of these autos also parked at the curb near my building every evening, so on the way home, I took to riding the car one block farther north and slipping into Kilkenny's for beer and sometimes dinner before heading back to my building and going in undetected–or so I thought–through the alley entrance and up the back stairway. I didn't like the idea of outfit guys patronizing the Killer's place, or even hanging around just outside keeping watch on me. Also because of the tail, or so I told myself, I put off visiting Nicolette Stover's apartment for the time being, lest I alert them as to her existence. She might be a murderer, but I was damned if I was going to be the one to finger her–at least not as some self-appointed judge, jury, and executioner all rolled into one.

It was drizzling on an early June evening when I ducked into the Killer's establishment, having ridden the usual block beyond my stop after seeing the Studie and its twin fedoras at the curb. I took a stool at the bar and nodded to the Killer. He returned the nod and slid a foamy stein of Schlitz along the mahogany. As usual, it came to a stop directly in front of me. I looked around and recognized several familiar faces, both at the bar and in the booths.

Several stools to my right were a couple of guys who looked to be in their late twenties or maybe early thirties, both husky, that I'd never seen before. The one closest to me was loud and laughing and slapping the bar top with a large palm to underscore the points he was making to those around him.

The Killer waddled down to where I was sitting and gave me a smirk. "Recognize him, Snap?" he asked, tipping is head in the direction of the talkative one down the bar.

I shrugged. "Can't say that I do. Should I?"

"Just thought you might, you being such a big Cub fan and all. That fellow, my earnest and hard-working scrivener friend, is none other than his eminence, Dizzy Dean."

"No shit?"

"To coin a crude phrase. He just sauntered in here after the game this afternoon, easy as you please–Cubs won, by the way–along with one of his teammates, Reynolds there."

"Carl Reynolds, the outfielder?"

"The self same. Used to be with the White Sox. Anyway, Ol' Diz came through the doorway, introduced himself, and said that he heard we serve some of the best steaks in town. Never one to hide my light under a bushel, as you well know, I responded by saying that we serve THE best steaks hands down, no question, no debate."

"Which of course you do. I know that because you've told me at least a hundred times."

"If memory serves, oh man of letters, you have enjoyed more than a few of our fine T-bones and filets here yourself, often at that very stool," the Killer responded good naturedly as he swiped at the surface of the bar with his ever-present rag. "And I cannot recall ever hearing a single complaint on the subject from your corner. Anyway, I'm getting Diz to send me an autographed picture that I can put up in the front window. Be a fine bit of publicity, and t'will serve to burnish our already sterling reputation as a culinary oasis. Under the picture I'll have a sign: 'The steaks preferred by Dizzy Dean.'"

"Might be even better for your business–and certainly for the Cubs' success as well–if you can find some way to repair Dean's arm," I observed, keeping my voice low. "You know as well as I do that he hasn't appeared in a game in several weeks now."

Kilkenny nodded somberly. "I do indeed, Snap. In fact, you'll be interested to hear that he was expounding on that very subject only minutes before you darkened my door."

"Is he drunk?" I asked. The noise level down the bar had if anything increased.

"By no means. In point of fact, Mr. Dean is apparently not much of a drinker. Lord, I even tried to buy him a shot of my best Irish–again, it's good business, you know. But he told me that he doesn't touch the hard stuff, only a beer or two. Says it helps him keep up his strength after a game, poor lad. Come on down the line, and I'll introduce you."

"Well, all right. Just don't say that I'm a newspaperman," I told the Killer. "Dean hasn't been all that happy with the way the local papers have gone on about him not playing– particularly the *Trib*."

"What career would you like to invent for yourself?" the Killer asked. "A salesman, perhaps?"

"Why not? If the subject even happens to come up," I told him as I rose, grabbed my beer, and walked over to where Dean and Reynolds were seated. Diz, big and square-faced and good-looking, with his brown hair slicked back, was turned sideways on his bar stool talking to Morty Easterly, one of the regulars in the Killer's establishment, who had stopped in to get an autograph and exchange a few words with the man who had only four seasons earlier won thirty games in a single season for the Cardinals.

"…so anyways," Dean was drawling, "this friend of mine, a night club comedian by name of Johnny Perkins, you may have heard of him, goes out to one of our games last year up there in Boston when I was still with the Cards, o' course. And listen to this: He bets me two bits that I can't strike out Vince DiMaggio–Joe's older brother, ya know. 'Cept he ain't near the hitter Joe is. I strike him out first time up, and Perkins yells to me from the stands that he wants to double the bet.

"I say okay, and I strike Vince out again. Perkins, he wants to raise the bet another two bits, and sure enough, I fan

Vince a third time. So now he's comin' to bat again in the ninth, and Perk and me raise it another quarter. Damned if this time Vince don't get ahold of a pitch and pops it up foul, toward the ol' backstop. Our catcher, Brusie Ogrodowski–we called him Ogie–chases after it and I yell for him to let the damn bawl drop. Well, he does let it drop, and shoot, I end up gettin' Vince to strike out again. Won me a whole dollar." Dean slapped his leg and let out a whoop, while the group that had clustered around him laughed its approval.

"Diz, I'd like to have you meet a grand old friend of mine, a first-rate fellow and a regular patron here, Steve Malek," the Killer said effusively. "We call him 'Snap' because he has this fondness for snap-brim hats, which he thinks make him look sophisticated. Some of us think otherwise, but that's neither here nor there. What's really important is, he loves the Cubs."

"So do I love these here Cubs now, Mr. Snap," Dean said with a wide grin, pumping my hand. "Glad to meetcha. Now you have yourself a seat on this stool right next to me. Over here, this is my teammate, Carl Reynolds, the best durn outfielder in the whole league, not to mention the way he can powder the ball. And he loves steaks as much as I do. Carl, meet Mr. Snap."

Reynolds nodded, smiled slightly, and lifted his beer in salute, then ordered another. "Good idea," Diz said. "I'll have another one of them St. Louis champagnes to go with my steak, which is cooking back there in the kitchen. St. Louis champagne, that's what we call Budweiser," he added, winking at me. "Can I buy ya one? It's better'n that there Schlitz."

I said sure, and the Killer set us up. "I saw you shut out the Cardinals at Wrigley that Sunday back in April," I told Dean. "That had to give you a lot of satisfaction."

"Doggone right it did," the big pitcher boomed. "Them Cards, they really screwed me up last year. After I got hurt– my busted toe in the All Star Game, y'know–Frisch had me out there pitching again too soon, way too soon. Mebbe I shouldn't blame Frankie all that much, though, he's jest the manager. He takes his orders from Mr. Rickey upstairs and also from

Breadon, that tightwad miser which owns the team. But somebody's gonna pay, I can tell ya that."

"Pay? How do you mean?" I asked.

He scratched his forehead, then nodded his approval as a plate with T-bone steak, baked potato, and salad was plunked in front of him on the bar by Doris, the Killer's sullen waitress.

"I ain't said so much on this subject yet, and I sure as heck wouldn't tell the papers in this town about it jest now, 'specially that *Trib*, the way they been ridin' me about not bein' able to pitch, as if it was my fault! Huh! But ah'm gonna sue the Cards and that Breadon for a quarter of a million bucks 'cause of the way they messed me up last year. A quarter of a million. And ah'm gonna give Mr. Wrigley a hunnert and some thousand of that for all the trouble's that's been caused. He's been good to me, that man has. Yessir, he has." Diz pumped a fist to underscore his feelings and then tore into his steak as if he hadn't had a decent meal in a week.

"When do you think you'll be able to pitch again?" I posed, trying to make the question sound nonchalant despite the knowledge that I'd just gotten a scoop handed to me–or at least to the paper.

"Next month–July," Dean said as he chewed his steak and nodded his approval. "My arm 'n shoulder are both feelin' a darn sight better now than they was, and I feel ah'm getting my rhythm back, too. Dontcha think so, Carl?"

The taciturn Reynolds nodded while tying into his own steak, but I didn't read any enthusiasm into his affirmative gesture. And nothing figured to make any Cub teammate more enthusiastic than to have a healthy Dizzy Dean back in the starting rotation, particularly with the way the club was sputtering in its attempt to keep pace with the Giants and now the Pirates, who were coming on strong, along with the Cincinnati club.

"So, when are you going to sue?" I asked, keeping the tone casual.

"Soon, real soon. Say, what line of business are ya in, Mr. Snap?"

"I'm in sales–steel."

"You out on the road a lot?"

"A fair amount, yeah."

Dean's wide face grew even wider as he broke into a grin that showed teeth as white as piano ivories. "With steel as your game, that would mean you'd get to Pittsburgh a lot, right? What with all them there mills they got sending up smoke and all."

"From time to time," I answered off-handedly.

"Good town, right, Carl?" Dean laughed and winked, getting another nod and nothing more from the impassive Reynolds, who was doing a trencherman's job on the steak.

"Yes sir, I shore do like Pittsburgh," the big pitcher went on. "Good steaks–not as good as these o'course–good night spots, good times. And a real tough team, them Pirates. Wouldn't surprise me to see us and them fighting it out right down to the very end this year. They got them there Waner boys, y'know, best damn pair of brothers that ever been on the same team–'ceptin' for me 'n Paul, o'course."

"That's right–what *is* your brother doin' these days?" a rotund bald-headed regular named Sunstrom asked.

"Paul's havin' himself kind of a tough time jest now," the more famous sibling said, his voice suddenly lower and his mind surely drifting back to those lost glories of 1934, when the strapping and colorful Dean boys together won a combined forty-nine games and a World Series for St. Louis. And they each won two of the four Cardinal victories in the Series.

"He's down there in that ol' Texas League," Dean continued, "tryin' to work out his arm troubles. Jest like I am. And he'll be back too, jest like I will. Heck, what am I *sayin'?*" Diz roared, his expansive self once more. "Shoot, I already am back, 'cause I never really been away! And now I'm a Cub, dammit, and proud of it, and we're gonna win us a pennant for these fine Chicago folks here, ain't we now, Carl?"

Reynolds nodded again, expressionless, and then actually spoke. He asked the Killer for another beer.

I hung around for another half hour or so, absorbing as

much of Dizzy Dean's bombastic but somehow endearing braggadocio as I could digest in a single session. As I started to edge out of the saloon, he was regaling his rapt assemblage about how before the seventh and deciding game of the '34 World Series he had told Hank Greenberg, the Detroit Tigers star, to relax. "Yore troubles are gonna be over in two hours, because ol' Diz is pitching. And shore 'nuff, about two hours later, we'd beaten those pore boys from Dee-troit by eleven to nothin.'"

"Snap, don't run off just yet," the Killer yelled above the rising noise level. "Did you ever get to talk to Dick Daley?"

"Oh, yeah, I did. Guess I forgot to tell you," I said as we huddled at the far end of the bar, where we could almost hear each other. "We met twice, once down in Springfield, once here, and he was, well…I'd say fairly helpful. Just between us, I don't believe the party had anything to do with Martindale's death. But understand, that's just me talking."

"I never thought they did. Did you by chance mention anything to him about how his father had never come in here?"

"Why?"

"Well, the great Dizzy Dean has not been the only new face around the premises lately," the bar owner said with his lopsided smile. "A few days back now–you weren't in here that night–who do you think strolls in but Mike Daley himself, as if he just stopped by every day as part of his routine. Told me that he'd been planning to visit me for ages. We had a fine talk, about everything from folks back in the Old Sod to Chicago politics to how his son is doing down in Springfield. And he said he'd be coming back again soon–even if I was located so far north."

"Interesting."

"Indeed it is interesting. And thanks, Snap," he said, clapping a big hand on my shoulder.

"For what?"

He smiled again and went back to the cluster of customers around the two ballplayers. The last thing I heard as I stepped out onto Clark Street was Diz's audience, begging for more stories. And the last thing I saw was the Killer's grinning face as he rushed to keep the glasses filled along the crowded bar.

My normal one-block trip home became two blocks because of my roundabout route down a side street and then in through the alley entrance to my building. Also, I'd taken to leaving a couple of my lamps on all day, and the Venetian blinds closed, so that the outfit boys stalking me couldn't tell when I got home. Once inside the apartment, I immediately telephoned Leo Cahill at home.

"Snap Malek! To what do I owe this nocturnal honor?"

"I've got a scoop for your sports section."

"You're getting a little far afield from your police world, aren't you?" he asked in a skeptical tone. News operations at the *Tribune*–and at all the other dailies in town as well–were rigidly territorial. Other than the top dogs, each editor worried about his own fiefdom and little else. And if you worked in one area of the paper, it was assumed that everything you did as a reporter would be for that area, or that section, and nobody else.

"A true reporter is never off duty, Leo, you should know that," I sighed in mock solemnity. "Anyway, here it is, on a silver platter. I just came home from a saloon where none other than Dizzy Dean says he's going to sue the Cardinals for 250,000 simoleons because they wrecked his arm when they made him pitch too soon after last year's All Star Game, where, as you may recall, he got banged up by that line drive. He also says he'll give at least a hundred thousand of that to Phil Wrigley as compensation for his lack of playing time with the Cubs so far this season."

"Dean told you all that?" Leo responded, surprised. "How come? I thought he was pissed off at the *Trib*."

"But he doesn't know I'm with the *Trib*. I told him I'm a salesman in the steel business."

"Uh-huh. Interesting. Well, it makes a nice anecdote to amuse your grandchildren with, Snap, but I can tell you that none of my editors would give that story even a column inch."

"Oh? And why not?"

"Snap, Snap, wake up, for God's sake, will you? You may be a whiz as a police and crime reporter, I'll give you that. But you're out of your league here; you don't know these guys. Dean's a bullshit artist–always has been. He's not gonna sue anybody. He's just thumping his chest and sounding off. The guy loves attention, can't live without it. And since he can't pitch anymore–probably never will again, in fact–he's going to make noise some other way. Mark what I say, Snap–the guy is a hundred and ten percent hot air. He's not going to file any suits or even suggest it. He'd get himself laughed out of town."

"He said just a few minutes ago that he'd be pitching again in July," I put in gamely.

" 'He said, he said, he said.' Snap, get off it, will you? I know I rag you a lot about the Cubs, because you're such an easy target. But this time, I actually feel sorry for you and all those other poor saps who pull for them. So, like I told you way back in the spring, Dean is washed up, through, done. Okay, so he got a little lucky and won…what? Two or three games right at the start of the season, when the hitters were still stiff. But what's he done since then? Nothing. I told you then and I'll tell you now–he won't win five games. Shoot, Dizzy Dean is done winning, period. End of story. Give it up, Snap."

There was no talking to Leo Cahill on the subject of Jay Hanna (Dizzy) Dean. Let the record show, however, that Leo was wrong on at least two counts. A month later, in mid-July, Diz really did pitch again–and he began to win. At about the same time, he announced publicly that he was suing the St. Louis Cardinals organization for that quarter of a million, and if he collected the money, he planned to give Cubs owner Philip K. Wrigley a sizeable chunk of the settlement.

Ultimately, however, baseball's crusty and dictatorial old commissioner, Judge Kenesaw Mountain Landis, said he felt the suit would be detrimental to baseball (whatever that meant), and he put pressure on Dean, who dropped the idea. But it turned out to be a hell of a story, and all of the Chicago papers carried the developments more or less simultaneously and with strong play–but there were no scoops.

There could have been a scoop, however, a full month earlier. Leo Cahill knew that, of course, but he never mentioned it within my hearing. And he never again brought up the subject of Dizzy Dean with me. But you can bet that I brought Dizzy up to him more than once in the weeks that lay ahead.

Chapter 17

It has always puzzled me that the outfit chose to expend so much time and manpower trying to monitor my activities during nonworking hours in the spring and summer of 1938. But whenever I looked around, there they were…each morning the car idling at the curb on Clark with two figures inside, each evening the same. I assumed they eventually figured out that when I got home, I entered the building through another door, but they made no attempt to intercept me for another of those "rides." And for my part, I continued to defer any attempt to see Nicolette Stover, either at Harding's again or up at her apartment on Grace Street, for fear that I might lead the goons to her.

My next contact with the syndicate was totally unexpected. I was working a crossword puzzle one July morning at my desk in Police Headquarters when my phone rang.

"Mr. Malek," the hoarse, familiar voice pronounced. It was "Mr. Left" of the night rides.

My hand tightened on the receiver. "Yes?"

"Have you read your own newspaper today?" he rasped. "The Three-Star Final?"

"More or less. Why?"

"Page 18, lower-left-hand corner."

"Hold on," I said, pressing the receiver to my left ear with a raised shoulder as I started flipping pages. "Uh, yeah, here it is," I said.

"Could be that there's more here than meets the eye, Mr. Malek," he said in his sandpaper voice, spacing the words.

"Could be, eh?"

"A lot more than meets the eye, Mr. Malek. Do I gather

that you did not write this?"

"You gather right. Not only did I not write it, I'm embarrassed to say I didn't even notice it on my first pass through the paper. It probably came from the City News Bureau and then was sent to all the dailies, which is not uncommon. Items like this usually come from City News."

"Far from complete reporting, whoever did it," came the dry response. "Have you made any progress on the matter that we previously discussed?"

"None at all, I'm sorry to say. The press of my day-to-day work—you know how it is."

"Good-bye, Mr. Malek," he said in that voice devoid of all emotion. The line went dead.

I turned back to the item he referred to. It was tucked away at the bottom of a column. At the *Trib*, a one-paragraph article like this one is referred to, for reasons unknown to me, as a "5 head." **"HOODLUM FOUND SLAIN**," it read. "Joseph Pariello, 37, a hoodlum with past convictions for bookmaking, was found beaten and shot to death yesterday in the Caldwell Woods forest preserve northwest of the city by a passerby. Cook County Sheriff's Police theorized that the crime syndicate was behind the killing of Pariello, a one-time driver for the imprisoned mob boss Al Capone. The victim was shot once in the head with a .32 caliber bullet, according to the sheriff's police."

Pariello of course figured to be the one that Mr. Left had mentioned to me earlier as the stooge the police were trying to hang the Martindale killing on. I turned to the City News reporter. "Hey, I'm sure we must have got this item from your guy on the North beat." I circled the paragraph and tossed the paper on his desk. "See if you can get his full file, will you?"

He nodded. "Sure, okay. You thinking of doing something more on it, or what?"

"Uh-uh." I waved the question away as I would a housefly. "Just curious. I went to grammar school with a guy named Joey Pariello, who would be exactly that age, and I figured maybe the full version of the story had more detail on him." City News, which covered most of the grittier crime news in town for the dailies (and the radio stations), usually gave the dailies more than they would ever use on this kind of story—when we printed the stuff at all. The kid started working the phone and came back to me a few minutes later.

"Okay, this Pariello was found in the Caldwell Woods yesterday morning around seven or so by a guy in the neighborhood who was walking his dog," he read from notes he had just taken. "The Sheriff's coppers said Pariello had been dead maybe twelve or fourteen hours. Single bullet went clean through the heart. He was also pretty badly beat up, too, according to the report. He musta done something that really pissed off the mob."

"He sure pissed off somebody," I allowed.

"Yeah. No details on his background, though, other than his record and that bit about his being a driver for Capone. Do you think this is the one that you went to school with?"

"Could be, but there's not much to go on. If I was to guess, I'd say it was him," I improvised.

"Hey, Snap, what kind of guys did you go to grammar school with, anyway?" Eddie Metz brayed, grinning through clenched teeth that gripped a cigarette.

"Guys who were a lot like you, Eddie, except maybe a little bit smarter," I responded, feigning irritability. "But I still don't know for sure that it really was the same Pariello."

"Come on, Snap, how many Joe—what was the name?— Pariellos do you think there are out there?" Packy Farmer put in. "Was the stiff your age?"

"Just about," I shrugged, pleased that I had established a personal reason for wanting more dope on the dead mobster. It looked like Mr. Left had it figured about right. The Chicago cops, pressured to solve the Martindale hit, had one way or another fastened onto this Pariello as their patsy. Chances are they took him someplace nice and private and worked him over, maybe for days, trying to wring a confession out of the poor, luckless bastard. Apparently that didn't work, so they got frustrated, shot him, and then dumped him in a forest preserve, outside the city limits of course, making no attempt to hide the body. But then, why should they?

When he was found, the Sheriff's men, probably not privy to what their city brothers had been up to, made the logical assumption, given Pariello's background, that he had fallen out of favor with the syndicate for some reason and had paid the ultimate price, which was hardly uncommon. It seemed like this was a good time for me to make another visit to the chief of detectives.

I got the usual toothy smile from Elsie Dugo and also the usual smart crack–this time a line from a movie. "Is that a pistol in your pocket, or are ya just glad to see me?" she quipped.

"Anybody ever take the time to tell you that you've got yourself a salty mouth, sister?"

"More than once, brother. I just tell 'em that I got that way from listening to the newspaper men who hang around my boss's office pretending to act tough."

"Huh. Well, at least you're a darn sight easier on the eyes than Mae West. Is the big cheese by chance hiding behind that closed door?" I made a gesture toward Fahey's office.

"He is indeed. And you're almost as easy on the eyes as Cary Grant–but not quite, to be totally candid. By the way, the man himself is grumpy, so enter at your own risk."

"You're all heart," I shot back. "And let the record show that Mr. Grant's real name, the one he was born with, is Archibald Leach. How, I ask you, how can any woman be interested in a joe who has a label like that?"

She gave a toss of her head and turned back to her typing. "A rose by any other name…"

"Yeah, yeah. But can he hit a curve ball?"

Elsie started to deliver another comeback, but I pushed on through to the sanctum, which gave me the last word in this particular sparring match. Fahey looked up and grimaced as I loomed over his horizon. "I see she's letting anybody get past her now."

"And a fine morning to you, too, sir," I responded,

slumping uninvited into a guest chair and lobbing my just-opened pack of Luckies onto his desk blotter. "You got five minutes for me?"

"Do I get a choice?"

I shrugged. "Hell, yes you do. You can call any one of those cretins down the hall who masquerade as sergeants. And then you can have one of them throw me out on my ear–which would no doubt result in a page one expose by none other than yours truly on how the Chicago Police take delight in bullying and otherwise intimidating duly authorized and certified representatives of the fourth estate, otherwise known as the press. Or…you can take relaxed and satisfying drags on some of my fine Virginia cigarettes–no charge–while we have an enlightening discussion about newly deceased mobsters."

Fahey's thick gray-white brows dropped low over his eyes as he considered me. "Meaning?"

"Meaning one Joe Pariello."

He lit one of the Luckies from my pack and flipped the matchbook aside absently. "You talking about that Capone wheelman found out northwest in the preserves? What about him?"

"Fergus, I'm real interested in Pariello, real interested," I replied with a smile as Elsie whisked in and set a mug of coffee on the corner of Fahey's desk for me. I nodded my thanks as she pivoted to leave.

"Hell, what's to be interested in?" Fahey snarled, taking a drag and leaning back, lacing his hands over his ample midsection. "The guy was strictly small potatoes, never anything more than a driver and lackey and a two-bit bookie, so far as we could tell from his record and from what we hear. May have been a numbers runner, too. Capone liked him, yeah, but so what? Al's long gone to the Rock–and apparently off his rocker, too, from what we gather–and Nitti and his boys call all the tunes now, you know that as well as I do, maybe better. We figure Pariello crossed one of 'em some way, most likely holding back dough. Happens all the time, you know that, too."

185

I sipped coffee, watching the chief. I'd known Fahey for almost ten years and liked to think I could read him. And if I was reading right, he was being straight with me on this. Still…

"So, if I were to suggest that someone other than the mob was responsible for Pariello's one-way trip to slumberland…" I let it hang in the air.

"What somebody?" Fahey said warily, grinding out his butt. "Like a jealous husband, maybe?"

"Maybe. Or maybe somebody who was trying to get him to talk."

The chief came slowly forward in his chair, resting on his elbows. "So you figure he was crossing the mob somehow, and they found out and made an example of him as a lesson about what happens to double-dealers, eh?"

"That's one possibility, yes. But here's another one–purely hypothetical, of course. Let's say for the sake of argument that somebody wanted Pariello to confess to a crime he didn't commit."

Fahey's eyes narrowed to slits. "Go on."

"Okay, our hypothetical somebodies work the hood over–maybe for days–but he won't spit out a confession. So they finally give up and croak him. They dump the body in the woods out to hell and gone, figuring it will look like it was a syndicate hit. But like I said, all this is purely hypothetical."

"And the hypothetical people who rubbed him out?" Fahey responded with a scowl.

I turned my palms up. "You fill in the blanks."

He snorted. "Sometimes I can be a little dense, but I get your drift, Malek." He only calls me that when he's sore at me.

"What drift is that?"

"Cut the crap. You've got a real fixation with the Martindale killing, don't you?" He lit another cigarette. "I think you dream about that murder. You've known me for what, ten or twelve years now? I don't claim to be a choir boy, and I've done more than a few things on this damn job that I've gone to confession about, but I've never–*never*–ordered anybody worked over. Got that?" Fahey slapped a fleshy palm on the desktop for emphasis.

"I didn't mean to suggest it was your doing, or that you even knew about it," I responded calmly.

"Well, thank you very damn much for that," he huffed, the veins in his square, map-of-Ireland face standing out. "I'm so relieved to hear it. But I'm really curious about what in God's name makes you think that anything like you suggest ever even happened."

"I've got a source–and it is not somebody on the force."

He made a deprecating noise. "Care to name this source?"

"Can't. Sorry."

"I've got a source, I've got a source," he mimicked in a rusty falsetto. "That's the tune you newspaper guys are always singing. You hide behind that damn phony line and act like you've all got secret information. Well, I think ninety percent of the time, maybe more, what you've really got is a load of bullshit and that you're on a fishing expedition to find out what we know."

"Fergus, I'm not going to quarrel with you except to say that I'm reasonably sure this belongs to that other ten percent of the time."

The chief appeared angry, but I felt that pose was at least in part a façade masking his concern about what I had told him. He was by all accounts an honest cop, most of the time, anyway, and he hated suggestions that not everybody on the force played by the same rules he did. Also, for all his blustering to the contrary, he had known me long enough to realize that my sources usually tended to be solid.

I now was virtually positive Fahey had no knowledge of how the minor-league mobster had met his end. But I wanted to be sure. "You ever hear of Pariello before this business?" I asked.

"Godammit, no!" he fired back, punishing his desk top with his fist again. "Like I said, he was small potatoes, a measly damn gopher. No reason I would have ever heard of him. You know, lately it seems like everybody's moaning about how we beat confessions out of people. Take for example that hammer moron who just got locked up."

"The one they say raped fifty women?"

Fahey lit another Lucky and made a face. "Yeah, and he used a hammer on some of 'em, too. In the courtroom he, or maybe it was his damn public defender, said we forced a confession out of him. Used the rubber hose and all, the whole business."

I nodded, recalling the case. "That claim didn't do him a hell of a lot of good, though, did it?"

"For once, no it didn't, thank the Lord!" he said. "But what if the jury had bought it?"

I drank the best coffee in the building and set the cup down, choosing my words. "Well, Fergus, you have to admit it *has* happened before–beatings by the force, I mean."

"Yeah, but dammit, never on my watch, at least as far as I ever knew," he said. "Not that I wouldn't mind seeing a few of the goons and morons and perverts we nail get the shit kicked out of 'em during, shall we say, an 'interrogation.' That's not my style, though–even when we're holding a suspected cop killer. Guess I must be turning into a softy, huh?"

"Many's the time I've said that very thing about you, Fergus."

He shrugged. "Well, I know more than a few around here–he made an arc with his arm as if taking in the whole building–who think I'm too soft for this job. Hellfire, they may be right. Mind if I keep these?" he asked, holding up the pack of Luckies.

"Why do you think I brought them in? I'm something of a softy myself, to say nothing of the bad habit I've developed of trying to curry favor with various public officials by supplying them with smokes."

"Get your butt out of here and do something productive like flirting with Elsie, will you? I've got work to do," he muttered, putting his head down and riffling through a six-inch-high stack of paperwork.

I did, and I did.

Chapter 18

"Will you be right here when I get back, Dad?" Peter asked, trying to make the question sound casual rather than pleading.

"Right here, at this very spot, two weeks from today," I assured him, pointing to the ornate, three-faced clock with Roman numerals that loomed directly above us. It was a muggy Saturday morning in July, and we were standing with Peter's suitcases in the columned, echo-filled concourse of the North Western Terminal on West Madison, waiting along with hundreds of other chattering adolescent boys and their parents for the announcement that the "Campers' Special" train to Wisconsin was ready for boarding.

Peter, who had never been to summer camp before, was not overjoyed with the prospect, which his mother had proposed. When I questioned her about it, she was adamant. "I need some time to myself, Steve," she said in that quiet-but-firm tone that always had an unspoken "don't argue with me" attachment.

"I need to get away for a little while, but I can't very well do that with Peter at home all day. And remember, you don't have any vacation coming until late September."

When I asked where she planned to go (hardly my business any more), she said to St. Joseph, Michigan, a small resort town around the southern end of Lake Michigan from Chicago.

"Alone?" (Again, no business of mine.)

She paused, an expression of irritation on her face. "No. A friend has a place over there."

"Who? Martin Baer?"

"I don't see that it's any concern of yours, Steve," she had answered evenly. In the dozen-plus years we had been married, I had never known Norma to raise her voice–one of the things that was at the same time both comforting and maddening about her.

"Well, if anything happens to Peter when he's up in Wisconsin, how will I get hold of you?" I countered with what I felt was irrefutable logic, although we both knew I was reaching.

"All right," she said, letting her shoulders drop. "It *is* Martin Baer. I'll give you the address and phone number over in St. Joe."

"So, just you and him, huh?"

Norma came as close to glaring as she ever does. "Again, Steve, it is hardly any concern of yours, but in fact, we will not be alone. Martin's mother will be there, too."

"A chaperone, eh?" I retorted, wishing in an instant that I could pull the words back. She did not respond, and we parted that day without warmth but also without overt rancor–much the way we related to each other during those last, listless days of our marriage. In all the times I had come home looped, for instance, I was never met with outright anger or hostility, but rather with a resigned disappointment. Even the night I missed Peter's seventh (or maybe eighth?) birthday and shambled into the apartment well after midnight, she turned over in bed when I walked into the darkened bedroom and asked if I was all right. When I told her I was, she said "Oh, good" as if she meant it and went back to sleep. Confrontation was not an element in our lives together.

By the time Peter boarded the camp-bound train, his mood had brightened somewhat, at least partially because of the anticipation of riding the brand new green-and-yellow North Western streamliner.

"How fast can it go, Dad?" he had asked, running his finger along the smooth yellow surface of the train as we walked along the platform, looking for his assigned coach.

"A hundred, easy," I improvised, having no idea. "Faster'n that Pennsylvania train you rode on when you visited your grandpa and grandma over in Fort Wayne last Christmas."

He liked that answer, uninformed as it was, and when I got him settled in next to an oversized and tinted window, I felt better about his being shipped off to the North Woods. "You'll meet some nice boys, meet a lot of new friends," I assured him, mouthing lines uncounted parents before me had used to hearten offspring who were facing the prospect of two weeks living in tents or spartan cabins, as well as other deprivations. I hugged him awkwardly and eased into the aisle to make way for the arrival of his seatmate, an acne-faced boy with straw-colored hair and an expression of doubt.

Within seconds, I learned from his parents that the newcomer's name was Robert, that he was twelve, lived in Des Plaines, suffered from hay fever, and had never gone to camp before. After introductions were made, the boys sized each other up and I said my good-byes.

As I left the train, the last words I heard came from Robert's mother, who gushed to her son: "See, now you've already met Peter here, and you haven't even left the station yet. You're going to make all kinds of friends when you're up there in those beautiful Wisconsin woods just like your father and I have been telling you. All that worrying you did was for nothing, wasn't it?"

Riding back to my place from the station on the Clark streetcar, I took stock of my feelings and my situation. On the one hand, I would truly miss seeing Peter over the next two weekends. On the other, I would have the time to myself. I felt guilty even thinking that–after all, I did only see my son for at most a day and a half a week, as was the agreement, while Norma was a full-time parent and a working one on top of it. Sure, I kicked in for alimony and child support, again as was the agreement, but she had to deal with most of the day-to-day stuff, like teacher conferences and buying school clothes and visits to the doctors and dentists and so on. She did all of this very efficiently and, as far as I could tell, very cheerfully.

But, so I rationalized, I had a job too, and I needed time to myself, same as Norma did. Besides, I was running out of things to do with Peter on weekends. After Riverview, the Lincoln Park Zoo, Wrigley Field, the Elevated and streetcar rides, and the big museums, there were only so many movies I felt comfortable taking him to. And of course, there was my current situation involving the mob and its interest in my activities.

That morning, for instance, when I left my apartment and went to Logan Square to pick Peter up, the car with its two fedora-lidded men was parked at the curb on Clark as usual. I slipped out through the alley and walked several blocks on side streets before flagging a cab on Belmont. Even then I wasn't completely sure that I'd ditched the tail. Because Peter had so much luggage, he and I took another cab from Norma's to the station, and on the way, I kept looking out the rear window of the hack, thinking I had recognized the tail car.

"How come you keep looking back, Dad?" Peter asked. "You think somebody's following us?"

I forced a laugh. "Of course not, Peter. Why would anybody want to do something like that?"

The thick-necked cabbie turned back and laughed too, but it wasn't forced. "Yeah, why would anybody be after us? It sure doesn't figure to be a copper, because, heck, I ain't even goin' the speed limit. There's just too doggone much traffic today."

I didn't look back again, although I was tempted to, so I never knew for sure if we were being dogged. And I didn't spot a tail when I left the North Western Station after seeing Peter off. But as the streetcar approached my building, the sedan and its two occupants was still (or again?) out in front, so I rode a block farther north and made straight for Kilkenny's.

The Killer had, as promised, added a touch to the outside: Next to the neon Pabst Blue Ribbon sign in the front window was an obviously posed black-and-white glossy photograph of a grinning Dizzy Dean in his Cub uniform, following through on a pitch with the empty Wrigley Field grandstands in the background. In the lower right-hand corner of the photo, Dean had scrawled "To my good friend Killer, who serves the best steaks in Chicago, bar none. Your pal, Diz."

Although I wasn't ready to call the Killer's steaks the best in the city, bar none, they were good, and Chicago's newest baseball luminary obviously agreed, as he'd become something of a regular since that night he had wandered in with Carl Reynolds. I'd even run into him there again myself, this time with another Cub pitcher, Clay Bryant, in tow, and I was surprised that Diz had remembered me."

"Ah, Snap, 'tis indeed fine to see your benign countenance this lovely day," the Killer boomed heartily, saluting as I walked into the nearly deserted public house that Saturday. "Will you be partaking of the usual nectar?"

I started to ask for coffee, then checked myself when I noticed that the clock behind the bar registered five past noon. "The usual nectar sounds good. I see, by the way, that you've got Dean's mug up in the window, as well as his written testimonial for your fine shoe leather."

"Shoe leather my sainted Uncle Liam!" he howled in mock anger as he slid a foam-capped stein of Schlitz along the bar to me. "You've had more than your share of both T-bones and filets at my groaning board, if I may be so bold as to remind you. And speaking of our Mr. Dean, he may not be much for partaking the juice, which is fine given his line of employment, but he does indeed know a good piece of beef when he gets his gums into it. And he's also pulled a few of the other Cubs in here with him, which doesn't exactly hurt business any."

The Killer grinned as he ran a rag over the bar. "He was in here with Billy Herman a few nights past, and he says he's bringing that Irish stalwart Gabby Hartnett next. To top it off, all sorts of new folks have been dropping by, hoping to meet some players and jaw with 'em. And look here–Diz even signed a ball to me." The Killer took a new Spaulding baseball from its place of honor on the back bar and proudly showed me Dean's signature.

"Well, just make sure you don't feed old Dizzy too much,"

I grumbled. "The guy's having enough trouble trying to throw as it is, so we sure don't want him to get fat on top of it. If he doesn't start playing soon, the Cubs will be as dead as last Sunday's paper, and about as interesting. And if the Cubs are dead, you know all too well that your newfound patronage will plummet like a brick in a pond, not to mention what will happen to every other saloon, restaurant, and shop within three or four blocks of the Wrigley playpen. And just remember, my Gaelic friend, if our Mr. Dean *does* begin pitching again, there's a guaranteed 40,000 in the old ball yard up the street every time he starts. And more than a few of them figure to stop in here–both before and after the game."

The Killer looked smug as he leaned on the bar and crossed his beefy arms. "Now don't go and get yourself all riled up, Snap. In point of fact, Diz is pitching next week, probably against the Boston gladiators. I bring you glad tidings that his wing's healthy again."

"Yeah, well, I've been hearing that for so long that it puts me to sleep. I'll believe it when I see it."

"'Tis really true this time," the barkeep avowed. "He mentioned that his wife's coming up from Dixie for a few days to see him pitch, and he says that always gives him a boost. Also, Charley Grimm told Diz he's ready to start him."

"Grimm better do something soon or Phil Wrigley's going to get himself a new manager and send Charley to the bush leagues," I remarked sourly.

"Diz'll be back in fine form, and real soon," Dean's new pal proclaimed, forming a circle with his thumb and forefinger. You can bank on that, my fourth-estate friend."

I wasn't willing to bank on much of anything these days, except that there would be a car with two hoods inside at the curb in front of the unimposing building I called home. And I was getting more than a little tired of having them around. As I walked south from the Killer's along the west side of Clark, I saw them yet again. But this time, instead of sneaking around to the alley door of the building, I pulled in air, approached the sedan from behind–it was the Studebaker this time, with its windows rolled down–and put a foot on the passenger-side running board.

"Hello there, boys. Waiting for anyone in particular?" I said amiably, touching the brim of my hat.

"Damn!" the thug in the passenger seat muttered, jumping as if he'd been slapped.

"Hey, I didn't mean to scare you," I told him, keeping my tone breezy and holding up a palm like the traffic cop at Clark and Madison. "It's just that I've noticed you fellows before–you're hard to miss–and I figured maybe you were looking for somebody in the neighborhood. I've lived around here for awhile now and thought maybe I could help you find who you're after."

"Goddamn you," the passenger growled, opening the door and starting to get out. "I'm gonna–"

"Shut the fuck up and sit down, Marko," the driver snapped. "I'll take care of this." He stepped out and circled around the front of the car toward me. He was at least six-four and 200 pounds, and the expression on his square, swarthy face raised scowling to an art form.

"You got yourself a problem, Mac?" he growled in a voice that suggested problems upset him.

"Not me," I told him, trying to generate enough saliva to swallow. "I'm just trying to be helpful, that's all."

"You're fulla crap, that's what you are. You know goddamn well why we're here. And don't think you're foolin' anybody with that sneakin' out the back way shit."

"Huh?" I put on a puzzled expression.

He loomed over me, creating a solar eclipse. "I'll spell it out, Mr. Newspaper Hotshot. If it was up to me and Marko here, you'd be sittin' up on some cloud strummin' a harp. And I could make that happen right now, right here, without a sound. Silencer, see?" He cackled and jabbed at the bulge under his 46 long blue pinstripe suit coat.

"Now I got better things to do than shadow some goddamn scribbler, but I also got my orders, and I follow orders. The Brother, he says to watch you, so I watch you, with Marko and his dumb-ass jokes to keep me from gettin' too bored. But the Brother is going to be pissed, real pissed, if he don't find out pretty damn soon who croaked Goody Two Shoes Martindale, and he says you're the guy what can find out for him—the cops sure can't. But so far, you ain't come up with shit—or have you?" I never saw the back of his right hand until it whacked my cheek, spinning me around. "Have you?" he repeated the question as I picked my hat up off the sidewalk and shook my head.

"No…I haven't."

His asthmatic laugh held only menace. "Didn't think so, pal. Just figured I'd see whether you was payin' attention. Now listen, listen good: the Brother, I know him pretty well, and I can see he's runnin' out of patience. If I was you, I'd be workin' real hard to find out who pulled the trigger."

"So your friend the Brother can croak *him*?" I responded in a weak attempt at bravado.

The driver laughed some more and rolled his eyes. "I wouldn't worry about what happens then. It ain't your affair, is it?"

I started to contradict him but quickly checked myself, rubbing a cheek that already was beginning to swell. Any satisfaction I might have derived from tossing off a clever remark would be more than offset by another reminder that I should be attentive.

The driver—although our paths would cross again, I never learned his name—gave an insolent salute, turned on his heel, and slid back behind the wheel but didn't start the Studebaker, while Marko leered at me over sunglasses balanced halfway down his Roman nose. I entered the building by the front door this time—there was no point to slinking around to the alley—and went up to my apartment to contemplate an ongoing existence in a fishbowl and how I might wriggle out of it.

I climbed out of bed at 9:15 on Sunday morning, having formulated a plan of sorts, nothing elaborate. Looking down onto Clark Street from my living room, I spotted the tail car, a black Dodge this time. Given the man-hours they were putting in, the organization placed a ton of faith in my detecting abilities–far more than I did myself. Once again, I had to wonder how smart they were, collectively. And although they had indeed been patient until now, I didn't need some oversized, pea-brained wheelman to tell me that their patience was wearing thin.

I could have brought in the cops any time during the last few weeks, of course, and had them knock out the surveillance. But the respite would only have been temporary...although I was a police reporter and as such unofficially entitled to protection beyond that received by the average citizen, the boys who wore brass buttons on their uniforms were not about to keep watch indefinitely. You could bet the farm that as soon as the prowl cars pulled back, the fedora-lids would return, watching and waiting. And there was another good reason for not calling in the law: They would want to know just *why* the mob was so interested in me, and for now I wanted to pursue the Martindale case alone and unfettered, and unquestioned by the police.

I strangled the juice out of a half grapefruit, then slurped two bowls of Rice Krispies with brown sugar and three cups of coffee at the kitchen table while reading the *Trib* and the *Examiner,* which I had begun subscribing to on Sundays. The line story on both papers was the death in a Paris subway station of old Sam Insull, who had been the grand poohbah of the public utilities in Chicago and across the whole of the Middle West until his electric empire came crashing down around him during the Depression. Sam skedaddled to Greece in the early '30s to avoid all kinds of investigations, and damned if he wasn't acquitted when they finally did have a trial in '35. The public, many of whom lost their shirts on his stocks, never acquitted him, though, and he was smart enough to spend the rest of his life on the far side of the Atlantic.

The *Examiner*, which like every Hearst paper was big on celebrity news, also had fun with the ongoing hit-and-miss romance between Hollywood's Katharine Hepburn and Howard

Hughes, the big-bucks aviator who had been setting all sorts of speed records in his souped-up aeroplane. The two were good at avoiding reporters, though, as both a news story and Damon Runyon's smart-alecky column reported with undertones of frustration.

I dumped my dishes in the sink and put on a white shirt and my newest summer suit, a light gray herringbone. After giving the hairbrush a workout and straightening my maroon-and-gray striped tie, I contemplated my image in the bathroom mirror. Despite the slight bruise on my right cheek where I'd gotten belted the day before, I looked respectable enough to be heading for Mass, which in fact I was.

Walking along Clark from my building, I kept my eyes straight ahead, paying no heed to the Dodge at curbside. I heard its motor start and knew that it had to be crawling along several yards behind me, which was fine. Standing as though I didn't have a care in the world, I turned east on Belmont and assumed the Dodge did as well. Both auto and pedestrian traffic increased as I neared Our Lady of Mount Carmel Church. It was the 11 o'clock Mass crowd.

I had been in the church only once before, for the funeral of a *Tribune* reporter about a half dozen years earlier, but I had a clear recollection of the layout. Not looking back, I joined the crowd of worshipers shuffling through the double doors, dipped my hand in the holy water from the font, and genuflected. I then made for the far right aisle and briskly moved toward the front of the sanctuary. I finally did risk a peek back, and only then from behind a knot of people pushing toward the pews. I saw no one who looked like a hoodlum, so I walked to the front of the nave and out through a door to the right of the altar. I found myself in a small, windowless room with three straight-backed wooden chairs, on one of which sat a young, dark-haired priest in his vestments who was praying aloud.

"Yes?" He looked up, startled, his eyes magnified by horned-rim glasses with thick lenses.

"This the way out?" I muttered, trying to look befuddled

and probably succeeding.

"Uh, yes…that is…if you want the alley?" he said, blinking and gesturing vaguely down a hallway. I thanked him and within seconds found myself in the alley that ran behind the church. No sign of the Dodge or of anybody following me. I turned west and eventually hailed a southbound Checker on Halsted. All the way downtown, I kept watch out the rear window–this was getting to be a habit. The cabbie didn't remark on it, although he gave me a questioning look when we pulled up in front of the LaSalle Street Station. "It's okay," I told him with a grin. "I'm only wanted for bookmaking and bunko, nothing rough like armed robbery or, heaven forbid, murder. Hell, I'm not even packing a rod."

Leaving him with a quarter tip and an open mouth, I went into the depot. Given the Sunday schedules, I had to wait almost an hour for a Rock Island local. As on my previous trip to Beverly Hills on this line, I was one of just a handful of passengers in my sooty coach. Stepping off the train into the sunlight at 103rd Street, I followed the route from my earlier visit except that once I reached Longwood Drive, my destination was not Edna Warburton's house but rather the massive brick-and-stone Victorian pile with all its chimneys that sat haughtily on a rise on the opposite side of the street.

I climbed the brick stairway cut into the embankment and marched up to an oaken door with leaded glass that was recessed in an archway on the front porch. I pushed the doorbell and heard chimes within. I waited a decent interval, then made the chimes sound again. This time, the thick door swung silently inward, revealing a broad-shouldered, somewhat hunched-over figure in a dark suit standing in the dark-paneled foyer. His oddly handsome triangular face, tapering to a pointed cleft chin, was without expression. "Yes?"

"Hello," I said cheerfully. "My name is Stephen Malek, from the *Tribune*." I held out my press card. "I apologize for not calling in advance. I am writing a long feature article for the newspaper saluting Lloyd Martindale for his accomplishments, and I would like very much to talk to his mother for a few minutes. I promise not to take too much of her time."

He frowned as he studied my card, then inhaled to speak when the shaky, querulous voice of a woman came from somewhere within. "Who is there, Preston?"

"Excuse me, sir," he said frostily, closing the door in my face. Either I had been dismissed or the dour Preston was receiving instructions, presumably from Mrs. Martindale, on how to deal with me. Ever the optimist, I waited, hat in hand. No more than a minute had elapsed when the door opened and the butler, if that was his role, reappeared.

"Sir, Mrs. Martindale regrets that she is indisposed and is unable to see you," he pronounced in a precise, well-modulated radio announcer-type tone that was as emotionless as his face was expressionless.

I nodded. "I certainly understand, of course, my coming on the spur-of-the-moment as I did. I should have made an appointment, sorry. Well, I would like to make one now–at Mrs. Martindale's convenience, of course."

Preston cocked his head and emitted a practiced throat-clearing sound, which they must teach in butler's school. "Sir, if you will permit me to be more specific: Mrs. Martindale is permanently indisposed. She is unable to see you *at any time whatever*."

"But, I–"

"Good day, sir," he said with the slightest of bows, his crisp tone contradicting his words as he closed the door with no further pretense of politeness.

Thus dismissed, I nodded to no one and executed an about-face, descending the steps to Longwood Drive and wondering how long the wait would be for a train back to the Loop.

Chapter 19

After a wait of well over an hour, I rode back north on another slow and grimy Rock Island local, contemplating my ill fortune and feeling more than a little sorry for myself. I had hoped to talk to Martindale's mother at least long enough to bring up the Stover name in general and Nicolette in particular to study her reaction. I thought about waiting a day or two and calling her, but I figured the stolid Preston probably answered the telephone as well as the door. Perhaps the old woman didn't even talk on the phone any more, I mused, although I was soon to be disabused of that speculation.

The next morning, Monday, I was settling in at my desk at Police Headquarters when my phone rang.

"Malek, you got anything hot going on there now?" It was Bob Lee, the managing editor.

"Not at the moment," I said taken aback and wondering if I'd blown a story. I didn't normally get calls here from anyone in the Tower above the assistant city editor level.

"Good!" he growled. "Then get up here now! I want you in my office in fifteen minutes."

I went outside and flagged a northbound cab on State Street, still puzzled by the summons. Why would Lee want to see me? Since he had succeeded Beck as managing editor last year, he and I hadn't exchanged a word, nor was there any reason we should. Police reporters rarely had dealings with managing editors–especially when the M.E. was no booster of the reporter to begin with.

Lee was talking on the phone in his glass-partitioned office along the north side of the local room when I got there, so I shot the breeze with Kirkpatrick, the best young general assignment reporter on the staff. We agreed that FDR would probably shoot for the third term in '40 and that Ed Kelly was almost a cinch to win next year's mayoral election.

"Malek!" Lee bellowed as he slammed down his receiver, jerking his head to summon me.

"Reporting as requested," I quipped, dropping into a chair in front of his mahogany desk. He stood and leaned forward, glowering at me for several seconds before speaking.

"What…the…hell…are…you…doing?" He came down on each word like a steam hammer.

"Huh? I don't get it. What do you mean?" I said, genuinely puzzled.

"I'll tell you what I mean," he snapped, jangling his key chain. "Beatrice Martindale happens to be a close personal friend of Colonel McCormick. Dates back to when her late husband and the Colonel were cronies. First thing this morning, she telephones the Colonel's office to complain that a *Tribune* reporter–guess who?–was banging on her door looking to get an interview for a feature he's doing on her recently deceased son. She read me your name off the business card you had left."

Lee paused for breath but kept rattling his damn keys. "Fortunately for you, the Colonel is out of the country, so Bessie had the call transferred down here. The lady was upset, Malek, very, very upset. She said she had always been willing to talk to our men before–even right after her son got killed. But she didn't understand why some reporter would show up unannounced on her doorstep. And she also didn't understand what more could be written about Lloyd Martindale that hadn't previously been covered. And dammit, Malek, I don't understand any of it either! I finally got her calmed down and said that I'd check the whole business out. After I got off the phone, I went to see Mike Kennedy in the Sunday Room, figuring he might have some sort of feature in the works on Martindale, and that you–for some reason–were the one writing it. But Mike didn't know anything about it, said that he'd never even met you. So here we are. What gives?"

"I was playing a hunch," I mumbled.

Lee pitched forward like an offensive lineman about to throw a block. "You were playing a hunch? Playing a hunch!" he roared as faces all over the cavernous local room turned toward us. "Since when do we give you a salary to play hunches?" I shrugged and made no reply.

The managing editor, as usual resplendent in a bright shirt–this one yellow–and a tweed, vested suit, sat down, crossed his arms, and leaned back, sending me a glare that told me he wished I'd disappear. "All right, Malek," he sighed. "What's this hunch?"

"I think Martindale was killed by somebody other than the mob," I answered quietly, realizing the words sounded ingenuous.

"Oh you do now, do you?" Lee snarled. "And what has caused you to formulate this theory?"

"Like I said, it's just a hunch," I told him, realizing that the conversation was at a dead end.

"And just who do your pals on the force down at 11th and State think murdered Lloyd Martindale?"

"They think it was a mob hit," I conceded.

Lee cocked his head, smirking. "The police believe it was a syndicate killing, the State's Attorney believes it was a syndicate killing–in fact, as far as I know, *everybody* believes it was a syndicate killing. But not you–oh no, because you've gone and got yourself a *hunch*." He hit the top of his desk with a fist, causing heads to turn again out in the big room. "Well, hunches are for swamis and fortune tellers. Around here, we happen to subscribe to the quaint old theory that facts are the basis of our reporting. Is that your understanding?"

I nodded.

"Good, good. Malek, I'm not going to pull any punches here–never do. As I think you're aware, I've never been a big fan of yours, and I'd be lying if I said I was. You may have done a good job on that Capone interview down in the Atlanta pen back in '34, but Christ, that was handed to you on a platter by his mouthpiece Ahern. Since then, I frankly haven't been all that impressed with your work. Oh, I understand you're pretty much off the booze now, which is all well and good. But among other things, you're too cocksure and headstrong for my taste–this latest Martindale business proves it."

"What are you telling me?" I asked, struggling to keep my voice even and wishing I had a glass of water.

"I'm telling you that as of right now–right this damn minute–you're on probation," Lee said. "I'm going to ask the city desk for weekly reports on your work. But more than that, I don't want to hear that you've bothered that poor, mourning Martindale woman ever again. One more complaint from her about you, and you're fired, gone, finished, through. His hand knifed through the air several times like a guillotine blade. "Are we clear on that?"

"Yes, I'd say you've made everything quite clear," I responded woodenly. "Anything else?"

"That's all," he snapped, turning to the telephone as if I were already nothing more than an unpleasant memory.

I steamed out of Lee's office in a cold rage, vaguely conscious of the stares and questioning looks from reporters and editors and copy boys who had seen and heard at least part of the managing editor's diatribe. Even at that moment, I reminded myself that Bob Lee was an able editor. And although I didn't by any means agree that my overall performance over the last several years warranted this probation, I knew the only reason I got slapped with it was that phone call to the Colonel's office from Beatrice Martindale. It seemed like when one of McCormick's friends sneezed–even if the Colonel himself didn't know it–the whole bloody *Tribune* ended up catching a cold.

Back at Police Headquarters, I spent the rest of the day mulling over my next move. I was still in a mulling mood that evening on the streetcar ride home, so much so that I totally forgot about my persistent shadows and got off the car at the stop in front of my building rather than a block north.

"Well, if it isn't Mr. Mouth himself, the guy who walks into a church and never comes out," a simpering Marko said from the front passenger seat of the Studebaker parked at the curb. "Got any more of your smart-assed comments for us today, Buddy?"

I should have ignored him, of course, but it had been a bad day, and I was in no mood to suffer fools gladly, even if they were mafia toughs. "Oh, put a lid on it, you baboon," I fired back, turning to enter the building.

"Why, you two-bit punk, I'll–"

"Marko," the driver barked. "Shaddup, will ya!" Marco did shut up, and I changed directions, opting for Kilkenny's rather than my apartment. It had been a day that called for a bracer or two.

The saloon was nosier than usual, and I soon found out why. "Snap, compadre!" the Killer boomed as I stepped across the threshold. "Diz here's got some splendid news for us."

The focal point of the crowd gathered at the bar, Dizzy Dean pivoted on his stool and gave me a wave and a thumbs-up. "Howdy there, Mr. Snap. Ah really don't know what all the fuss is about."

"Sure he does, Malek," Morty Easterly hollered, holding his beer stein aloft. "He's pitching tomorrow against Boston. And his arm feels great again, doesn't it, Diz?"

"Ah'm plannin' to mow them Bees down awright," Dean affirmed with a broad grin, patting his right arm. "And this here steak'll give me all the strength I need, shore 'nuff." He pointed with his fork at the T-bone on the plate in front of him, "Mr. Snap, say hello to Augie Galan here, a fine outfielder and a durn fine hitter, too. I oughta know–he had the whammy on me when I was with the Cards. And he's also the only guy whatever hit himself a homer both left-handed and right-handed in the same game. And now, him and me, we're gonna play as teammates in the World Series this year. That's a guarantee."

I reached across Dean and shook hands with the dark-haired Galan, also seated at the bar, who'd been playing with the Cubs since the early '30s. He smiled and turned his attention back to his own steak, content to let Dizzy do the talking–as if he could have gotten a word in edgewise anyway.

Returning to the end of the bar closest to the door, I started in on a beer when a hand came down hard on my shoulder. It was Marko.

"Let's go, punk. We're gonna take ourselves a nice long ride. Nobody calls me a baboon and then walks away. You got yourself one heap of trouble."

"No thanks, anyway," I replied, pulling back and looking around the noisy room for some help.

He lowered his voice still further. "I said *let's go.*" He began backing me toward the door, his hand pushing against my chest, and I was vaguely aware that the room had gotten quiet. Over Marko's shoulder, I could see Dizzy Dean, suddenly alert, getting to his feet and gesturing silently toward the back bar. The Killer nodded and flipped him the autographed baseball, which Diz plucked effortlessly out of the air in his right hand, cocking his arm in the same fluid motion. It's difficult to describe the next sound I heard, the closest I can come is when my mother used to take the rugs out into our little back yard in Pilsen and beat them with a broom handle. The ball hit Marko in the back of the head, making that same "whap," and the pupils of his eyes rolled up and out of sight in the sockets before he sputtered with a wheeze and crumpled to the wooden floor.

"Jesus, Mary, and Joseph," the Killer pronounced as the room became even more silent and Marko rolled over onto his back, his now open suit coat revealing a shoulder holster and an automatic. "Who the hell is he, Snap?"

"Marko for starters, I don't know the last name," I told him, picking the baseball up off the floor and tossing it back to Dean. "Thanks, Diz," I said as I realized my hand was shaking.

"Lord above, this is terrible," the Killer said. "This is just..." He halted in mid-sentence because of the figure who loomed in the doorway–the driver of the Studebaker.

"What the shit!" the hoodlum spat, gaping at Marko's prone and unconscious figure and reaching inside his coat. Then came that sound again. This time, the ball fired by Dizzy Dean was a frontal shot, hitting the driver in the right temple.

He went down without a murmur, and the revolver he'd already drawn skittered along the hardwood, coming to rest at Morty Easterly's feet.

"Call the police–right now!" I ordered the Killer. "And get Dizzy outta here. If the cops want to know what happened, tell them some guy you never saw before popped both these hoods with a club and then ducked out the door. But for God's sake, make sure that nobody mentions Dean. Now I need a car, fast."

"I got mine parked right outside," Augie Galan volunteered. "Where do you want to go?"

"Just a few blocks. What about Diz?"

"You okay?" Galan turned to his famous teammate. Dizzy Dean, back on his barstool and more than a tad shaken, nodded, stroking his arm. "When I got traded, the boys on the Cards said this town wouldn't be like St. Looie, and they was right," Dean drawled, shaking his head. "But it shore as heck is interesting."

"Okay, where we headed?" Galan asked once we were rolling in his new Lincoln Zephyr.

"A bar over on Diversey, it's just a few doors west of Clark. I'll show you the way."

"That was amazing–what happened back there in the saloon," Galan pronounced as we drove south on Clark. "Dizzy had this reputation with the Cardinals for making a lot of noise and then always ducking out or hiding when the fight actually started. But tonight…look what happened. He must really think a lot of you."

"We don't really know each other all that well," I said. "It's the Killer's steaks he thinks a lot of."

Galan pulled up in front of the Centurion. "Wait here," I told the outfielder, who seemed remarkably calm through all of this. "I should be back in fifteen minutes. If I'm not, call the police and tell them that a *Tribune* reporter named Steve Malek went into the Centurion and never came out."

He nodded like this was something he did every day. I went inside. The place, decorated in red and black Moderne style, was dark and the jukebox was loud. Within seconds after I'd eased onto a chrome stool close to the door, and before I could get the bartender's attention, a blonde in black patent spike heels, spangles, and an acre of creamy cleavage teetered over, rubbing an ample hip against me. "Hey, how 'bout buying a girl a drink?" she cooed.

"Love to, but I'm here on business. I need to see the Brother. Now."

She jumped as if she'd been goosed with a cattle prod. "Why din't you say so, mister? I'll get him," she replied, probably as earnestly as she knew how. She swivel-hipped to the other end of the bar and leaned across it, cupping her hand and saying something to the bartender. He looked toward me, nodded, and picked up the phone on the back bar, mouthing words into the instrument. He then told me that the Brother was "on his way."

He must not have had far to come, because within three minutes he materialized next to me. It was the first time I'd gotten a look at him in the light, and I was surprised at his appearance. The dark, wavy air had liberal doses of gray mixed in and his long face, dominated by that Roman nose, was deeply lined. I mentally added ten years to his age.

"Hello, again, Mr. Malek," the Brother said in that now-familiar high voice. "You have something for me?"

"I'm afraid it's not what you want," I answered somberly as he sat on the stool next to mine. "You–or the organization–have had a tail on me for weeks now, right?"

His thin mouth formed what he probably thought was a smile, and he nodded. "Perhaps."

"Not perhaps," I contradicted. "Well, something's happened to a couple of your men–at least I assume they're your men–and I wanted you to hear it straight from me."

The Brother's hint of a smile disappeared. "Go on."

"I'll start with day before yesterday–Saturday. Your driver–I don't know his name–thought it would be good sport to whack me across the face, which he did." I indicated the vestige of a bruise. "Then tonight, when I got off the streetcar from work, Marko sat in the surveillance car outside my place and started riding me. I called him a baboon, which pissed him off. The upshot was that I was in this saloon a few minutes later when Marko–he'd followed me there–came in and tried to drag me out. Said he was going to take me for a long ride, which isn't hard to translate as the last ride I ever make.

"Well, some folks who I'd never seen in the saloon before didn't take too kindly to this attitude of Marko's and they cold-cocked him from behind. Then the guy I call the Driver because I don't know his name came in looking for Marko with his automatic drawn and got the same treatment."

"It appears they were careless," the Brother observed impassively.

"Among other failings. Anyway, the reason I tore over here is to ask you not to take it out on the bar. Those people were just protecting me, and your boys were out of line all the way."

He nodded grimly. "Unfortunately, Marko *is* a baboon. I would expect something like this from him. But the one that you call 'the Driver,' he has more sense than he apparently showed."

"Yeah? Maybe, but it didn't make a whole lot of sense for him to take that swipe at me the other day."

The Brother drummed manicured fingernails on the polished surface of the streamlined bar. "What condition are they now in?"

"Your guys? I can't say for sure, but they're probably going to have king-sized headaches for several days. And when I left the saloon a few minutes ago to come here, the cops were on their way over."

The smile crept back. "It will be a lesson well-learned," the Brother said quietly. "Mr. Malek, you may not value my word, but others do. I say this: I am prepared to guarantee that neither of those men will ever set foot in that establishment again, wherever it is. And they will not get revenge against you, your friends, or the establishment."

"Well, I appreciate that."

"You should. And now, to ensure my guarantee, I want *your* word on something as well."

"There's always a catch, isn't there?"

His smile broadened, then disappeared as if it had been erased. "We have discussed this matter before. May I assume that you continue to search for the killer of Lloyd Martindale?"

"Yeah…and still without success."

"But you plan to continue?"

I raised my shoulders and turned my palms up. "Yes…if I don't get myself fired first."

He scowled. "For one who has your experience and your ability, that seems unlikely."

"Don't be too sure. But that's my problem, not yours. Make your play."

"It's as I said to you before, Mr. Malek. If you discover the identity of the murderer, my organization wants to know before the police, and before it appears in your newspaper."

"I still don't get it," I told him as frosted pilsener glasses of beer were placed on coasters in front of us by the bartender. "You've got your net out all over town, and way beyond. And it's got to be a damn good net. Christ, you ought to be able to find out who knocked off Martindale a lot easier than I can."

It was his turn to gesture with his shoulders. "To use your own words, don't be too sure."

"And you obviously don't place much faith in the ability of the police to find the killer?"

Although he didn't open his mouth or alter his expression, the Brother made a noise that actually sounded like a laugh, and I knew why. In the last two months, there had been at least nine mob killings in Chicago, most of them execution-style, and not one had been solved. (Business as usual in the city that Capone made infamous.) Despite this, the syndicate was upset because, or so the Brother intimated, they were being unfairly tagged with the Martindale rubout.

"Okay, so I keep looking, and if I learn something, I tell you first, right?" He nodded.

"And your men stay away from that saloon and my

friends, right?" Another nod.

"One more thing," I said as I got up to leave. "Am I still going to have a tail?"

"You ask a lot of questions, Mr. Malek," he replied, adjusting the knot of his silk tie. "Good night."

Augie Galan was still parked outside in his gleaming Lincoln Zephyr. "I was just about to come in. You okay?" he asked as we pulled away from the curb.

"Yeah, under the circumstances. I'm as okay as anybody who just made a deal with the devil."

Galan looked over at me, rolling his eyes, and I didn't blame him.

Chapter 20

The next day at Headquarters was blessedly uneventful–and I heard nothing from Bob Lee, who apparently had put things right with Bernice Martindale after I left his office. After work, I rode the Clark car one stop north of my apartment building, although I did not spot a mob car parked anywhere along the block. Either they had gotten sneakier or the Brother had ordered the surveillance dropped–which I doubted.

It was just past 6:30 when I walked into Kilkenny's, surprisingly almost deserted except for a half dozen guys at the far end of the bar, none of whom I'd ever seen before. "Hey, where is everybody?" I asked the Killer, who wore a disgruntled expression.

"And where in Hades d'ya think they be, after last night's little contretemps? They've all probably been scared away for a while. Police came in here maybe ten minutes after you left, and they took those two thugs away, both of 'em by this time moaning like mourners at an Irish funeral and holding their heads.

"The cops didn't question us much," he continued. "They just wondered who knocked them out, and I said it was me, with the baseball bat I keep behind the bar, which I showed to them. We all said we never saw the thugs before–which is the truth, of course–and that they just came in looking for trouble. One of the cops seemed to recognize the second guy who had walked in, the one Diz plunked just as he came through the door. Diz was hiding upstairs in the storeroom all the while, like I told him to. At least nothing about this got into the papers, so the only ones who know about it are the ones who were in here last night. That's mostly regulars, so they'll all be back, I hope. What was it all about, Snap?" he asked, softening

213

the tone and lowering his voice. "You in some trouble with...*them*?"

"Damn, I'm sorry about what happened, Killer. It's a long story, but I can tell you this much: They won't be back in here, either of them. After Galan dropped me off at home last night, did he come back for Dean?"

"Yeah, and by then, the gendarmes were long gone with those goons and their headaches; it's a wonder one of 'em wasn't killed by those balls. As it is, they both probably have concussions. I told Diz it might be a good idea to stay away from here for a couple of days until things blew over, and– hey!–did you hear about this afternoon's game?" He jerked a thumb toward the small radio on the back bar.

"No, how'd it go?"

The Killer slapped the top of the bar. "Friend, I'm about to tell you how it went. Diz shut down the Bees 3 to 1, went the distance. Gents broadcasting the game said he looked sharp, good control."

"Well, we know there's sure nothing wrong with his accuracy, judging by the two pitches he threw in here last night. But what about his speed? That fast ball still just a memory?"

"Ah, about that I'm afraid you're right, Snap. They said on the radio that he was getting Boston out with nothing but the slow stuff, junk, you know? But he's still got it up here, where it really counts." The Killer tapped his forehead.

"How many wins does that make for him?" I asked, thinking about the Cub-hating Leo Cahill and his insistence that Dean was washed up.

"Still only four, but he hasn't been beat yet, so that's four wins the Cubs wouldn't have had without him. Lord, I know our boys are only bouncing between third and fourth place, but they're not all that far back of the others. And the way Bill Lee and Bryant've been cranking, if Diz can start winning a few down the stretch, we've got ourselves a pennant and a date to the prom with those cursed Yankees."

I resisted throwing cold water on the Killer's enthusiasm,

but I had to figure the chances of Dean's winning a few more down the stretch were about the same as me getting invited to the managing editor's house for Sunday dinner. And as far as the Cubs winning the pennant, I'd already kissed good-bye to the fifty smackers that I'd bet with Leo Cahill.

Rather than go home, I stayed at the Killer's for dinner–a steak, of course. The place never did fill up much that night, other than those guys at the far end of the bar. They turned out to be Cub fans who had drifted in after the game hoping to meet Dean or some of the other players. They were disappointed, but that didn't stop them from hanging around celebrating Dean's victory, buying each other rounds of boilermakers, and singing songs that would make even a sailor blush.

It was ten past 8:00 when I left the bar and started walking north on Clark in the summer twilight. My destination: the Grace Street address of Nicolette Stover. I looked back to see if I was being followed and spotted no tail, although I double-checked by ducking into a half dozen alleys along my route.

Her apartment building was one of those big, U-shaped four-story brick walk-ups with a grassy courtyard, a style that you find by the hundreds all over Chicago–north, south, west. Her doorway was on the right side of the courtyard. I went into the foyer and punched the buzzer for STOVER, 2-B. No answer, but then I hadn't expected one. The night I had stopped at Harding's on Wabash for dinner, she didn't leave until after 8:00 and it was now only 8:30. Assuming she took a bus or streetcar home, she probably wouldn't get here for another few minutes, maybe even a half hour.

I sauntered across the street and leaned against a tree, from which I had a clear view of the building. It being a warm, clear night, there was a steady flow of pedestrian traffic along the residential block–couples walking arm-in-arm, clusters of noisy teenagers in bathing suits coming back from the Lake Michigan beaches a few blocks east, and the occasional panhandler drifting over from Halsted Street. One old specimen in a scraggly white beard, wearing raggedy clothes and a knapsack, fastened onto me like Coleridge's Ancient Mariner glomming onto the wedding guest. With a gnarled hand clutching my arm, he spun a tale of how he'd ridden the rails in from California.

"Been on the road eight weeks now, Bo," he said in a sandpapery voice, spitting tobacco into the gutter. "L.A. on down to Tucson in a dust storm, where a railroad bull for the Espee line threw me off into a gully. I luckily didn't break no bones, though I sure coulda. Then back on the rods over to Gallup and Amarillo, where it were a hunnert-ten in the shade. Came north through Oklahoma to Wichita in an empty boxcar, where another damn bull hit me upside the head with a bar, like to knock me silly, before he tossed me off the train. I stayed in a hobo camp outside Wichita, gettin' myself mended up for a week 'n some, then I come up through St. Looie and 'crost Illinois to git here. And y'know why, Bo? 'Twas to see my sister, Francine, in an apartment over on Clarendon, who I hain't laid eyes on fer near onto twenny years now. So what happens? I come to find she hain't lived there since '34, and them what's in the place now say to me they got no idea where she's up and gone to. So here I be in this damn big town, biggest one I ever seen, with no kin and no grubstake. It's a helluva life, Bo."

"It is that, but it could be worse—could be winter here," I said, slipping him two quarters, more than I'd ever given a panhandler before. But then, he'd related quite a saga, true or otherwise.

"Thankee, brother, thankee, and God bless ye and all yer loved ones," he cackled, slapping me on the shoulder and loping off to find another sympathetic ear and, with luck, some more loose change.

No sooner had the well-traveled hobo dissolved into the Chicago night than I heard the clicking of heels on the sidewalk on the opposite side of the street. It was Nicolette Stover, approaching her building and carrying a sack of what appeared to be groceries.

I walked stealthily across the street, staying behind her

and getting to the foyer just as she opened the inner door with her key. She spun around, eyes wide, and drew in air as if to scream.

"Not a sound, not a peep," I ordered, placing a palm lightly against her lips. "Don't make me use this." I gestured to the bulge under my suit coat caused by a wadded up newspaper–something I had picked up from a second-rate gangster film, I forget which one.

"I remember you from Harding's. Why can't you just leave me alone?" she whisper-yelled as we climbed the creaking, carpeted steps in a stairwell reeking with a mixture of cooking aromas, none of them appetizing.

"I just want to talk to you–that's all, just talk. I am not going to hurt you," I murmured as she unlocked the door to her apartment and I pushed in behind her. She spun toward me, hyperventilating. "Then what's the gun for?" she demanded in a shaky voice.

"It's not really a gun, see?" I said in a lighthearted tone, opening my coat and pulling out the rolled-up newspaper, which happened to be that evening's *Times*. "Look, like I told you in Harding's, I'm a reporter, doing a feature on Lloyd Martindale, remember?" I whipped out the very same dog-eared calling card that I'd showed her in the restaurant, the one identifying me as the ethereal (read nonexistent) Bob MacNeal of the *American*. I was especially glad after the set-to involving Martindale's mother that I hadn't told her who I really was. A second complaint to Bob Lee and I'd be out trying to find an unoccupied street corner where I could hawk pencils or apples or both.

Nicolette's hands were shaking as she set the grocery sack on the end table in her small living room and switched on a lamp. "There's nothing I know that can help you with your story. Please leave," she beseeched, folding thin, white arms across her chest and giving me a pleading, almost tearful look.

"I have just a few questions for you–won't take much time," I persisted. "First of all, how long–"

She tensed, now turning hostile. "Where did you get my

name?" she demanded. "What makes you even think I knew this…what is his name?"

"A neighbor in Beverly Hills mentioned several families that lived close to the Martindales, and yours happened to be one of them. And that included you. That's all." I spread my arms in a gesture meant to convey honesty.

"Me? My God," she cried, her own arms now thrown out awkwardly as if to encompass–what, her whole existence to this point? "I was only a child when we lived on Longwood Drive all those years ago. There's nothing I can tell you about him, nothing."

"I'm not so sure of that," I said as we faced each other in the dismal room made even more so by the sepia aura cast against stuccoed walls by the light of a single lamp with a depressing brown shade and a low-wattage bulb. "Let's sit down and talk about it."

I dropped into the wing chair behind me and took my eyes off Nicolette for no more than two or three seconds, but that was enough to prove that I wasn't anywhere near ready to hire on either with Fergus Fahey's boys on the detective detail or with the Pinkerton boys.

By the time my backside had sunk into the cushion, I found myself looking into the working end of a what appeared to be a .32-caliber automatic in the none-too-steady hand of one none-too-steady Nicolette Stover, whose purse lay open on the end table beside her. Score one for the "terrified" woman.

"Now, Mr. O'Neill, or whatever your name is," she blurted, running the words together as she waggled the gun, "I want you out of here, out of here. And if you don't go, if you don't…if you don't, I'll shoot!"

"I held up a palm. "Wait, I–"

"I mean it, I'll shoot, shoot, shoot!" She seemed to be in a state of near-hysteria, and although that could have been an act, I was not about to put it to a test. "I will shoot," she repeated, her eyes open wider than I had seen previously and her hands, both of which gripped the pistol, were unnervingly steady. Now I was truly frightened.

"I'll tell them you were attacking me," she spat. Yes, yes I will. I'll tell them that you forced your way in here! I'll tear my clothes!" Now she was screeching. She ripped her dress at one shoulder, exposing a peach-colored brassiere strap. "Now get out, you low-life bastard!" Her eyes were glazed, her body tensed as if she were about to explode. And worse, from my standpoint, the veins stood out on the back of the thin white hand that gripped the automatic.

My mouth was as dry as the Oklahoma Dust Bowl. "Take it easy," I said gently, edging toward the front door. "I'm leaving." I took a deliberate step backward, then another and another, until my groping and sweaty hand fastened on the doorknob. I wasn't about to turn my back on her, figuring it would be harder for her to shoot me as long as I held eye contact. Neither of us blinked while I eased the door open and backed into the hallway.

Once out of the apartment, I slammed the door and flattened myself against the wall lest she start pumping bullets through the door, which wouldn't have surprised me. As I caught my breath, I heard the click of her door lock, followed by sobbing.

I raced down the stairs to the street, feeling a rush of euphoria at simply being out of that apartment. The exhilaration quickly gave way to frustration, though, when I had settled down enough to tally the events of the last several days: One whack in the face; one dressing down from the managing editor, followed by probation that could lead to the loss of my job; one attempted kidnapping (of me) from my favorite saloon; and now one gun drawn on me by a half-crazed woman who may or may not be new to trigger-pulling.

I started trudging south through the warm night toward that favorite saloon of mine. More than anything else, I needed a drink, and tonight, it would have to be something stronger than beer.

Chapter 21

When I stumbled out of bed in the morning, my head pounded, and this time–unlike New Year's Day–with good reason. After having been routed by Nicolette Stover, I had beat a retreat to Kilkenny's, which was still less crowded than normal, and I knocked down four–maybe five–scotches.

"Better go easy on that Gaelic elixir, Snap," the Killer had cautioned, genuine concern showing on his broad, ruddy face. "You aren't used to it anymore, and it can bite you good." In fact, he had tried to talk me into having a beer when I came in, but gave up when he saw my overall state. "Want to talk?" he asked, which is the closest he ever comes to putting his nose into the business of his regulars.

"No, but if and when that time comes, you will undoubtedly be the one I spill my guts to, and then I'll run off at the mouth so much that you'll beg me to shut up," I responded as I dove into the first scotch. I probably didn't utter more than a dozen words the rest of the night, and when I finally tottered back to my place, I was in no condition to know–or even care–if my moves were being watched.

I felt practically sober and hangover-free when I got to my desk in the Headquarters pressroom, although I apparently wore the ravages of the previous night.

"Christ, Snap, you look like the wrath of the gods," Packy Farmer boomed, clearly amused. "I don't know what it was you did last night, but you must have had a good time doin' it."

"Not very damn much," I grumbled. "I hope nobody around here plans to do any loud talking today–I'm not up to it."

"Hangover alert!" Dirk O'Farrell pronounced in his version (which wasn't bad) of radio announcer tones. "This room is now officially designated as a quiet zone until further notice, or until Mr. Malek of the noble and revered *Chicago Tribune* passes out. Which, judging from his appearance, could be at almost any moment now."

"Very funny," I snorted. "See what kind of sympathy you get from me the next time you come dragging in here on a Monday morning looking like a cadaver, as you surely will."

O'Farrell had started to respond when Eddie Metz, who had been hunched over his phone, cradled the receiver and announced that he'd just gotten word from somebody in the *Times* sports department that Phil Wrigley had fired Charlie Grimm as Cubs manager.

"I'm not surprised, the way they've been staggering along. Who's taking over?" Farmer asked.

"Guess," Metz smirked. It wasn't often that Eddie got information of any kind first in the pressroom, so he was making the most of it.

"Let's not play guessing games around here," O'Farrell groused.

Eddie giggled. "Give you a hint. The new guy's already a Cub and a player, too."

Anson Masters cleared his throat, always a prelude to a proclamation. "That would be Billy Herman, of course," he pronounced in an oracular tone. "He's got the maturity for the job."

"Wrong," Metz cackled. "Anybody else?"

"If it's not Herman, then it's got to be Augie Galan," the City News kid weighed in.

"Wrong again. How 'bout you, Snap?" Eddie asked.

"I can barely talk right now, let alone think," I muttered. "Hell, what about Hartnett?"

"Bingo!" Eddie barked. "Ol' Gabby's going to be the skipper now."

"Sounds like a decent choice at that," Farmer said. "He already has to be able to handle the pitchers, right? So why not let him handle the whole team? Is he going to keep playing, too?"

"My guy at the office didn't know," Metz answered, his moment in the spotlight quickly slipping away.

"I don't see why he wouldn't," O'Farrell said between drags on his cigarette. "From back of the plate, you can see all of your men and the whole damn field–ideal spot for a manager."

"Well, I just hope Gabby doesn't head the team in the wrong direction, like that Corrigan guy who landed his plane in Ireland yesterday thinking it was California," Farmer said. "His compass was frozen and the sky jockey thought he was flying west from New York, 'stead of east."

"Cyril, if you believe him, I've got a big bridge in Brooklyn that I would like to sell you," Anson Masters rumbled. "According to the wire service reports, the aviation authority banned him from flying across the Atlantic because his plane wasn't safe. It's clear that he thumbed his nose at them."

"I dunno, maybe his compass really was froze," Metz volunteered.

"Eduardo, Eduardo," Masters scolded. "I don't care how dark or cloudy Corrigan said the conditions were; in a 3,000-mile flight, you're going to see the sun and the earth sooner or later. And you're not going to tell me that an experienced aviator did not at some point along the way notice the position of the sun and also the interesting fact that there was water–lots and lots of water–under him instead of the Iowa cornfields and Kansas wheat and Rocky Mountains that should have been down below."

Metz turned his palms up. "Say what you want, Anson–he's a hero at the moment."

"Heroes is something we can use more of on the Cubs right now," Farmer observed dryly. "Like for instance maybe Mr. Big-Bucks Dizzy Dean."

"Hey, go easy on Diz," I said, opting to not share that I knew the pitcher. "He pitched a helluva game against Boston the other day."

Dirk O'Farrell scowled. "And about time, too. What's

that make it, now, four wins for him? Which means that each one of them's been worth–what?–about forty-five grand."

"He'll get more," I said with a confidence I didn't feel. "He's at his best under pressure."

O'Farrell looked doubtful. "Well, he'd better win some more, or they'll never catch the Pirates. Bill Lee can't pitch every day."

"They'll never catch 'em anyway," Metz declared, trying to sound like an authority.

The baseball discussion rambled on in a desultory fashion for several more minutes and was running out of steam when my phone squawked. It was Catherine Reed.

"Hi, how have you been?" I said brightly, hoping that I sounded like I was glad to hear from her. For weeks, I'd thought about phoning Catherine, but I always found some reason for not calling. Because of what she had told me about that depraved son of a bitch of an uncle, which was followed immediately by her plea that I walk away from the Martindale murder, I was reluctant to see her. She might not ask again about my progress on the so-called investigation, but one question would always hover over us, even if unspoken: Are you still hounding that poor woman?

"I've been fine, Steve," Catherine said with what sounded to me like strained enthusiasm. "Just fine. I realize this is late notice, but I thought maybe you would like to come to dinner tonight. I know Daddy would enjoy it."

"How is he?"

"About the same as last time you saw him. Some days are better than others, but he does seem to perk up around company, what little we get. And he particularly liked it when you were here, what with all your newspaper stories."

"A few of which are actually true," I said. "That is a capital invitation, and I accept."

"Wonderful! Around 6:30 again?"

At 6:35 that evening, I climbed the steps of the stucco house in Oak Park. Catherine looked more bright-eyed and animated than I remembered as she swung the door open, accepting my box of chocolates with a curtsy.

"Daddy, Steve Malek's here," she called out as we walked into the sitting room where Steel Trap Bascomb obviously spent most of his waking hours. "How'ya?" he asked from his armchair, raising a hand in greeting.

"Keeping ahead of my creditors, Steel Trap, but just barely. You too?"

"Damn right, damn right. Bastards, all 'em."

I took the chair opposite him that Catherine gestured me to. "What do you think about Hitler?" I asked, pointing to the copy of the *Daily News* resting on Bascomb's lap–its headline: HITLER MAY MOVE AGAINST CZECHS.

"Bastard," he muttered. "Ought to be shot. Or strung up."

"Daddy!" Catherine gasped. "What a thing to say about anybody–even *him*."

He turned and looked at his daughter defiantly. "S'true. He's a prick, greedy. Wantsa whole world."

"I agree," I put in. "And the way the English and the French are pussyfooting around these days, it seems like they're willing to hand it over to him."

"Damn right," he nodded, his lined face and rheumy eyes sending Catherine a "So there!" expression.

"Let's go on into the dining room now," she said.

"Damn right," Steel Trap seconded.

I did the best I could as a raconteur while we devoured the ham and au gratin potatoes, remembering from my previous dinner with them that Steel Trap didn't like to talk while he was eating. But he didn't mind listening. His facial expressions indicated that he enjoyed my stories, particularly the one–and it was true–about the pickpocket who got nabbed in the act of lifting a wallet by a house dick at Marshall Field's. "When they handed him over to the precinct for fingerprinting, it turned out that this dip had an extra finger on his right hand," I said.

"Oh, now, really!" Catherine scoffed as Steel Trap made a chuckling noise deep in his throat. "You're making that up, Steve," she insisted.

"It's God's truth," I swore, holding up a hand like I was

taking an oath. "The precinct guys were so impressed they even took photographs of his hand. It was as if he had two ring fingers. Claimed he was born that way, which I suppose must have been true. How else would it have happened? His left hand was normal. He claimed his moniker was 'Eleven Fingers.'"

"Knew one like 'at," Steel Trap put in. "'Cept with two thumbs onna same hand."

"Oh, go on, the both of you!" Catherine chided, her eyes moving from me to her father and back again as she tried to look reproving. But it seemed she was obviously entertained. "I don't know whether to believe a single word that either one of you says."

"Hey, it's a weird and wacky world out there, Lady," I cracked. "I don't make the news, I just report it."

"Well, that was a good enough story, true or not, to earn you some apple pie a la mode–that is, if you're interested," she said.

"I could get real interested real fast," I responded, and I did. After he finished his wedge of pie with ice cream, Steel Trap got to his feet without a word to either of us and shuffled back into the sitting room.

"It's Tuesday, and that means 'Fibber McGee and Molly.' Daddy never misses it," Catherine explained.

"So he can still enjoy stuff like that, huh?" I asked as I heard static coming from the sitting room. Steel Trap was warming up the radio.

"Well, he seems to laugh in all the right places," she said. "And he really loves it when Fibber opens that hall closet of his and everything comes crashing down around him."

"For that matter, so do I," I admitted. "Sure, the program's corny and predictable, but it's funny anyway. Besides, I've got a closet that's sort of like Fibber's myself."

"Shame on you," Catherine teased, drinking the last of her coffee and folding her linen napkin into a neat rectangle. "Steve, it's a beautiful night, and I thought we might go for a walk around the neighborhood–unless of course you want to stay and listen to the radio with Daddy."

"Well…seeing as how I'm not really in the mood for corny jokes, you've twisted my arm. Let's go."

The sky was clear and the air still dispensed that freshness from the rains earlier in the day. After having lived on Clark Street for two years, I'd forgotten what quiet was like. And Catherine's neighborhood was quiet, so much so you could hear the crickets rubbing their legs together, or however they make that noise. Nobody was out driving, or even walking. Maybe they were all inside tonight listening to Molly groan at Fibber's gags and puns.

"Seems really peaceful here," I commented as we passed under elm trees that filtered the glow from street lamps, making dappled patterns on the sidewalks.

"It is," Catherine agreed. "Have you ever lived in the suburbs, Steve?"

"Never. Closest was Logan Square, back when I was married. But there, people sat out on their front steps on nights like this. You could walk down the block and stop three or four times to chat. Sometimes you'd even get a bottle of beer handed to you if you were lucky."

"There's not much of that around here. Oh, our neighbors are all very nice, but everybody pretty much keeps to themselves. Sometimes, I really wish there *were* more people sitting out on their front steps or porches."

"I understand, but I believe that most of those folks back in Logan Square would trade places with you in the flick of a cigarette lighter. This is pretty nice living."

She nodded. "Oh, I know, and I'm not really complaining. It's just that sometimes it gets so…lonesome."

We walked for a half-block before I responded. "I mean no disrespect to him, Catherine, but I suppose your Dad really isn't much company for you most of the time, is he?"

"No…but that's not really his fault. I don't mind looking after him at all." Another half-block of silence. "I had hoped you would have called sometime," she said tentatively.

"It's been busy at work, and–"

"Oh, I'm sure it has." Now her tone was apologetic. "Of all people, I should know how hectic a reporter's life can be, shouldn't I? Having been around Daddy all those years."

"Yeah, sometimes it can get pretty crazy."

"Did you ever locate that girl—except she really isn't a girl any more of course, is she?"

"Huh? Oh, you mean the one who had lived next door to Lloyd Martindale," I said, feigning puzzlement, then sudden realization. "Yes. Yes, I did see her, but very briefly. She didn't want to talk to me, though, and nothing ever came of it."

"I thought maybe you were angry with me for what I said when you were here before."

"Angry? Why?"

"Because I suggested that you not try to find her, that you just let her be, which I had no business doing. And when I did bring it up, it seemed like you were irritated, which is understandable."

"I wasn't irritated—not at all," I lied. "In fact, I'd forgotten all about it, Catherine."

"Well, all right. That's good," she pronounced with finality, although I sensed just then that she would have liked it better if I had said I remembered at least *something* of our earlier conversation.

We had now covered perhaps a half dozen residential blocks in Oak Park and had yet to encounter another person on the sidewalks. "Well, it's getting late," I told her, showing my wristwatch as confirmation as we passed under a streetlight. "I'll walk you home and then head for the El."

"That's not necessary, Steve," she protested. "We're closer to the station right now than we are to our house. That would make an unnecessary round trip for you."

"Hey, it's late. You shouldn't be walking home alone," I insisted.

We had stopped at an intersection, and I could see her puckish expression as we stood in the blue-white nimbus cast by a street lamp. "You mean those crowded and dangerous streets, with all the ruffians and brigands lurking behind every tree?" she asked.

"Okay, so maybe I won't need a sword and a club to protect you from ruffians and brigands, after all. I still want to walk you home, though."

"But I don't want to be walked home," Catherine insisted, a new resilience evident in her voice. "Good night, Steve," she said, holding out a hand with formality and, I sensed, finality.

I grasped her hand, returning her firm grip and forcing a smile. I felt pulled in two directions, but only for a few moments, then whatever struggle I was having passed.

Catherine returned my smile, saying nothing, then pivoted gracefully and walked off in the direction of her house. I stood and watched until she blended into Oak Park's still and gentle July darkness; then I started toward the Elevated station and the ride back into the city.

Chapter 22

Norma was over in Michigan with Martin Baer and, presumably, his mother. Peter was at camp in the North Woods of Wisconsin, and I was on probation at the *Tribune*. Welcome to midsummer in the Middle West.

On the positive side, the Cubs were beginning to show signs of life. Dizzy Dean went out and pitched another complete game–his second in a week–beating the Giants, who scored only one run. That gave him five victories, a long way from his glory days in St. Louis but encouraging for the Chicago boys and their new manager, Hartnett.

After staying away from Kilkenny's for a few days following his beaning of the two hoodlums, Diz was around again, drawn back by the lure of the T-bones and filets–and maybe the camaraderie and the adulation of the regulars. The Killer himself was alert to further incursions from the mob, though, and had bought a revolver–he showed it to me very quickly and quietly one evening–that he kept on a shelf under the cash register. I found the idea of his keeping a loaded gun in the joint unsettling, but after what had happened, in part because of me, there wasn't anything I could say.

On the evening of the Cubs' victory against New York, Dean and Augie Galan were at the bar eating when I sauntered in, while the usual knot of regulars hovered around the players.

"Hey, Mr. Snap, how ya doin'?" Diz boomed, waving me over. (It would only be later, and in far different circumstances, that he would briefly raise the subject of the most exciting night Kilkenny's had ever seen.)

"Just fine," I answered, "and it sounds like you are, too, from what I've been hearing about the way things went out at Wrigley this afternoon."

He made a face and shrugged. "I didn't have much on the ball, but them Giants was patsies, real patsies."

"Don't let Diz fool you with that kind of talk," Augie Galan said to me between bites of his filet. "He was plenty tough out there today. I'm glad I wasn't batting against him."

"Yeah, sure," Dean said. "The way you tagged me over the years, you'da put one on Sheffield Avenue, or maybe even two." He swiveled toward me. "My wing's like t'drop off now, Mr. Snap," he brayed as he flexed his right arm. "Hurts to beat all heck."

"You should be home soaking it or something," I told him. "That's two good games in a row you've tossed, and you need to keep it up. And you're also making a monkey out of a guy I know who works for the *Tribune*."

His face went from puzzlement to a frown. "How'dya happen to know somebody from that doggone paper, Mr. Snap?"

"Uh, I've known him for years…from my old neighborhood," I improvised, hoping nobody around us would give me away. They didn't.

Dean rubbed his chin. "Hmm. And you say that ah'm makin' a monkey outta him?"

"In spades, Diz, bless you. He's a copyreader in the Sports Department, name of Leo Cahill, and he said in the spring that there was no way that you'd win even five games. And now…"

The Killer raised one bushy eyebrow. "Did you have occasion to speak to this Cahill individual today?" he asked as he served me a beer.

"No, why?"

"Let us now give this misguided fellow, Irish though he may be with that surname, a call forthwith and remind him of the comment he made," the barkeep said, eyes twinkling. "Do you suppose he's still at work?" (The Killer knew that I was keeping my employer a secret from Dean and wasn't going to mess things up.)

I checked my watch. "Yeah, he's there for another hour or so, if he's on his usual shift."

"Hey, I got an idea," Morty Easterly piped up from his stool down the bar (he, too, knew I was keeping my job from Diz). "Go ahead and give this guy a call, Snap, and then put Diz on the line. See what kind of tune he sings then."

I liked the idea, and so did Dean. He and I went around behind the bar, and I called the Sports Department, asking for Cahill. "Hi, Leo, it's Malek. Got a friend who'd like to talk to you. Let me put him on." I handed the receiver to Diz.

"Howdy there, Mr. Cahill, this's Dizzy Dean on this end. My friend Mr. Snap here tells me you didn't think ah'd win me even five games this year. Well, ah'm gonna win more than that, and when we get us into the World Series, ah'll... Yes sir, yes, ah'm him all right. Ya don't believe me? Well, now, it's God's own truth that ah'm Jay Hanna Dean–some folks call me Jerome Herman, but truth is I was born Jay Hanna on the 16th of January 'way back down there in little ol' Lucas, Arkansas, sir. Well, ah'm sorry you feel that way, sir. Yes sir...yes." Dean handed the phone to me and shook his head. ""He wants to talk to you."

"Yes, Leo?" I said coolly.

"Steve, where in blazes are you, and what's going on? Stop playing games, will you? Just who was that you put on the line?"

"It was exactly who he said he was, Leo. We are currently in a convivial establishment not three blocks from Wrigley Field–Kilkenny's by name; I think you've heard me speak fondly of it. And two fine gentlemen by name of Mr. Dean and Mr. Galan are having a well-earned steak dinner here–some of the best steaks in town, by the way. I hope you weren't rude to Mr. Dean, who put in a very strenuous day at work against a bunch of boys from New York." That brought guffaws and a chant of "DIZ-ee, DIZ-ee, DIZ-ee" from the customers lining the bar.

There was a pause before Cahill spoke. "Mother of God," he murmured. "It really *was* him?"

"That's what I said, Leo. Weren't you listening to me? And if you don't believe me, look up the phone number of

Kilkenny's–it's on Clark–and call here to check up on us. I'm sure Mr. Dean would be happy to speak to you again and hear your apology."

"Damn. Well, I got to get back to work," he huffed. "On deadline." He hung up.

"Sorry about his manners," I told Dean. "He doesn't like to be proven wrong."

"Pore feller," he said absently, shaking his head as he returned with gusto to his steak and potatoes.

When I walked into my apartment that night a few minutes past 9:00, the phone was ringing. It was Norma, from Michigan, and the connection was bad.

"What is it?" I asked tightly, figuring that the call must have something to do with Peter.

"I just wanted to tell you that Martin and I have decided to get married, in September." Her words were punctuated by static on the line. "I felt you should know before anyone else, Steve. Steve…are you there?"

"Yeah, thanks for the alert," I replied, unable to think of anything else to say.

"And Steve, I have a favor to ask. When you pick Peter up from camp at the depot next weekend, please don't tell him about this, all right? I'd like to be the one to do that, if you don't mind."

"I don't mind," I said woodenly.

"Are you…all right?" Norma asked.

"Sure. I figured this was coming," I told her truthfully.

"Well, I want you to know that as far as I'm concerned, this will not in any way affect how often you and Peter see each other."

"Fine," I grunted, wishing there were some graceful way I could end the conversation. But now Norma couldn't seem to stop talking.

"And Steve, I think it would be a good idea if you met Martin some time soon, since Peter will after all be living with us."

"After all," I repeated. "Yes, I suppose I'll have to meet him."

"Oh, Steve, please don't be that way. You and I both have known for ages that we weren't ever going to get back together again."

"No, we didn't both know it," I wanted to shout into the mouthpiece. I also wanted to ask Norma how magnanimous she would be if I were calling to tell her that I was getting hitched again. But instead I conceded that "I'm sure I'll be meeting your Martin soon enough, whether by choice or otherwise."

That put the brakes on Norma's attempt at being chatty, but I got no satisfaction from stifling her. She was, I grudgingly appreciated, trying hard to keep the understandable happiness out of her voice.

"Hey, I'm sorry, that was rude, to say nothing of childish," I told her gently. "You're right of course–we were through a long time ago. And I'm glad for you, I really am. Congratulations."

"I appreciate that, Steve," she said, and I thought I detected a sniffle, but given the connection we had, it was hard to tell. I thanked her for the call and hung up, staring at the receiver in my hand. I had not had any dinner, so I should have been hungry, but I wasn't. I was thirsty, though, so I turned, went back out, and headed for Kilkenny's.

Chapter 23

Back in the '20s when I worked for the City News Bureau, another police reporter, Doherty of the *Tribune*, referred to me as having "street smarts." I don't remember the context in which he made the remark, but at the time I took it as a high compliment, especially given the source. And in the years since, I have flattered myself that those two words captured my defining characteristic as a newspaperman. I was glad Doherty wasn't looking over my shoulder the last week of July to see just how far off the mark he had been in his appraisal of me.

I had been home from work that Thursday night for about an hour and was having scrambled eggs and tomato soup at the kitchen table when the phone rang.

"Mr. Malek?" a vaguely familiar voice asked. "You may not remember me...I'm Preston. I work for Mrs. Martindale. I'm the one who answered the door when you were here at the house awhile back."

"I remember you," I said coolly.

"Well, Mrs. Martindale got to feeling badly about declining to see you when you came to the house, and also about that call she made to your newspaper to complain."

"Oh?"

He made the same throat-clearing noise I remembered from our meeting at the front door of the Martindale house. "Yes, well, she wants to make it up to you now. She wishes to talk to you about her son...for that feature of yours."

"Really? And why the change of heart?"

"As I said, she feels badly about what happened, and she is interested in seeing an article that talks about what her son was really like, from her own perspective. She would like to see you tonight–if it is convenient, of course."

"Why didn't she telephone me herself?"

More throat clearing. "Well, sir," he said in a lowered voice, suggesting that he might be overheard, "to be honest, sir, she is embarrassed about her behavior. She asked me to make the call."

"But she won't be embarrassed to talk to me?"

"No, sir, I do not believe so."

"Uh-huh. And she can see me tonight, you say?"

"Yes, sir. I should not be speaking for her, of course, but I believe I can honestly say she feels that the newspapers have not written enough about her son's life and his contributions. She has so many remembrances of him. Her moods, sir, have been, well, up and down, shall we say, which I am sure you can appreciate. And right now, she feels talkative."

I thought about my probation at the *Trib* and hesitated. If I came up with a strong interview, how could Bob Lee possibly be angry, especially with that interview coming at Beatrice Martindale's invitation? And maybe, just maybe, there was a way of getting at the subject of Lloyd Martindale and the children who once lived next door, although that was a real long shot. "All right, where should I meet her?" I asked.

"At the house, of course," Preston said, his tone suggesting that any other location was unthinkable. "I can pick you up at your place and drive you here."

"Not necessary. I could catch the Rock Island and…"

"By the time you got downtown and then on and off the trains, it would be much too late for Mrs. Martindale, sir, given that she prefers to retire quite early. I can be at your residence in a short time. I took the liberty of getting your address from the telephone directory."

"Uh, well, okay, sure." I told Preston that I'd be waiting out in front of my building on Clark Street.

About half an hour later, a simonized dark blue Packard limousine with Preston at the wheel rolled up to the curb in the summer twilight. He got out and walked around the car, opening the front passenger side door for me in the manner of a well-trained chauffeur. And he looked the part as well: dark, perfectly tailored suit, white shirt, dark tie. He must have been somewhere in his fifties, although there were no traces of gray in the slicked down black hair resting atop the triangular face that tapered to its pointed chin. He was maybe an inch taller than me, but his slouch made him seem shorter.

"Would you mind riding up front, sir?" he asked flashing an engaging smile. "I would like the company, if you don't mind."

"Not at all," I told him, deciding that he wasn't such a bad sort after all. "I'd feel funny sitting in the back, what with that glass panel and all," I said eyeing the light blue velvet seats and padded foot rests.

As Preston turned left into Belmont, then east and onto Lake Shore Drive, I snuck a few brief glances over my shoulder and saw no indication of a tail. Apparently the mob had given up on shadowing me. We rolled south along the shore past Grant Park with its picnics and softball games just winding up in the near darkness and the dramatic backdrop of the downtown skyscrapers lining Michigan Avenue to the west. I broke the silence as we approached the hulking, colonnaded silhouette of Soldier Field.

"I was surprised to get your call," I said with a vague but growing unease that I could not explain.

"Yes, sir," Preston replied, hands kneading the wheel and eyes fixed firmly on the road.

"What exactly were Mrs. Martindale's words when she asked you to telephone me?"

The chauffeur, or butler, or whatever his roles were in the old Martindale mansion, frowned and screwed up his face as if searching for a reply. "As I said to you on the telephone, sir, she told me she was sorry–that's the word she used–sorry if she caused you any grief with her call to your superiors at the newspaper. And she also said that she was willing to give you an hour or so of her time. I believe that was it, sir."

It was totally dark as we turned off Lake Shore Drive and wound through Jackson Park past the Rosenwald Museum, or the Museum of Science and Industry as they were now calling it, and then over to Stony Island Avenue. Another few miles of driving south, and we were in the suburban atmosphere of Beverly Hills. We crossed the Rock Island tracks and, at Longwood Drive, Preston made a right turn.

"I thought the house was to the left," I told him.

"But we are not going to the house, Mr. Malek," he answered with a quiet and well-modulated firmness as he produced an automatic and pointed it in my direction while steering with his left hand. I reached for the door handle but found that it wouldn't budge.

"Don't bother trying to get out, Mr. Malek," he said sharply. "You can't, not from the inside. I took care of that with a screwdriver and a wrench."

Now my so-called street smarts kicked in, about an hour too late. The questions that had been festering in my subconscious now burst through to the surface, where they should have been all along: Why didn't Beatrice Martindale call me herself? Why was Preston so intent on picking me up? How did he get to my apartment so relatively quickly if he was phoning from Beverly Hills? There were probably others as well, although I was too busy gauging my chances of wrestling the gun from him.

I slid my left hand slowly along the plush surface of the seat, but Preston must have had good peripheral vision, because he slammed the pistol down on my fingers while never turning his head in my direction. "Please keep your hands in your lap, sir," he said in the same tone he likely used every day when asking Beatrice Martindale if she was ready for her afternoon tea or her ride in the limousine around Jackson and Washington Parks. The pain was momentarily searing, but I was damned if I was going to let him know it. I rubbed my fingers, none of them apparently broken, and asked where we were going.

"We're almost there," was the non-answer as we left the residential area and the car's headlamps knifed into thick woods that I later learned was a forest preserve. We drove perhaps a quarter of a mile on a twin-rutted path to a grassy clearing, where Preston eased to a stop. There was no light and no sign of anyone within shouting distance. He had picked his spot well. Wordlessly, he got out and walked around to my door, pulling it open and gesturing to me with the automatic.

"What the hell is this all about?" I barked, hoping my burst of anger would somehow throw him off stride.

"What this is about is nosiness, Mr. Malek," Preston said tightly as we faced each other about twenty feet apart in the wedge of light thrown by the Packard's headlamps while he kept the gun leveled at my chest. "You insisted on poking around."

"Poking around? How?"

"Huh! Your visit to that prying old Warburton biddy across the street from us," he snapped, his voice rising. "She couldn't wait to call Madam and tell her a *Tribune* reporter had called on her. And your tale about doing a feature on Beverly Hills–hokum! That sounded fishy enough by itself, but when the Warburton hag told Madam that you had asked a lot of questions about the family and about Lloyd, I smelled something. I called the *Tribune* switchboard and found out you were a police reporter–that was easy. Mr. Malek, I'm no Albert Einstein, but I do know enough about newspapers to realize that police reporters rarely if ever go around writing cute feature stories on quiet neighborhoods where nothing ever happens. If that visit to the Warburton place had been the last of it, though, I might have let things drop. But then you came to the house, and I knew what had to be done."

"I guess I don't understand," I said, figuring that as long as I could keep Preston talking, I was buying time. "Since when is being curious a crime? As you said, I'm a reporter."

"It's what you were curious *about*," he said tightly, keeping the automatic leveled at me with a steady hand.

"Oh…you mean Lloyd Martindale's murder, don't you?" I responded with what I hoped seemed like genuine surprise, hoping to divert him with my ingenuousness. "Well, sure, I was curious about it, who wouldn't be? I never totally bought the theory that the syndicate boys killed him, did you?"

Preston's jaw tightened and he drew in air, still holding the automatic steady. This time, there was no Dizzy Dean in the wings preparing to fire a beanball. "For a while, I actually figured the Democrats might have shot him," I jabbered, groping for ways to keep the conversation alive, one-sided though it was. "What do you think of that?"

"You really are pathetic, Mr. Malek," the dark-suited man chuckled dryly. "And I'm getting…"

The next sound from Preston was somewhere between a scream and a cough as he toppled over on one side, dropping the gun and clutching his left knee with both hands. His face was distorted and he was drooling as I covered the distance between us in long strides and picked up his automatic from the grass. He looked up in pop-eyed terror, but his eyes weren't focused on me. I turned to see a familiar figure, revolver in hand, stride into the clearing.

"Who is he?" the Brother snapped, motioning his gun toward the writhing butler-chauffeur.

"Name's Preston. He works for Mrs. Martindale, the mother, that is," I replied numbly.

"Better let me have that," he ordered, prying the gun from my hand and wiping the handle with his handkerchief. "The way you're shaking, you could blow your goddamn foot off. Good thing we kept watching you, huh? And good thing I decided to be part of the tail tonight."

"I didn't see any tail."

"When I'm the one doing the tailing, nobody ever does," he said without a hint of bragging in his voice. "And this clown here"–he motioned to the groaning Preston–"he wouldn't know how to spot one. We were never more than two blocks behind you. Call it a hunch that I showed up, and then you getting into a limousine, that was a tip-off of something, shall we say, unusual. Now what's with him?"

"He telephoned me at home, said that Mrs. Martindale was willing to talk to me about her son. I had tried once before to see her, but they wouldn't let me in the house."

"How'd you expect to find out who killed the guy from his mother?" the Brother asked, eyes narrowed.

"I have hunches, too," I said, feeling slightly dizzy.

The Brother's laugh was satanic. "We figured it had to be an inside hit."

"Huh?"

He ignored my puzzlement and knelt on one knee next to Preston. "You got him, didn't you. Mac?"

"Please, my knee, my leg," Preston sobbed. A dark stain was visible on his pants.

"Yeah, your leg, right," the Brother mimicked, pressing an automatic similar to the one that had been aimed at me against the wounded man's temple. "Let's hear your story. I'm feelin' real twitchy."

"What, what…"

"Cut the shit! You were ready to blow this man away. Why'd you off Martindale?" He jabbed Preston's sweat-soaked forehead with the silencer-equipped barrel of his gun.

"Madam, she…"

"Who's Madam?" the Brother demanded.

"Beatrice Martindale, Lloyd's mother," I put in.

"Go on," the hoodlum prodded Preston.

"She got a call a few months back…from a woman…" He paused, grimacing. "This woman…she said Lloyd had fooled around with her…when she was just a little girl."

The Brother looked up at me and scowled. "Shit, the guy was a pervert? Did you know about this?"

"This was my hunch," I said, leaving it at that.

"This woman," Preston went on laboriously after another sharp nudge with the gun, "she said that…if Lloyd ran for mayor, she would tell all the newspapers what he did to her back then."

"Why didn't she say that to Martindale himself?"

"She…wanted to punish Madam too…because she said that Madam had known all along what Lloyd liked to do. But I don't believe that…I don't believe she ever knew…" Preston, who was now lying on his side in a fetal position, groaned again, louder, and kept clutching the injured leg.

"So why didn't you kill this other woman instead of

Martindale?" the Brother asked, continuing to shine the beam of his flashlight on Preston's contorted, sweating face.

"Madam wouldn't tell me her name, and all this happened years ago...before I worked for the family. I asked her more than once...who it was. But all she would say was that if it got out...about Lloyd...she was going to kill herself."

"And you believed her?"

"Oh yes...she would have," Preston mumbled, again pleading for help.

"And why'd you want to kill this guy?" the Brother asked him, jabbing his automatic in my direction.

"Because he was poking around and I think he would have found out...about everything."

The gunman turned and looked up at me. "You know who the girl was that Martindale fooled with?"

"No," I lied, unblinking. "I never got that far."

"Then where'd you get that 'hunch' of yours?"

"An old-time newspaperman, he's long retired, said he remembered hearing that Martindale liked little kids...*that way*. But he didn't have any specifics." The second lie is always easier.

"You got paper and something to write with?" the Brother asked me.

I nodded and handed him my spiral-bound reporter's notebook and a pencil. He tore out a couple of sheets from the middle and used the cardboard cover as backing. "Now, Mac," he ordered, giving the paper and pencil to Preston, "you're going to take some dictation from me, got it?"

"My leg...oh my God! My God!"

"We'll take care of that leg, but first, you're going to write. Malek, go sit in the car with Mel–you remember him, from when all of us took a couple rides around your neighborhood together."

"But, I..."

"Goddamn it, go and sit in the car!" he commanded. Still shaking, I walked gingerly through the darkness for a couple of hundred yards to where the Cadillac was parked, its lights and engine off.

I opened the front passenger door and started to climb in. "In the back," Mel muttered.

I was in no condition to argue. I slid into the back seat of the big car, where I had been before, although this time I had it all to myself. "Okay, Mel, where were you guys watching me on Clark tonight? Just curious."

"Don't be curious. Bad habit."

"Okay, all right." We sat in silence and darkness for maybe fifteen minutes. When the single shot sounded, I jumped, but Mel was impassive. "Jesus Christ," I shout-whispered.

"It's copasetic," he said, yawning and grinding out his cigarette in the ashtray. "The Brother'll be along now."

And he was, within seconds. He slid in next to me, adjusting the knot on his silk tie. "Let's roll," he calmly ordered.

"And what about Preston?" I asked, knowing the answer.

"His leg doesn't hurt him anymore," the Brother said.

"So…just like that?"

"Hey, the fucker was about to kill you, Mr. Newspaperman. Also just like that." He snapped a finger and a thumb.

"He really did shoot Martindale then, didn't he?" I said as the reality began to sink in.

"Goddamn right. Showed his loyalty, and probably his love, for the old lady by knocking off her son."

"And he figured that you guys—well, the organization— would get the blame, eh?"

"Goddamn right again."

"Wait a minute. I heard the shot, but your automatic's got a silencer."

I thought I detected a fleeting smile on the Brother's face as we passed under a streetlamp. "You're not as dumb as you sometimes act, Malek," he said. "The poor depressed bastard plugged himself with his own .32."

"The one I picked up after you shot him in the leg. That

means–"

"That means nothin', except that when they dust the roscoe he's still holding, the only fingerprints they find on it will be his."

"But what about the shot in his leg? Done with a different gun–yours. How will that get explained?"

"You're filled with questions tonight. So happens, call it good fortune, that my friend here"–he tapped the bulge in his suit coat–"is also a .32. Seems it took Preston two shots to end it all. He was so nervous the first time that he plugged himself in the leg."

I leaned back and exhaled deeply as Mel drove north up Stony Island.

"You gotta be philosophical sometimes," the Brother said, smoothing the sleeve of his suit coat.

"Yeah? How's that?"

"Well, you lost yourself a scoop here, now didn't you? I mean, you can't very well write about what happened here tonight, can you?" His tone was not threatening, just matter-of-fact.

"Not if I want to stay healthy," I observed ruefully.

"But that isn't really so bad, is it? We took away your scoop, but we gave you something in return."

"Yeah. My life."

"Strikes me as a pretty fair swap," the Brother observed, gazing out into the dark waters of Lake Michigan as we slid onto the northbound Lake Shore Drive.

Chapter 24

Preston's "suicide" was big news, with every daily in town giving it an all-caps Page One screamer. The *Tribune* got a slight jump on the others, though. After the Brother and Mel dropped me off at home, I raced upstairs and called my own desk in the Police Headquarters pressroom, getting our lazy overnight man, Corcoran.

"Here's a hot one for you to check out, pal," I said hoarsely, muffling my voice with the old handkerchief-over-the-mouthpiece stunt. "A body in the forest preserve in Beverly Hills, lying near a Packard. Shot. Figures to be a connection with the Martindale murder."

"Who is this?" Corcoran bellowed as I cradled the receiver. That should give him a slight head start, I figured. If I couldn't get a scoop, at least maybe the paper would have one.

Our story the next morning was the most complete, although the *Examiner* had a long piece too, and the p.m.'s all came out with early extra editions. I read them as eagerly as everyone else in town–maybe more so. The *Trib* version, in part, said: "**MARTINDALE MURDERER KILLS SELF! Family chauffeur leaves confession.** The murder in February of civic reformer and potential Republican mayoral candidate Lloyd Martindale appears to have been solved with the suicide of a long-time Martindale family retainer.

"Everett Arthur Preston, 58, was found shot to death in the forest preserve on the north end of the Beverly Hills neighborhood late last night by police after the *Tribune* received an anonymous telephone tip that a body was in the forest preserve.

"Preston, who had been employed as a chauffeur by Martindale's mother, Mrs. Edgar Martindale, of Longwood

Drive in Beverly Hills, apparently shot himself twice, the first time in the leg, the second time fatally, through the heart. His body was found near an auto licensed to Mrs. Martindale, along with a note in which Preston confessed to the killing of Lloyd Martindale.

"In the note, which the police made public, Preston blamed Martindale for 'ignoring his mother for years, refusing to call or visit her. She suffered terribly because of this lack of consideration.'

"Police confirmed that the handwriting in the note was that of Mr. Preston. 'This closes the book on a sad chapter on our city's history,' said Police Commissioner Allman.

"Both Mrs. Edgar Martindale and Lloyd Martindale's widow, Carla, of North Lake Shore Drive, were too distraught to comment."

Later that day I got a phone call in the Headquarters pressroom from the Brother. "I see that you managed to tip your people off," he growled.

"Hey, I didn't give anything away," I said in a low voice, cupping my hand over the mouthpiece.

"I know you didn't," he conceded. "Just checking up, that's all."

"As far as I'm concerned, the whole business is over," I assured him. "And by the way, that was an interesting note Preston wrote–about how Martindale neglected his mother and all."

The Brother grunted. "Bastard sure didn't want to write it, but I wasn't going to let him tell the true story. That would have made him look like some kind of damn hero, shooting a pervert and all. Besides, the pervert was already dead, and this Preston and me, we had a score to settle."

"About Pariello?"

He grunted again. "The cops killed Joe, but the way we figure it, so did Preston."

"Yes, I guess that's true, in a sense. While you're on the line, I've got a question."

"Yeah?"

"What happened to those two guys, the ones who got roughed up in…"

"In that saloon? They got transferred."

"Where. To Hades?"

"To K.C., not that it's any of your business. We had a coupla openings down there. Change'll be good for them. And don't get yourself all worked up–they won't be coming back."

"Remind me never to go to Kansas City. I got one last question. When you guys first started talking to me just after Martindale got shot, you said Capone was still calling the shots, or at least some of them, from out in Alcatraz. That really true?"

"Way back before he went to stir, Alphonse mentioned you once to me, said you were a good reporter, that you covered his trial fair and all. I remembered. Helps to have a good memory."

"So you really haven't been in touch with him at all?"

I thought the line had gone dead, but after several heartbeats, the Brother spoke. "Alphonse," he murmured, "is as nutty as a fruitcake."

I never saw or spoke to the Brother again, never even learned his name, all of which was jake with me and I'm sure with him as well. I've always wanted to see loose ends tied up, though, so I wasn't ready just yet to walk away from the Martindale story. Two nights later, I stood outside Harding's on Wabash. At a little past 8:30, Nicolette Stover came out alone through the revolving door.

"Evening," I said, doffing my hat.

"You!" She backed away, hunching her shoulders.

"Now hold on," I urged, showing her my palms in mock surrender. "I only want a minute of your time, and you'll want to hear what I have to say."

"Go…away. Go…away." Her dark eyes were wide with terror. I hoped she wasn't carrying the automatic in her purse, but this time I was ready if she started to reach for it.

"No, I won't go away. Listen to me, Nicolette, it's all over," I said, stepping up my pace to keep even with her as she walked north. "Nobody knows anything about that call you made to Beatrice Martindale. Even Everett Preston, the man who killed himself–and murdered Lloyd Martindale–never knew your name."

"You know it. She knows it," Nicolette gasped, now almost running despite her high-heeled shoes.

"I'll go to my grave with that knowledge," I said. "And I'm sure Mrs. Martindale will, too."

"She'll get me, she'll get me," Nicolette Stover keened as she started running away, her heels making sounds like horses' hoofs on the dark sidewalk.

Three weeks later, the second half of my final comment to Nicolette came to pass. Here was how the *Tribune* reported it:

"MARTINDALE'S MOTHER KILLS SELF; Despondent over recent deaths

"Mrs. Edgar Martindale, 79, widow of the late steel magnate Edgar Martindale and mother of the late Lloyd Martindale, died of gas poisoning yesterday in her Beverly Hills home.

"A maid arriving for duty found Mrs. Martindale's body on the kitchen floor of the 18-room Victorian mansion. The gas jets on the nearby stove were all open, and the Negro maid, Jessie Lake, was very nearly overcome herself.

"Marsha Weathers, a niece of the dead woman, said that Beatrice Martindale had been despondent since the shooting death in February of her son, a civic reformer and a Republican mayoral hopeful. This despondence, Miss Weathers said, intensified when the family chauffeur, Everett Preston, killed himself last month and left a note confessing to Lloyd Martindale's murder.

"Although police said that Mrs. Martindale also left a handwritten note, they declined to reveal its specific contents. But one officer who would not be identified told the *Tribune* that 'The contents (of the note) left no doubt that the woman meant to do away with herself.'"

There was more, mostly about how star-crossed the Martindale family had been in the last several months. But as dramatic as the paper made it all sound, whoever wrote the piece did not know the half of it.

The trusted family retainer, in an attempt to keep the dowager from killing herself, had dispatched the son, thereby setting in motion the chain of events that led to her suicide anyway. Three deaths, and yet perhaps a greater tragedy than any of them was that of the tormented woman whose life two of the three had helped to shatter.

Chapter 25

One story, the Martindale saga, was over, but another continued–the 1938 National League pennant race which, thanks in part to Dizzy Dean, was to become a chapter in Chicago sports lore.

As the season ground toward its finish, the Cubs passed the Giants and the Reds in the standings and kept picking up ground on the Pirates. Dizzy's arm went bad again, so he wasn't much of a factor in the team's success in August or most of September, but Bill Lee and Clay Bryant were nearly unbeatable, and the hitters came to life, too.

The Cubs were six games back of Pittsburgh, then four, then three. And when the Pirates rolled into Chicago for three games the last week in September, the local boys were riding a seven-game winning streak and now trailed by only a game and a half.

Through good fortune and my own lack of planning, my vacation fell on the last week of September and the first week of October. My plan early in the year had been to get some time off in the middle of summer so Peter and I could do things together around the city. I was slow putting in my request, though, and other reporters, some of them with less seniority than I, grabbed off the choice June and July weeks. So I was left with what was to become an ideal time away from the job for a Cub fan–which I had been since they lost the 1918 World Series in six games to the Boston Red Sox and their young pitcher, Babe Ruth.

The first game of the Pirate series was on Tuesday, and Gabby Hartnett surprised the whole town by announcing that he would start Dean, who hadn't pitched in nine days and hadn't won a game in five weeks. Monday night in Kilkenny's, Dean was in grand, chest-thumping, pre-game form, though, affirming that the manager, Gabby Hartnett, was getting smarter by the day.

"Who else would he pick to beat those jerks but Old Diz?" he proclaimed to the whoops and applause of the habitués as he polished off a T-bone at his usual place at the bar, washing it down with a Budweiser.

After Dean left—"to get a good night's sleep so I can whup them Pirates in style"—the Killer leaned across the bar and whispered to me that Diz had left four tickets for each of the first two games of the Pittsburgh series. "He said he loves coming in here, both for the food and the friendliness. He also said he was sorry he probably wouldn't be able to get any tickets for us when—that's what he said, *when*—the Cubs get into the World Series, but he did leave these, and he wanted me to hand them out to whoever I wanted. So I'm offering you the first crack, scrivener friend. You can have one for either day—take your pick."

"That's really swell of him and of you, too, Killer, thanks. Damn, I wish I could see Diz pitch tomorrow, but I've got this dentist appointment I've had for weeks, so how 'bout Wednesday?"

"You now have ownership," the Killer said, slipping a ticket from an envelope and sliding it to me. "That's when I'm going as well, compadre. I couldn't get Grady to spell me here tomorrow, but he's coming in the day after to serve the thirsty public." The barkeep then moved down the bar, discreetly huddling one-on-one with other regulars and slyly doling out the balance of the tickets that Diz had given him.

I wanted to kick myself Tuesday afternoon for missing what surely had been the game of the year. Dean made Hartnett look like a genius by beating the Pirates, 2 to 1, although Bill Lee had to come in to get the last Pittsburgh batter in the ninth when Diz's arm gave out. That night in Kilkenny's the hero of the day stopped by, but only for a few minutes.

"Arm's so sore ah can barely lift it," Diz groaned, gripping the elbow with his other hand. "But ah wasn't gonna let that stop me from winnin' the greatest game of mah life. The Lord was right there with me." Now the bar was really rocking with cheers, the only sobering element being the news that Augie Galan wrenched his knee during the game and had to be carried off the field. He was probably through for the season.

The next day, the Killer, Morty Easterly, Ed Dugan, and I found ourselves in third-row box seats down the left field line near the bullpen. "Damned if this ain't the best seat I've had in twenty years coming to this ball yard," Morty marveled, shaking his head. "That Diz, he's a prince. Killer, next time he comes in, I want to pick up the check for his steak, got that?"

"You'll have to fight me for it," Dugan put in, but the Killer insisted that Dean's next few meals at the bar would be on the house. "By patronizing my humble oasis, he and his noble teammates have brought in so much other new business that I ought to cut Mr. J.H. Dean in on a piece of the action."

During the pre-game warm-ups, Dean was jogging with several other players on the left-field grass when he spotted us and came over to the brick wall. "Howdy Killer, Mr. Snap, Morty, Ed," he grinned, tipping his dark blue cap to us. "Seats okay for you?"

"More than okay!" Morty fired back.

"Well, we're gonna get y'all another win today and push them Pirates down into second place, where they belong!" That drew applause and a few whoops of "Yea, Diz!" from fans in our section as Dean trotted back to the dugout.

Because of the way the game ended, I've forgotten almost every detail about it, although I think I have the scorecard tucked away in a drawer somewhere. I do remember that there was a lot of hitting–the pitchers on both teams got pounded pretty good and, going into the ninth inning, the score was 5 to 5. It was past 5 o'clock and getting dark, and the umpires held a conference at home plate, probably trying to figure out how much longer to play.

"This will be the last inning," the Killer pronounced with assurance.

"What happens if the thing's tied and they have to call it?" Dugan posed. "The pennant's on the line."

"They'll probably pick up tomorrow where they left off," I speculated. "Start in the 10th inning, finish that game, then play another one."

"God, so on the one day we can come out here, we see a lousy tie," Easterly fumed.

"Ah, but 'tis not over yet, Morty, me lad," the Killer said with the assurance that only a bartender can summon.

The Pirates went out in the top of the ninth without scoring. The first two Cubs went down in their half of the inning, and the squat Gabby Hartnett lumbered to the plate in the near darkness. He had been an unqualified success since taking over as manager two months before, but at age thirty-eight, his days as both catcher and hitter were about over. Mace Brown, the Pirate pitcher, got two quick strikes over, and on the next pitch, Hartnett swung hard.

I heard the crack of the bat, but in the twilight, I lost the ball somewhere in the air. Everybody stood, though, and I stood with them. "Yes, yes indeed!" the Killer bellowed, his outstretched arm and pointed index finger moving in an arc from right to left across the darkening sky, following the trajectory. I finally picked up the round speck, just before it cleared the high brick left-field wall and disappeared into the bleachers as 40,000 spectators roared in unison.

The barrel-shaped player-manager slowly trundled around the bases, but by the time he reached third, there was such a mob surging onto the field–players, fans, ushers–that it seemed liked he'd never get to complete the full circuit. The crowd pressed in on him as flashbulbs popped, until we lost sight of Gabby somewhere between third and home. He must have made it, though, because the 5 for the Cubs on the big scoreboard had changed to a 6, and they were in first place, where they would stay.

Two days later, after the Cubs had clinched the pennant, I got a call at home from Cahill.

"Leo! I've been expecting to hear from you," I said with

bonhomie. "How's things?"

"Yeah, go ahead and gloat while you can," he groused.

"Me, gloat? Why would I want to do that?"

"Look, how 'bout us going double or nothing on the Series?" he asked plaintively.

"Are you kidding? You know what kind of favorites the Yankees are? It's something like 14 to 5, last time I checked."

"I'll give you those odds–or more." He sounded desperate.

"No thanks, Leo."

"But I got a problem."

"Yeah. How so?"

"Damn, Snap, I can't spare fifty bucks. Not now."

"Oh, I see," I said, savoring a moment I had been anticipating–and rehearsing–for days. "Well…I have a solution to that 'little problem' of yours. You guys in the Sports Department get tickets to everything–tickets you usually don't want to share with your co-workers in other areas of the paper. I know very well that you do, so don't bother trying to deny it. How 'bout you give me two seats for one of the Series games? Then I'll consider our bet paid off."

"Darn, Snap, that's tough, that's really tough to do."

I paused for effect before responding. "Let me make sure that I've got this straight, Leo. You don't want to pay me the fifty simoleons, is that right? And you don't want to get me the tickets, which together wouldn't cost anywhere near the fifty clams I wagered in good faith–and in fact, those tickets probably wouldn't cost you a copper Lincoln.

"What it really comes down to is this, Leo. A grumpy White Sox fan whose own woebegone team has not been in the series in almost twenty years–and they threw that one–can't stand it because the Cubs got in again. This same petulant White Sox fan who insisted Dizzy Dean wouldn't win five games, and wouldn't even pitch after June…now let's see, Dizzy has won…"

"All right, all right," Leo sighed. "Now look here, Snap, I can't get you a thing for the opener on Wednesday–everybody from the governor and the mayor on down to precinct workers wants to be out there, posing for the cameras down in front with that damn red, white, and blue bunting. But I'm pretty sure I can get you a pair for Thursday."

"*Pretty sure*, Leo?"

"Okay, dammit. I *will* get you two seats for Thursday's game. That's a promise."

"Good seats?"

He sighed again. "Very good seats, third-base side, couple rows back of the Cubs dugout."

"One more thing. I'm taking my boy, and I want a pass that gets us into the Cubs clubhouse after the game."

"Now wait a minute, Snap…"

"No, you wait a minute Leo," I said without warmth. "None of what I'm asking is costing you a damn single dollar. I'm letting you off the hook in a big way, and this is what I want in return."

Silence. "All right," he finally said, his voice tight. "You can pick everything up in the Sports Department the day before the game. Martha'll have an envelope with your name on it."

"I knew I could count on you, Leo. Thanks." I cradled the receiver and leaned back in my one living room chair, feeling smug. Norma and Martin Baer had gotten married two weeks before, and Peter told me Baer had said he would take them to Miami Beach around the holidays. "Is it okay with you if I go?" Peter had asked in an uncertain tone.

"Sure, why not? Never pass up the chance to get out of the cold weather here. Besides, you've never been to Florida; be a good experience."

"But you'll be all alone for Christmas," he said with what I knew was genuine concern.

"That's okay, Son. You and I can have our Christmas when you get back. Just the two of us."

"Yeah, I'd like that, just us. This trip will cost plenty, won't it, Dad? The train tickets and hotels and stuff?"

"Well, it sounds like Mr. Baer's got the money to do it," I told him. "And it's nice that he's taking you along."

Such was my outward benevolent stance to Peter

regarding Martin Baer. I was jealous of the man's wherewithal to show my son places I'd never been able to take him. This was a big part of the reason I decided to pry those World Series tickets and clubhouse passes out of Leo in lieu of the money that he couldn't afford to part with. Let Baer try to match that.

The Cubs sent their best pitcher, Bill Lee, against the Yankees in the opener, which I caught on the radio. Big Bill pitched well, but Red Ruffing threw better, and the Yankees won, 3 to 1. During the game, the broadcasters reported the speculation that Hartnett had decided to gamble on starting Dean rather than Clay Bryant in the second game, even though Bryant had won nineteen during the season.

Despite the cold, cloudy, and windy weather, Peter and I were in our seats the next day more than an hour before game time, watching the teams warm up. Getting him out of school for the afternoon wasn't as hard as I thought it would be: It turned out that his teacher, a tall, skinny, and warm-hearted spinster named Forsythe, was a Cub fan who seemed genuinely happy that Peter could see the game. And we promised to bring her a program and a pennant, which really sealed the deal.

"Are the Yankees as good as when Babe Ruth was with them?" Peter asked, as the swaggering New Yorkers took batting practice, pounding pitch after pitch over the left and right field walls.

"I think if anything, they're even better," I told him. "They won the Series the last two years against the Giants, and they've got Joe DiMaggio–that's him right there, Number 5, stepping into the batter's box–who's only about twenty-three and he's already hit over .300 all three years he's been in the big leagues. And the rest of their lineup is terrific, too, although Lou Gehrig's slowing down now. But at least you can tell your grandchildren you saw Gehrig play; he's one of the great ones."

"Do you think the Cubs have a chance, Dad?"

"Not much of one, Peter. Five guys on the Yankees hit over twenty home runs this year, and you can see the way they're whacking 'em now in practice. And do you know who led the Cubs in homers? Rip Collins, the one with his hands on his hips over there in front of the dugout, who had a grand total of thirteen."

But once the game started, the Yankees didn't seem much like killers. Dizzy Dean, throwing his slow, sidearm "nothing ball," was fooling the Bronx boys on pitches I was sure I could hit.   Unfortunately, the Cubs weren't playing so well themselves. They did take a 1 to 0 lead in the first inning, but in the Yankee second, DiMaggio led off with a single and Gehrig walked. Then after Diz got the next two batters to pop up, Joe Gordon hit a ground ball that either third baseman Stan Hack or shortstop Billy Jurges could have fielded easily. But they banged into each other, falling down like a couple of bumbling Keystone Kops, and both runners scored.

Chicago grabbed the lead back in the fourth when Joe Marty, their best hitter in the series, drove home two runs. And that's the way it stayed–the Cubs and Dizzy Dean ahead 3 to 2, as the Yankees went down one-two-three in the fifth, sixth, and seventh innings against the "nothing ball." Then in the eighth, with one man on base, the Yanks' Frank Crosetti came to bat and took a smooth swing at one of Dean's slow, slow pitches. Unlike Hartnett's home run the week before, I saw this one all the way, watching it as it fell into the left-field bleachers. As Crosetti rounded the bases, Diz came off the mound and yelled something at him that we couldn't hear despite the sudden silence in the ballpark, and the Yankee stopped in the baseline to reply to him.

In the ninth, DiMaggio also teed off against Dean, and the Yankees had a 6 to 3 lead…and the game. Hartnett went to the mound and took the ball from Diz, giving him a pat on the back. As the pitcher trudged slowly off the field toward the dugout, clusters of fans rose to clap, then more followed, and soon the entire crowd was on its feet in salute. The applause and whistling went on for more than a minute, as the Cubs in the field, hands on hips, looked down at the ground or made idle patterns in the infield dirt with their cleats.

"Why is everybody cheering him so much, Dad?" Peter

shouted over the din as we stood and clapped. "They hit two homers off him."

"Eventually they did, but he pitched awfully well for a long time," I said. "And people will do this when they know they've seen somebody give the very best they can." Also, I might have added, these cheers were in effect a hail and farewell to a legend, who at the age of only twenty-eight was leaving the spotlight for probably the final time.

The Cubs clubhouse was crowded, but there was no noise above the level of murmurs. Players sat half-dressed and dejected in front of their cubicles as reporters knelt down asking questions in lowered voices. "Nice hitting today, Joe," one said to Marty, who only shook his head and scowled. "You'll get 'em in New York on Saturday," another said to Stan Hack, whose wooden smile and nodding response carried little conviction.

As Peter and I weaved our way through the funereal gloom, I spotted Dizzy Dean, still dressed in his uniform pants and cleats but stripped to his undershirt, sweating and slumped on a bench, his street clothes hanging on pegs behind him. Three reporters, one of them from the *Trib*, stood above him scribbling in their notebooks.

"What did you say to Crosetti when he hit the homer?" one asked.

"Ah told him he wouldn't of got a loud foul off me two years ago," the pitcher said.

"Did he say something back?" another scribbler posed.

"He said I was right," Diz responded in a tired voice, and the reporters dispersed to get quotes from other players.

A tall, thin, erect figure in a dark suit and white hair stepped out of the shadows and planted himself in front of Dean, holding out a gnarled hand. I recognized him from newspaper photographs: Connie Mack, now probably seventy-five years old and the manager of the Philadelphia Athletics since before I was born. "Son, you pitched a great game out there with what you had on the ball," Mack said with quiet conviction.

Diz looked up and forced a smile. "Thanks, Mr. Mack, 'preciate it. And yore right…Ah didn't have nothin' out there today, 'cept maybe heart."

"You had plenty of that," Connie Mack told Diz, patting him on the shoulder and leaving.

Peter and I stood a respectful two paces away, not wanting to disturb the reverie as Diz watched baseball's Grand Old Man depart. Then Dean turned, saw me, and actually grinned.

"Well, Mr. Snap! Nice of ya to stop by." He stood and we shook hands.

"Diz, this is my son, Peter. We were cheering for you all the way today."

"Hey, Peter, pleasure to meet you," Diz said, pumping his hand. "You got yourself a great dad, but ya already know that, dontcha?"

"Yes, sir, I do," Peter said. If he was awed, he didn't show it, and that made me proud of him. "We're sorry about…sorry you lost today."

"Yeah, well, like I told Mr. Mack just now, and them reporters what were here before him, I didn't have nothin' on the ball. Fooled 'em for seven innings, though, didn't I, Peter?"

"Yes, sir, you did. Could I…" He held out his program and a pencil.

"Peter, I don't think Mr. Dean is in the mood to sign any autographs just now," I whispered.

"Hey, Ah'm *always* ready to sign, win or lose," Diz said, taking the pencil and writing at length on Peter's program. "You play ball yourself, son?"

Peter hunched his shoulders. "Sorta. Second base. I'm not very good, though."

"Hey, Rogers Hornsby played second base, and he was the best hitter there ever was, anywhere. Well, you keep at it, promise?" the pitcher boomed, tousling Peter's hair and turning to me. "Mr. Snap, is everything okay? I mean…" he looked to see if Peter was listening, but saw he was engrossed in reading Dean's handwritten message to him… "about them two thugs what came barging into Killer's place that night," he said in a lowered voice.

"They're gone, Diz, and they won't be back," I said. "I never properly thanked you for your accurate pitching that night."

He raised his shoulders and let them drop. "Glad to help. Don't know if Ah'll be back, either. If Ah'm traded or I hang up my spikes, give all them fine fellas at the Killer's mah very best, and tell 'em they shore made ol' Diz feel welcome, will ya?"

"I'll do that, Diz, and that's a promise," I said as we shook hands. "Be seein' you. So long."

Peter and I left the somber clubhouse and walked out onto Clark Street. Most of the crowd had dispersed, but whistle-blowing cops were still directing traffic at the intersection with Addison and vendors kept hawking souvenirs from their carts, aware that the Chicago portion of the World Series was probably over so this was their last chance to make sales. I bought two Cub pennants, one for Peter, the other for his teacher, and I also handed him the extra program I had bought for her. "Don't forget to give this stuff to Miss Forsythe," I said. "It's always best to stay on their good side."

"Today was really fun, Dad," he said, smiling up at me, "even if the Cubs did lose. You sure have a lot of famous friends, don't you?"

"I don't know if they're all what you would call friends, although I sure do like Dizzy Dean, and some day I'll tell you how much he helped me once. But meeting well-known people, that's just what happens when you're a newspaper reporter, Peter. You naturally run into people who make news."

"Mama says you're different, though."

"Oh, does she now?"

"Yeah. What does 'essential brashness' mean?"

I gave him my interpretation of that phrase as we walked south on Clark to my apartment. We would have frankfurters and potato salad for supper there before I took him in a taxi to

his new home, the duplex on Lake Shore Drive where he lived
with Mr. and Mrs. Martin Baer.

Epilogue

The preceding is a work of fiction, and all of its principal characters, other than those mentioned below, exist solely in the mind of the author. Also, all of the episodes in which these historical figures interact with fictional ones are products of the author's hyperactive imagination.

Helen Hayes, who completed her storied run (more than 900 performances) as Queen Victoria in "Victoria Regina" in 1939, continued to be a prominent and popular figure on the Broadway and London stage until the early 1970s. She also acted in films, most notably "Anastasia" (1956) and "Airport" (1970). In the latter, she won an Oscar for her performance as an impish stowaway. It was her second Academy Award, the other being for "The Sin of Madelon Claudet" (1931).

Miss Hayes' daughter, Mary, died of polio in 1949, and her husband, author and playwright Charles MacArthur, died in 1956. The actress, known as the "First Lady of the American Stage," died in March 1993, at the age of ninety-three.

Al Capone, terminally ill from the effects of syphilis and its later manifestation, paresis, was released from prison in November 1939 and spent most of the rest of his days in seclusion with his family at their home in Florida, where he suffered from both physical and mental deterioration and periods of intense depression. No longer a factor in the world of organized crime, he died in January 1947, eight days after his forty-eighth birthday.

Michael Ahern, who first made his name as a defense attorney in celebrated criminal cases in the 1920s (including the murder of a Chicago policeman), concentrated largely on civil law in the years following the Capone tax trial. Ahern, who also taught law at his alma mater, Chicago's Loyola University, died in September 1943, at the age of fifty-six.

Dizzy Dean's baseball career was to all intents finished after the 1938 season, although in some ways that year was his grittiest and gutsiest, given that, despite a burned-out arm, he managed to win seven games while losing only one and posted a superb 1.81 earned-run average. He hung on with the Cubs for three more years, but won only nine games in that span. He did, however, develop a second successful career as a baseball broadcaster on radio and later on television. His fractured syntax and malapropisms (Sample: "slud" for "slid") endeared him to fans but bedeviled English teachers across the land. He was inducted into baseball's Hall of Fame in 1953 and died in 1974, at the age of sixty-three.

Augie Galan batted only twice in the four games of the 1938 World Series because of the injury he sustained late in the season. He played for the Cubs until 1940, when he was sent to the Brooklyn Dodgers, where he enjoyed some of his most productive years. His last season in the major leagues was 1949. He died in December 1993, at the age of eighty-one.

Col. Robert R. McCormick continued to head the *Chicago Tribune* as its editor and publisher until his death in 1955 at seventy-four. He remained a staunch conservative and Republican throughout his life, vigorously opposing Franklin D. Roosevelt and the New Deal, Harry Truman and the Fair Deal, and foreign aid to countries including the United Kingdom (he was a fierce Anglophobe) and China.

Robert M. Lee had an all-too-brief career as managing editor of McCormick's *Tribune*. Taking the reins of the paper's news operation on the retirement of the venerable and esteemed Edward Scott Beck in 1937, the flamboyant, imaginative Lee served only two years before dying of a heart attack in January 1939. He was fifty-five.

Edward J. Kelly was victorious in the Chicago mayoral election of 1939, defeating Republican candidate Dwight Green. Kelly went on to serve as mayor until 1947. (Green later was elected, and re-elected, governor of Illinois, serving from 1941 to 1949.)

Richard J. Daley moved from the Illinois State Legislature in Springfield to numerous other governmental posts, including Cook County Deputy Controller, Illinois Revenue Director, and Cook County Clerk before being elected mayor of Chicago in 1955, a post he would hold until his death in 1976 at the age of seventy-four. During his more than two decades as mayor, he exercised firm control over the city and state Democratic organizations. He received national notoriety in 1968 during the Democratic National Convention in Chicago. When police beat youthful demonstrators in the streets, Sen. Abraham Ribicoff of Connecticut ripped what he called these "Gestapo tactics" from the rostrum. Daley, a member of the Illinois delegation, rose on the convention floor and angrily berated Ribicoff before a national television audience.

The late mayor's son, Richard M. Daley, who had served as Cook County State's Attorney, was himself elected Chicago mayor in 1989. He was re-elected by comfortable margins in 1991, 1995, 1999, and 2003.

Three Strikes You're Dead

Bibliography

Barrow, Kenneth. *Helen Hayes: First Lady of the American Theatre*. Garden City, N.Y.: Doubleday & Co., 1985.

Gies, Joseph. The *Colonel of Chicago*. New York: E.P. Dutton, 1979.

Gregory, Robert. *Diz: Dizzy Dean and Baseball During the Great Depression*, New York: Viking Penguin, 1992.

Hayes, Helen with Katherine Hatch. *My Life in Three Acts*. New York: Harcourt Brace Jovanovich, 1990.

Hecht, Ben. *Charlie: The Improbable Life and Times of Charles MacArthur*. New York: Harper & Brothers, 1957.

Kennedy, Eugene. *Himself! The Life and Times of Mayor Richard J. Daley*. New York: Viking Press, 1978.

Kobler, John. *Capone: The Life and World of Al Capone*. New York: G.P. Putnam's Sons, 1971.

Royko, Mike. *Boss: Richard J. Daley of Chicago*. New York: E.P. Dutton & Co., 1971.

Schoenberg, Robert J. *Mr. Capone*. New York: William Morrow & Co., 1992.

Smith, Richard Norton. *The Colonel: The Life and Legend of Robert R. McCormick*. Boston: Houghton Mifflin, 1997.

Spiering, Frank. *The Man Who Got Capone*. Indianapolis: The Bobbs-Merrill Co., 1976.

Staten, Vince. *Ol' Diz*. New York: HarperCollins, 1992.

Waldrop, Frank C. *McCormick of Chicago*. Englewood Cliffs, N.J.: Prentice-Hall, 1966.

Wendt, Lloyd. *Chicago Tribune: The Rise of a Great American Newspaper*. Chicago: Rand-McNally & Co., 1979.

Wlodarczyk, Chuck. *Riverview, Gone But Not Forgotten, a Photohistory, 1904–1967*. Evanston, Ill.: Schori Press, 1977.

Meet the author:

In his early teens, Robert Goldsborough began reading Rex Stout's Nero Wolfe mysteries. This started when he complained to his mother one summer day that he had "nothing to do." An avid reader of the Wolfe stories, she gave him a magazine serialization, and he became hooked on the adventures of the corpulent Nero and his irreverent sidekick, Archie Goodwin.

Through his school years and beyond, Goldsborough devoured virtually all of the 70-plus Wolfe mysteries. It was during his tenure with the *Chicago Tribune* that the paper printed the obituary of Rex Stout. On reading it, his mother lamented that "Now there won't be any more Nero Wolfe stories."

"There might be *one* more," Goldsborough mused, and began writing an original Wolfe novel for his mother. As a bound typescript, this story, ***Murder in E Minor***, became a Christmas present to her in 1978. For years, that's all the story was—a typescript. But in the mid-'80s, Goldsborough received permission from the Stout estate to publish "E Minor," which appeared as a Bantam hardcover, then paperback. Six more Wolfe novels followed, to favorable reviews.

As much as he enjoyed writing these books, Goldsborough longed to create his own characters, which he has done in ***Three Strikes You're Dead***, set in the gang-ridden Chicago of the late 1930s and narrated by a *Tribune* police reporter.

Goldsborough, a lifelong Chicagoan who has logged 45 years as a writer and editor with the *Tribune* and with marketing journal *Advertising Age*, says it was "Probably inevitable that I would end up using a newspaperman as my protagonist."

www.robertgoldsborough.com

I sank the dagger deep into his inconsistent blubber and seethed. For he laughed at me even as his blood pooled at my feet. Then his evil soul slipped free.

Alas, the deed was fruitless. I knew it before the cold sting of forged steel severed my head. The demon held the advantage.

My lifeless body lay twisted and foreign beneath me as my soul rose, already fashioning apology and plea. For failure served no one and meant only more pain. How would my mission be fulfilled?

Chicago 2096

Jaden Michaels splashed the last of her best merlot into the only clean glass in the kitchen. Presentation didn't matter when a woman only needed to rinse the taste of a poor lover from her lips. Poor he'd been, but useful. He reported to another in the criminal food chain who could bring her closer to her target.

She swirled the wine in the glass and her mind flashed with timeless, bloody memories. Tossing back the last swallow, she imagined the day when she could rest. She prayed this life would break the cycle.

She stripped the sheets from the bed, unwilling to sleep amidst the smells of a sweaty bar fly. Cocooning herself into a clean blanket she closed her eyes, hoping her elusive quarry would behave himself tonight.

Then the crying began. The frightened, jittery tears of an innocent child pushed into a new world of horrors. Jaden tried to tune out the echoes of pain and terror that sounded in her mind each time he struck, but she knew anyway. And the residual grief she'd share with the victim come morning is what fueled her to keep slogging her way through the bottom dwellers, the middle men, the lieutenants and body guards until she could take the head off the beast - permanently.

Available

February 2005

Justice has a new name…

Regan Black

Justice Incarnate

Women's Adventure

Whoever said you only live once…didn't know Jaden Michaels!